A TIME TO SEEK

THE TIME TRAVEL JOURNALS OF SAHARA ALDRIDGE, JOURNAL ONE

TRACY HIGLEY

D1596592

STONEWATER BOOKS

PROLOGUE

The past is a foreign country: they do things differently there.

~L.P. Hartley

April, 2021

*T*he first time I watched the television series *Downton Abbey*, I wept.

Not for the characters. Not for the story set in that magnificent place, in that far-off time.

No, I wept for my story. For my time. The story of my life, in which Highclere Castle was the place I sometimes called home.

Long before the *Downton Abbey* creators set up cameras at the real-life family estate of Highclere, home to eight successive generations of Earls, the scenes of my own story were unfolding there at that estate, amidst those who had taken me in and called me family.

What a decade. The Roaring Twenties, they call it now. In hindsight, part of that slip of time between two great wars. But we were heedless of the horrors that were coming and only felt relief for what was past. Relief that spilled out into a throaty roar

1

of freedom, into glittering decadence and gluttony, into smoky jazz clubs and mobsters dealing Prohibition-outlawed alcohol in American speakeasies tucked into alleys.

Some of this wildness touched us in the English countryside of Highclere, of course, but it was a frivolity restrained into house parties lasting a week, into fox hunts and duck-shooting excursions and dancing into the night. My heart was never in any of it. My heart longed for only one place — the parched and sand-blown stretch of Egypt known as the Valley of the Kings.

In the early months of 1922, my fourth winter season digging in Egypt was finally getting underway after a late start. It was to be the last season before the discovery that would change Egyptology forever, but again, only hindsight tells me that. On that first day of digging in February, I had no idea that I was about to make my own life-changing discovery. Not a discovery in the sand. Rather in a bit of old paper, brought in the hands of a friend...

CHAPTER ONE

February 8, 1922
Valley of the Kings, Egypt

hree hours into the season, and already tightness gripped my lower back. I straightened, jammed my pick into the ground, then my thumbs into the muscles weakened by a year of suffering through dinner parties and garden walks.

Before me, a desert jumble of bleached tunics and dark skin climbed over miniature peaks and valleys. The swarm of hired Egyptian men sang and dug as though their lives depended on how much sand they moved.

I grabbed the pick again. No one would have reason to think me less capable than any Egyptian laborer. Or than the dig's director, Howard Carter, himself.

"Alsahra', here!"

I shaded my eyes against the morning sun and followed the chirp of the youthful voice, calling out my Arabic name.

Across the digsite, young Nadeem was jumping and waving. "Here, Alsahra', come!"

A thrill bloomed in my chest. So soon?

I glanced across the sand for Howard, past scattered ivory canvas tents glowing under the blinding sun. Past sagging canopies stretching shade over worktables. Where was he? Nadeem must have found something of interest. But it was too good to be true, this early into the season.

The boy's enthusiasm slowed the line of men hauling baskets of rubble on their shoulders out to the growing pile at the edge of our grid.

I strode across the site, pulse pounding, to the grinning boy.

"What is it, Nadeem?"

"It is good, *Sayida!*" He tugged me toward a trench. A rickety ladder disappeared into its depth.

I peered over the edge. Four meters below, several laborers stood around what appeared to be the lip of a jug poking from the orange sand. It bore the characteristic blue-green of Egyptian faience.

"Good, yes?" Nadeem's head bobbed.

His gap-toothed grin was contagious.

I wrapped one arm around his shoulder. "*Na'am jayid.*"

"English, my lady! English!"

I ruffled his wavy hair. He'd grown at least ten centimeters since last season, as his too-short tunic attested, and was hungry to learn.

"Yes, it's good, Nadeem. But we must wait for Mr. Carter."

He puffed his chest, then yelled down to the men, as authoritative as a foreman. "*Yjb 'an nantazir!*" We must wait.

Yes, we must wait. And probably far too long.

The dig director must have sensed the interest spreading across the sand. He was at our side a moment later.

"What is it?" The question was more of a grunt, aimed at no one. Though nearly fifty, Howard's full hair and trimmed mustache were still dark, his physique still lean from years of digging his life's work out of the Egyptian desert. And his manner hadn't softened since my childhood.

"*Sayidi!*" Nadeem took Howard's hand in his own and pointed it toward the jug. "We have found!"

"I told Nadeem we should wait for you. But perhaps—"

"Yes, we'll let Porchy dig it out. He'll love that. And a find on the first day. Lucky omen, and all that."

"Indeed. But incentive enough for Porchy to keep the money flowing?"

He huffed. "Don't count on it. But they'll be here soon enough."

I dragged myself to the shade of a tent to wait out the frustrating interval, and sketched a few scenes in the smooth leather-bound sketchbook Porchy had given me last Christmas. I needed to finish the drawings soon.

Lord Carnarvon, formerly styled Lord Porchester, had gained the nickname Porchy in childhood. He soon arrived, roaring into the digsite in a hired dust-raising, clankety Model T with its top pulled back, a shabby imitation of one of his sleek roadsters back in England.

Howard stood beside me at the worktable strewn with small finds, under the dirty canopy propped up by poles. He scanned each of my sketches with half-lidded eyes, shrugged, and said nothing.

I rose from my chair, but remained with fingertips braced on the table, avoiding the automobile's sandstorm. "The man does love to move fast. It's a mystery to me how he tolerates the snail's pace of this work."

Howard responded to my comment with silence. Howard was a man of few words, and had made it clear he resented Porchy's insistence I be allowed to dig. Too young, too female. After four dig seasons, I was still an outsider, still trying to prove myself worthy. Still trying to find my place and purpose in this inhospitable world.

"He's brought the Countess." My spine straightened.

The Lady Almina Carnarvon sat beside her husband, furiously batting at the kicked-up desert that threatened to descend on her head. Porchy's wife typically preferred the opulence and service of the Winter Palace Hotel, on the other side of the Nile in Luxor, to the sandy grit of the digsite.

Their daughter, Lady Evelyn, sat upright in the seat behind her parents, but bounded out of the car nearly before it stopped. She wore a lemon-yellow beaded dress with a low-waisted sash and fashionable matching cap, and looked like a golden-petaled Narcissus blooming in a hostile wasteland.

"Oh, Sahara, I am *so* glad to see you!" Her embrace nearly knocked me flat, despite her feeling as petite as a child, next to me.

I pulled away. "Eve, I only left England three weeks ago!" She smelled of perfume and I was conscious of what the heat had already done to my morning bath, and of the riding breeches and men's shirt I wore.

"I know, but, my dear—" her voice lowered to a whisper and she clutched my arm—"I have *so much* to tell you! It's about your—"

"It'll have to wait." I inclined my head toward this morning's excitement. "We have something to show you."

Her eyes widened, and she covered a tiny gasp with gloved fingertips. "You've found something!"

"Come and see."

"I'll come, but Sahara—it's about your *parents.*"

We were already walking, and I nodded a greeting to Lord and Lady Carnarvon, who were slower to remove themselves from the automobile. The Earl still leaned heavily on a cane for support.

But Eve's words ricocheted off the inside of my skull. What could she possibly have to tell me about my parents?

At our approach to the trench, the laborers on the surface parted like the Red Sea.

They enjoyed calling me Alsahra'—the Arabic name of the Great Desert. Probably believed I didn't catch the elbow jabs and smirks and whispers. *Barren as the desert, eh?* Apparently it was their only explanation for why a single woman of my age would be dressed as a man and digging in a trench. Yes, women got the vote in England four years ago, but I had yet to earn the respect of a dig crew.

Behind us, Howard hailed Lord Carnarvon with a shrug. "A bit of a find, nothing more."

Porchy grunted. "Hoping for more than a bit this season, old man."

Eve and I crossed the digsite to the sound of the men singing as their trowels scraped and dug. The mournful chant always sounded funerary—appropriate for our grim work, searching for tombs. Above us, the wide blue sky went on forever, and the orange sand under our feet stretched out to meet it.

Eve ran ahead, one hand holding her cap against the hot wind.

"Darling, do be careful!" Lady Almina cupped a red-and-white-striped parasol above her head. "Your English-winter skin will freckle terribly under this Egyptian sun!"

But *careful* was not something the young Lady Evelyn thought much about. At the edge of the site, the sand crumbled under her heeled leather boots, and in one fluid motion she sank into the trench as though it were quicksand.

"Eve!" I was at the trench in a moment, heart thudding in my chest and half-expecting to see her lying dead at the bottom.

Instead, she had one arm hooked around the rung of the ladder, tiny leather boots flying free, and three Egyptian men staring up in terror at the underside of her flounced dress.

CHAPTER TWO

*E*ve was screaming. Well, to be fair, it was more of a squeal.

It took only a moment for the men below to scatter like ants to the end of the trench, far from the immodesty of an English woman's undergarments.

I lurched at the wobbly top rungs of the ladder and braced it against the side of the trench before Eve's leg-kicking pulled it backward.

Her cap had fallen to the sand, and her hair, newly bobbed short but still possessing all its curls, fanned out around her head like a dark cloud.

My first wave of protectiveness fled, and my jaw tightened. "Eve! What were you thinking?"

Sometimes it became clear she was only twenty. Nearly twelve years my junior.

She was too far down to clasp my outstretched hand, and with her right arm hooked on the ladder, her left arm was out of reach.

"Grab the ladder and pull yourself up."

She blinked away tears. "I can't!"

"Get her out of there!" Howard's command in my ear.

An unnecessary command. I was already stepping aside to give him access to the ladder. "Hold it steady."

He took my place and tightened his hands against the two rails.

I spun and scrambled down, careful to avoid Eve's arm.

At the bottom, I positioned myself under the girl, her kicking boots just above my head.

"Let go, Eve. I'll catch you!"

"What? No! I couldn't—"

"Let go, Eve!"

Despite my being technically American, our friendship began when she was a toddler and I was conscripted as her babysitter, while our parents dined and smoked and chatted. Perhaps she felt a remnant of that long-ago obedience. She released her hold on the ladder and tumbled downward into my arms.

The force of her weight pushed me backward and down, but I had broken her fall.

And the faience jug, I suspected, had broken mine.

"Oh, Sahara!" Eve hugged my neck. "You saved my life!"

Not exactly. But no need to correct her.

"Evelyn Herbert, you come out of that trench at once!" Lady Almina, still holding her parasol, glared down at us, in all her elegant and horrified glory.

Behind her, in a line of white tunics, were more than a dozen Egyptian laborers, equally horrified yet curious.

Eve regained her feet, and her cap. She smashed the cap over her curls and scurried up the ladder, perhaps a bit rebuked. Perhaps not.

I shifted my position in the sand and felt the displaced artifact shift with me. There was a bite of pain in my left palm.

As I feared, the jug was in pieces.

"Sahara, your hand!" Lord Carnarvon pointed his silver-tipped cane at the blood.

I glanced at the wound, jagged but not deep. I'd seen far worse during the war.

"It's nothing. Toss me a rag to wrap it, and I'll be right up." I scooted sideways, revealing the find in the sand. "I'm afraid our treasure did not fare so well."

My hand throbbed. The stupid injury had better not get in the way of my work this season.

While waiting for the rag, I bent to examine the jug and brush the sand away with careful fingertips. The clay bore symbols. Untranslated hieroglyphs were a perplexing question dangled like bait. "And bring a tray and a brush," I called upward. "I'll get this piece out, too." Porchy would have to wait for another treasure to dig up. This one was mine.

By the time I reached the surface, tray braced against my hip, Eve had been whisked away to Howard's tent with her mother, to sip lemonade and recover from her ordeal.

And the laborers had already begun a rant about women being allowed on the digsite.

It was a familiar grudge, and a fair one. In previous seasons, there'd been a parade of women in candyfloss-pink or royal blue dresses, parasols twirling and laced ankleboots punching little holes in the sand, coming to watch the work. In the hundred-plus years since Napoleon invaded Egypt, sparking "Egyptomania" in both scholarly and popular culture, the fever hadn't waned.

And it wasn't only the public. Egyptologists were coming and going all the time, and often had wives in tow. There were even swanky dinner parties held in the recesses of empty tombs, complete with fine linens and bone china. For a professional like Howard, whose very identity was bound up in the work, the popularity served only to annoy.

Howard's raised hands staved off the flood of Arabic.

I joined him, waiting to be castigated with the rest of the world's women.

But Ahmed Gerigar, the foreman, was shaking his head toward me. "Alsahra' — she is not like the others." He turned to the workers. "She works like man. She is married only to her work, yes?"

Grudging assent from a few of them.

I shrugged. *"Rudhkar, alsahra' ymkn 'an tuqtal rajul fi yawmayn."* Remember, the Sahara can kill a man in two days.

The angry rant turned to uproarious laughter at my joke. Or perhaps at my pronunciation. It was always hard to tell.

I wanted to grill Eve on her comment about my parents, but Howard was doing his duty, touring the family around the site, pointing out the grid plan for this season.

It wasn't long before the ladies were covering delicate yawns and asking to return to their hotel.

"Sahara," Eve pulled me aside as her parents approached the Model T. "You must come tonight for dinner. I have something so important to show you." An unusual furrow creased her smooth forehead.

"Can't you tell me now? Is something wrong?"

She shrugged one petite shoulder. "Not wrong, no. But... odd. I don't want to talk about it here."

I had little time for gossip, but sensed more than a morsel of society scandal in Eve's evasion. "I'll be there."

The Winter Palace Hotel glowed in yellow-stuccoed glory on the east bank of the Nile. European in style and grand in scale, it offered travelers the luxury to which they were accustomed, while enjoying the warm and sunny climate of southern Egypt.

It was that warm climate that first brought Porchy here, nearly twenty years ago, to ease the pain in his leg after his terrible automobile accident. Characteristically, the accident had not muted his passion for automobiles—only sparked a new love for Egyptology.

From the busy street of Luxor, I walked the white-railed balustrade to the front entrance of the hotel and entered into the marble, silk, and gilded elegance of the lobby. I'd cleaned up after the days' work in my room at the Met's dig house.

The Metropolitan Museum of Art in New York City, sponsoring an Egyptian Expedition, had built their own dig house, practically a hotel, and called The American House by most. Porchy secured me lodging there, arguing "the girl's an American, after all." My quiet room there, surrounded by my books, was always a welcome respite after the hot and dirty days of digging.

But no matter how much I cleaned up, I was not up to snuff in this place.

Eve's ominous hints had me curious, but I would have preferred to avoid the social scene here at the hotel. My injured hand would draw attention, and I had work to do back in my room, to meet the deadline I'd been given.

A quick check at the massive mahogany front desk, and then I climbed the main staircase with its spiraling ironwork, to the third floor where Eve had a spacious bedroom in the central rooms of the hotel, with an adjoining room for her lady's maid, Marcelle, of course.

She met me at the door, already outfitted in a dress I'd never seen—a slim white satin, with wide sleeves embroidered in exotic red. She whisked me into the coolness of her room with a scandalized glance at my trousers. "My dear, we must get you into something more suitable!"

I groaned. "I know you think it's better to appear at dinner in one of your dresses than bear the looks of the other guests. But I have no one to impress."

"Well, just because you dig like a man doesn't mean you have to look like one!"

I ignored the jab. Despite our age difference, Eve was one of the only friends I'd allowed into my world.

I knew her well enough to be certain she would't elaborate on her "news" until she had me transformed. "Fine. What have you got?" Attired in one of Eve's gowns, I would fit in with the wealthy as easily as I did with the laborers while wearing my breeches. But I balked at the frothy lace-and-pearls thing her lady's maid pulled from the wardrobe as a first suggestion.

Eve laughed. "Marcelle, perhaps find something… less girly?"

I nodded. "Uh, yes."

"How about this?" Eve chose a sleek emerald-green jacket and skirt, tailored and belted.

"That'll do."

I shrugged off my clothes, slipped into the skirt, and eyed my legs. Though I didn't have her curves, I could still fit into Eve's clothes, but my taller height resulted in a hemline too high on my calves to be fashionable. Oh, well.

Marcelle brushed a sharp part into my wavy, shoulder-length brown hair, and tried unsuccessfully to keep a stray curl from tickling my eyelashes.

Once Eve had my injured hand rewrapped in fresh gauze, she sent her maid away and pulled me to an orange-brocade sofa beside the window.

"Now, before we go down to dinner, I must show you what I brought." She pulled a leather-bound book from the end table. Her personal journal, similar to the less-expensive sketchbook her father had given me.

She opened the latch and slipped a sheet of paper from it, the size of her own journal's pages. It had been crumpled and pressed smooth. She held it to me, wordless.

Every muscle in my body slackened. I knew the handwriting at once.

CHAPTER THREE

I snatched the page from Eve. "Where—where did you get this?" The paper trembled in my hand.

"In the Library, at Highclere. It was shoved back inside the drawer of the writing desk. You can see—" she pointed to creases in the paper—"it was all scrunched, as though other items pushed it back years ago."

A journal page, written in my mother's hand. It was enough to see her handwriting after all these years, but the date! The date left me somehow both cold and hot at the same time.

I pressed the back of my hand against my eyes.

Eve was pointing to the first line. "You see when it was written, of course?"

June 8, 1905.

The words blurred. I spread the sheet flat on my leg to better read it.

We leave tomorrow for Venice. It will take more than a day by train. How tiresome not to be able to travel faster. But considering where we will go next, I suppose I should not complain!

We hope, of course, to intercept Belzoni before his impressive, yet destructive, work begins. Though Alexander is still fighting me on whether we will try to change Belzoni's methods or subvert him entirely.

We should be back long before the birth. We've told no one here at Highclere about the baby, since they would likely try to convince us to stay.

One day, when Sahara is older and we have explained everything, she will understand our little lies. Until then, she is safe here with those we love, who also love her.

I read it twice. There was so much, even in those few lines, that I didn't understand. The uncertainty curled inside me, like something alive and unpleasant.

"What does it mean?" Eve pointed to the third paragraph. "What baby? There was no birth at Highclere that year. Was it one of your parents' friends, perhaps?"

"I think she was—she must have been—pregnant. My mother. Before they left."

"Pregnant!" Eve repeated the word as though I'd spoken vulgarity. "But she was—old!"

My lips twitched downward. "She was only six years older than I am, Eve."

Eve clutched my arm. "Oh, I didn't mean you—of course *you* are not old. I'm certain you will someday be in the family way..."

I ignored her reassurances.

Had my mother died while carrying my sibling?

But there was more in these lines, much more, that made no sense.

I should have felt joy at having something new of my mother's to cherish. I had so very little left of family. But the paper filled me with an inexplicable dread. And one crushing question about myself.

I folded the paper into a careful square, tucked it into the tiny beaded bag Eve lent me for dinner, and steeled my voice. "We should go down. Your parents will be waiting."

How I wished I could instead escape back to my little book-lined room at the American House, to settle the questions plaguing me, to puzzle it out. But perhaps I could get a partial answer downstairs.

Eve studied my eyes for a moment, gripped my cold fingers, but friend that she was, she had sense enough to let it drop. For now.

Eve's parents, Porchy and Lady Almina, were sipping *aperitifs* among potted palms on the verandah with Herbert Winlock from the Met and Dr. Johnnie, Porchy's physician. Despite years of ill health, Porchy modeled tenacity and grace in the face of pain, and simply brought Dr. Johnnie as a companion on every trip, to monitor his ongoing health concerns.

Each of the travelers had their chair turned outward, watching the blue-green ribbon of the Nile, speckled with boats, from flat-bottomed wooden *dahabeyah* houseboats carrying wealthy and leisurely travelers, to Thomas Cook steamers puffing past with ordinary tourists. Tiny, white-sailed feluccas bobbed among the larger ships, searching for a good catch.

Against that backdrop, in his pinstriped suit and cravat, Lord Carnarvon looked like a portrait of wealth and elegance.

Porchy was the reason I was here in the Valley of the Kings, digging for buried treasure. He'd saved the poor American orphan from being turned out into the streets of London as a teen, begging for my next meal. He seemed fond of me, but I tried not to love him. I was not his daughter.

And intimidating as she was, Lady Almina had been the closest thing to a mother to me, all those summers at Highclere, after my parents' strange death.

June 8, 1905.

My skin tingled uncomfortably, and I shook off the dark thoughts. Almina had taught me much, especially during the war, about what it meant to be a lady of both grace and strength. We had worked side-by-side then, along with Dr. Johnnie, to offer help to wounded soldiers. Now, here in Egypt, I hoped to one day make her proud. What would she say of the suspicion pounding behind my eyes?

Eve placed a hand on her father's shoulder and bent to brush a kiss against his cheek. "You look positively better in this sun, Pugs."

"Ah, there you are, girls." Porchy patted Eve's hand. "I was just telling Winlock here how good it is to be back. This is going to be the year, I can feel it."

I turned away from the father-daughter affection, including Eve's silly nickname for Porchy, to nod a greeting to Winlock.

We seated ourselves at the linen-covered table. An attendant in a red fez was beside us at once, filling our glasses from a cut-glass decanter.

Almina's gaze traveled to my bare ankles. A raised eyebrow, but she was too gracious to make a public comment.

Herbert Winlock was a bit older than me—late thirties, perhaps—but already nearly bald, with a high forehead that gave his head an egg-like appearance, and a bushy mustache hiding thin lips.

He smiled knowingly and winked at me. "We shall see, Porchy. We shall see."

I warmed to Winlock's acknowledgment but looked away.

"Many an adventurer has thought the same," Winlock said. "But if anyone can prove old Davis was wrong, and the Valley's not dug out, it'll be you and Carter."

"We'll be a team for the history books, I promise you." He raised a glass. "Carter and Carnarvon. A legacy in the sand."

Winlock chuckled. "Sounds like you have your next book title."

"Speaking of legacies," I twirled my glass and kept my voice light. "I've been thinking lately about Belzoni." I bumped Eve with my leg under the table to keep her quiet. "How long did he dig before he made his first big find?"

It had been nearly ten years since I finished my Egyptian studies at Oxford, and famous names, like Giovanni Battista Belzoni, remained in my memory, along with dates that never seemed to grow fuzzy. I had an odd ability to retain that sort of thing, and disliked appearing unknowledgeable. But I needed to get the conversation started.

"Belzoni?" Winlock raised his eyebrows. "Haven't thought about that chap in years. Hmm, that big, bumbling fool was only here a year or two before he started tripping over tombs at every turn, I believe."

"Yes, of course, and that was in…"

"1817 or thereabouts, I believe. At least when he found KV17."

"Did he have children? A son, or grandson maybe, who continued his work?"

Winlock squinted, then shook his head. "He had a passel of children, I believe, but none who ever worked here."

I nodded and took a sip of my chilled white wine with trembling fingers.

Dr. Johnnie remained silent, but watched my shaking hand with a quizzical look.

Eve would no doubt be even more confused by my mother's hint that they would be meeting Belzoni in person.

My brain was making sense of it.

And it was a shock. A shock that went down into my chest, colder than the wine, and then heated my belly.

No longer able to remain nonchalant, I blinked back stinging tears and shoved my chair back from the table.

"Excuse me, please."

I fled the verandah, and didn't stop through the lobby, carried by a deep need for the safety and privacy of my room.

Eve might feel confusion.

But I had just been given the most ground-shaking information of my life.

A revelation that changed everything I knew about my parents. Everything I knew about myself.

A revelation that resurfaced an episode eight years ago that still had the power to frighten me.

∿

Even eight years later, I knew what I had to do.

The irrational suspicion took root in my mind and wouldn't let me go.

I spent a restless night in my room at the American House, the words of my mother's journal page pulsing in my head.

A trip to Venice, with hints she would *meet* Belzoni, who had been dead over eighty years by that time. I double-checked.

Was it possible? Could that experience on my first day in the tomb of Seti eight years ago have been real? If my parents could visit Giovanni Belzoni in Venice, could I have visited a Nineteenth Dynasty funeral in Egypt?

Should I talk it out with Eve? An objective voice would be welcome, but could I trust anyone with something so bizarre?

There was only one way to know. I had to try again.

When dawn finally lit the lower edge of my window frame, I read my mother's journal page for the hundredth time, though it was nearly memorized. Then, avoiding the dining room where the Burtons and the Mace family typically took an early breakfast, I slipped out of the American House.

A few Egyptian men were always hanging about with a broken-down car, or even a horse or donkey, hoping to catch an American willing to pay for a ride to a digsite. This morning I got lucky and found one of my favorites, Chefren, in the dirt road in front of the building, leaning against his dusty '07 Fiat and smoking. He straightened at my exit from the verandah, tossed the stubbed cigar to the ground, and opened the rear door with a flourish fit for a queen.

"King's Valley, Chefren. KV17."

"Indeed, my lady."

As the crow flies, the American House was probably only a kilometer from Seti's tomb. But the narrow valleys between limestone cliffs necessitated a route so circuitous it quadrupled the distance. I checked my pocket watch twice as we threaded through the cliffs. I needed to be back early, to perfect the last touches on the sketches Albert Lythgoe, head of the Met's Egyptian Expedition, had promised to review this afternoon, and this jaunt would likely make me late to work. Howard hated lateness.

When we reached the entrance at last, I left Chefren and trekked down into the recesses of the longest tomb ever excavated in the Valley.

Six hundred kilometers to the north, the pyramids in Lower Egypt were built to house the mummies of pharaohs and were already a thousand years old when Egyptians began digging elaborate tombs underground here in the Theban valley, in hopes of better preservation. Egypt defined itself through its pharaohs, but how many slaves had labored here, pouring out the resources of their lives? Had they been the Israelite slaves of Old Testament fame?

Seti's tomb sported a metal grille at the entrance, but it was never locked. The tomb had been emptied long ago, and contained nothing to steal.

Down multiple descending stone corridors, followed by steeper steps cut into the rocks. My swinging lantern illuminated the still-vivid blues and golds and reds of mural-coated walls. When Belzoni discovered the tomb over a hundred years ago, some of the artists' paints and brushes still littered the floor.

By the time I reached the echoing burial chamber, I was having second thoughts.

Eight years ago, on my first day in Egypt as scholar rather than student, I stood in this very place, my back against a painted wall, and experienced a terrifying hallucination.

Was trying to recreate that moment the worst idea of my life?

I was wasting valuable time on this insane notion.

Or worse, about to embark on something utterly inconceivable.

CHAPTER FOUR

October 21, 1914
Eight Years Earlier
Valley of the Kings, Egypt

*M*y first day in Egypt as a bona fide Egyptologist.
I breathed in the silence of the tomb, a sacredness that extended like an unbroken chain from antiquity to this day.

This day, more than six years in the making. Through my university studies, through two years waiting for Howard Carter to agree.

I had dressed this morning in clothes arranged last night, trembling fingers fumbling at the buttons of the starched white shirt, then jammed the shirttails into a pair of brown men's trousers, and laced my sturdy boots. Positioned a tan fedora that had been my father's over my unruly dark hair. Pocketed a log journal in the inner recess of my leather jerkin.

The effect, when I had glanced in the mirror, had seemed official enough.

Behind me in the tomb, Howard was pointing out some

feature of the wall-paintings, but the words didn't penetrate the buzz of adrenaline in my head.

KV17. Belzoni's Tomb. I was truly here.

Over sixty tombs had been found in the King's Valley, with a numbering system dating back almost a hundred years. Belzoni had found several of them, but this tomb of Seti I, a Nineteenth Dynasty pharaoh, was his first.

And my first.

We had descended four separate sets of stairs connected by three long corridors, and crossed a six-pillared hall to reach the vaulted burial crypt, deep in the heart of the earth. Now, the tomb stretched behind me over one hundred meters, every wall of its eleven chambers and side rooms covered with such well-preserved paintings, they still looked fresh.

I turned a slow circle in the center of the celestial vault, shaky hand holding the lantern high above my head to reveal the vibrant blue of the faraway ceiling, spattered with bright gold constellations. The sarcophagus resided in a London museum, but the chamber still held the hush of death.

Howard poked a finger toward the top of the wall. "The goddess Ma'at."

Her outstretched blue and green wings spread truth and justice over the lower registers of paneled paintings.

I reached a tentative hand to touch the Esna shale wall. At its cool solidity, a chill swept over me, electric with connection. I kept my fingertips on the rock, half-listening to Howard talk of the damage done by Champollion a century ago, when he removed a wall panel.

I didn't want a lecture. I'd heard years of lectures. I wanted to *experience.* I wanted to see and feel, to taste and smell and hear the past. To let it run through me like a current.

Something caught my eye in the sand. Had it been here when this place was new? With my hand still braced on the wall, I bent to retrieve it. Oh, how I wished I could have been here then, to get one last glimpse of Seti I's gloriously-wrapped mummy, before it was hidden for three millennia.

As I bent, Howard was saying "This blasted war is going to ruin our efforts."

My fingers closed around the tiny object. But then it blurred and surged, warped and twisted, like waves rising off hot sand. My stomach surged with it. My vision blanked for a fraction and then cleared. I righted myself quickly, carefully. Praying I wouldn't be sick here in an empty ancient tomb, in front of Howard, on my first day.

But Howard was gone. And the tomb was not empty.

Around me, a crowd of women, dressed in tightly-fitting white linen dresses, keened and wailed around an open granite sarcophagus. Their kohl-painted eye makeup ran down olive cheeks.

I looked down to the object in my hand, but it was only a smooth, black stone. Dark against the unfamiliar white linen of my own tight dress. *Dress?* My head swam and stomach surged again. My breath was a shallow pant, my ears rang with the sound of the wailing. Nostrils filled with the sharp spice of burning incense and the tang of fresh blood.

What is this? What...?

A deep-throated recitation began behind me. I spun to the looming presence of a horrible black jackal.

No, not a jackal. A priest with jackal-headed mask, incanting from the Book of the Dead.

The incense lay thick on my tongue and stung my eyes. I swallowed and blinked. It all remained. A dream, but I could not wake. My chest constricted around my breath, trembled like a palm frond in a sandstorm.

I needed to get out. Outside, where I could breathe and think.

My feet were rooted to the sand. Fear and confusion rendered me immobile.

Until the crowd surged, and thrust me against the open sarcophagus.

My elbow scraped stone. I clutched at the pain and felt a sticky wetness.

The women swayed. The wailing and singing crescendoed and the mob pushed inward.

I would be crushed.

The urge to flee swept me like a cold wave, and the jostling unmoored me from my position.

I pushed outward, wove through the crowd, along the corridors, retracing the multiple sets of stairs. Finally, out into the night air.

Beyond a cluster of crying women, the tomb opened to the silk-purple sky, strewn with a sprinkling of silver stars. Another crowd of mourners gathered, some singing and others bending to sweep up dirt with their fingers and fling it over their heads.

A pair of oxen loitered with a wooden sledge harnessed behind them, presumably the way the massive sarcophagus had been moved into the tomb.

I backed away, kept retreating, until I brushed against the lip of the tomb entrance.

This was no better. I had to understand. Needed answers.

Needed to make all of this *stop*.

I shoved back against the clot of women behind me, fueled by irrational anger. Or maybe rational. I was in no position to judge.

Back down, down to the vaulted burial chamber, searching for logic.

The crowd yielded against the pressure and a way opened for me to reach the wall where it began. I lurched for it, spun, and pressed my back against the painted stone. Braced both hands against it, head bent downward. Closed my eyes. Repeated a single word like a chant. *Stop.*

The sharp-pitched wails, the creepy recitation, the hum of a mob, it all ceased, like a knob on the wireless clicked off, leaving a hollow silence. Light flashed against my closed eyes, illuminating snatches of muddled scenes, like someone else's memories. The skirt of a red dress. My mother's. Her hand crushing mine. The spinning vertigo returned, along with the nausea.

I tightened my own hands into fists. Breathed the first vague prayer I'd said since childhood. Opened my eyes.

Something caught my eye in the sand.

"This blasted war is going to ruin our efforts."

I blinked. Ignored the small black stone. There was no way I was going to pick that thing up again.

But why had Howard said it — those words about the war — twice?

Had he repeated himself?

What seemed more true was that the bizarre, perhaps psychotic, episode had cranked the film of my life backward a frame or two.

I reached for my injured elbow.

The skin was unbroken. There was no pain.

None of it had been real. *It was not real.*

Some kind of... waking dream... brought on by the excitement of my first official day on a dig.

"Miss Aldridge? What's wrong? You'd best not be overcome by the work expected of you."

I licked dry lips, shook my head, and turned to Howard with a smile. "Nothing. Just happy to be here. A little — overwhelmed — I suppose."

Howard grunted, his usual mixture of acknowledgment and disapproval.

It was not real.

I was in Egypt, yes. But not ancient Egypt. Not at the burial of Seti I, Nineteenth Century pharaoh. That was madness, and I was not mad.

I refused to let my love for this place be my undoing.

And yet, the fear... the fear remained.

❧

February 9, 1922

As it turned out, the blasted war *did* ruin our efforts in Egypt.

Only a week after arriving, fresh-faced and confident I'd be useful, then terrified by the "incident," in Seti's tomb, I was bustled back to England. Japan was attacking China and the Germans were calculating the use of poison gas. Demonstration marches in London demanded rights for women to serve in war industries. But my dream was put on hold for almost four long years, years spent in part at Highclere-turned-hospital, nursing wounded soldiers.

Now, in our fourth season digging since the war, Carter had found almost nothing, Porchy's funding was running out, and I had convinced myself the episode in the tomb eight years earlier was the product of an over-eager young scholar beginning her life's work at last.

The foolish girl had receded into memory.

The moments in this tomb that October day had not. Nor my suspicion that more than simple imagination was involved.

Today, alone in Seti's tomb, with Chefren waiting far above, I tried to recreate everything my memory held. Stood in the same position, flattened a palm against the shale wall, bent to pluck something from the sand. Focused my mind on my desire to see Seti's mummy before it was lost for centuries.

But there was nothing.

I pulled myself to standing.

Tried again.

Foolish girl. Did I really think coming here was going to... what? Take me back in time?

I'd read a shiny paperback copy of H.G. Wells' *The Time Machine* when I was a kid, a few years after it was published. My father gave it to me as a Christmas gift. The idea captured my imagination, along with the imagination of everyone who read it. What if we truly could climb into a machine and travel through time?

Now, standing in this silent tomb with chilled fingers, thinking of my dead parents and the Egyptian mummy who'd lain here, it seemed all the silliness of a wishful girl who grew up to be a wishful woman.

Ridiculous.

CHAPTER FIVE

Summer, 1922
Highclere Castle, Hampshire, England

*A*nd so I put aside my mother's journal page, and my preposterous conjecture, and went back to work, striving for the excellence necessary to make a name for myself.

The Carnarvon family returned to England.

Howard and I dug in the sand for another six weeks. Found nothing. Again.

The dig season drew to a close in April as the sun grew hot, and I was back at Highclere for the summer, taking advantage yet again of the generous hospitality of Lord Carnarvon and Lady Almina. And once more putting my dream to carve out a place of value in the world on hold.

During one of my first free afternoons, I slipped away to one of the rarely-used bedrooms on the third floor and knelt in front of a locked trunk.

When my parents abandoned me here at age fifteen, to take their trip to Venice in '05, they promised to be back in three months. They took clothing and personal items, but left the rest behind at Highclere Castle, in the rooms where Lord Carnarvon and the Countess had welcomed them, and me, for so many years.

They never returned.

Eventually Lady Almina and I donated their clothing to some of the poor tenants on the estate. The rest of it had been locked away in a trunk and stashed in this room.

This afternoon, I slotted the key into its narrow hole, lifted the lid, and then piece by piece, gently removed and set aside each fragment of my parents' lives, as I had done many times over the seventeen years since they'd died.

My mother's hairbrush, which she had loved and must have been sad to discover missing from her luggage after they left. A pretty glass bottle of her favorite perfume. I pulled the stopper and dabbed a tiny bit on my wrist, as I always did when looking through this trunk, and inhaled the scent of her. I set the perfume aside and pulled out a few well-loved books—*Gulliver's Travels*, a few by Rudyard Kipling. The tarnished metal tag worn by my father's favorite dog, with the engraved "Tarzan" still readable. A picture of my mother, looking so young, her name written in elegant script below the image.

And a tiny black-covered notebook, filled with tiny scribbles in two different hands, one young and one older. I paged through it, throat tight with emotion, scanning the special coded drawings no one but my father and I could decipher.

Holding the notebook, I relived that day years ago begging my parents not to leave me, to take me with them to Venice. My father's cold refusal, my mother's silence. The car rolling away, across the gravel curve of Highclere Castle.

I shook off the memory and set the book aside. It was the twine-tied bundle of letters that brought me to the trunk today.

Some of the correspondence was between one of my parents and colleagues in London or New York. These I set aside, at least for now, and pulled out a smaller packet of letters bound with a pink ribbon I had never felt free to untie.

Letters between the two of them, written during the infrequent separations when my father was teaching summer term at

Oxford and my mother remained in the cool confines of High-clere. I rubbed at the back of my neck and shifted position. What would it do to my heart, to read the affection between them? To read, perhaps, some mention of me. Or more painfully, no mention of me.

With my back braced against the wall beneath a stately window, and the afternoon sunlight warming my legs, I read them all within an hour or two, an occasional twinge of guilt interrupting my reading. But the letters were all I had left of their hearts.

When the reading was done, there was only one line, in one letter, that held any clue.

"I am missing you fiercely," my father wrote, "and our adventures. When I return, perhaps we can make our once-in-a-lifetime visit to Hatshepsut. I know it has always been your fondest wish, despite the dangers to mind and body."

Slight evidence, but enough to set the letter aside, and upon re-reading to feel the flutter of excitement in my chest.

He had not said "a visit to Hatshepsut's Mortuary Temple," as one would expect. Besides, by 1905 they had both worked with the archaeologist Édouard Naville, near the famous female pharaoh's temple at Deir el Bahri for three seasons. No, my father had said it would be a visit *to Hatshepsut.*

The phrase, including the idea the proposed visit would happen only once for them, cast a new light on my episode in Seti's tomb eight years ago, as well as the single page Eve had brought me in February.

Could this be the reason I was not able to recreate the experience in Seti's tomb? Was it possible to slip back past the centuries, but also true that time was like a river with many docks, and one could only visit a certain dock once in a lifetime?

Was I truly making this leap of logic? That my parents could travel through time? Or—even more unbelievable—that it was possible for me, as well?

And yet, somehow, I had always known. That moment in Seti's tomb. It was simply too real.

I knelt before the trunk again and ran my fingers over the metal latches, cool to the touch. I blinked away tears, silly after all this time.

"What secrets did you have, Mother? Father?"

And why did you take your secrets, but not your daughter, to Venice?

Questions with no answers. And unanswered questions never failed to aggravate me beyond reason.

But there was one question I *could* answer, as soon as I returned to Egypt.

If it were true that one could travel to the past, would it be possible for me to travel through the millennia again, if my chosen destination were different than the last time? If I chose a new "dock" at which to land?

I swiped away the useless emotion and placed the meager remnants of my parents' lives back into the trunk. Next season's digging, if we began in January as usual, was months away. What was I to do until then?

I had the wedding of Eve's brother, called "Porchy" like his father, to distract me in July. It was a splendid affair at Seamore Place in London, the house Almina's father, banking tycoon Alfred de Rothschild, had left her in his will a few years ago. Over a thousand people were invited to the bash.

But although the younger Porchy's new wife Catherine was an American like Lady Almina, the similarity ended there. Almina had brought the Rothschild money to her marriage. Catherine had no money. And it was that sad fact that led to the afternoon which was the first time I ever heard Howard Carter and the Earl yell at each other.

We were all at Newbury Races, watching horses with names like Weathervane and Poisoned Arrow, through a summer drizzle that left everyone's nerves frayed. For some reason, Lord Carnarvon had picked today to tell Howard he was giving up. Giving up Egypt and their shared dream of finding the illusive, and perhaps illusionary, pharaoh called Tut-ankh-amun.

I sat with Eve and her mother, just behind the two men, and could see Howard's ears grow pink with anger.

"So, that's it, then? You're just calling it quits?"

Porchy dropped his chin to his chest. "I simply can't afford it, old man. I've spent a fortune—" at this, he barely glanced backward at Lady Almina, whose father's money it mostly was— "more than fifty thousand pounds at this point. It's been fifteen years. When are we going to face the truth—"

"Tommyrot!" Howard's favorite expression erupted from between clenched teeth. "He's out there!" He pounded a fist into his palm, his racing form crumpled between tight fingers. "I know it. We have to give it more—"

"More! I've sold three houses, man. Egypt's a sovereign state now the war's over, and all the excavation concessions are going to the museums and the government. What more can we give?"

But Howard was shaking his head. "There is still more to dig. Under KV9. The workmen's huts. You know there is. All those embalming goods Davis found years ago."

"And perhaps Davis is right. He's already found our pharaoh, plundered in KV54."

"KV54's not a tomb! It's a pit! And how do you explain the faience cup ten years ago, with Tut-ankh-amun's name, near KV9—"

"Fine. Let's say he's still there, under KV9. How are we going to dig it? Ramesses VI is covered in tourists for the entire season."

"We'll start early. Autumn, even. Beat the tourist crowd."

The Earl sighed. "I am sorry, Howard. You know it's been my dream as much as yours. But I must think of my family."

"Then I'll fund it myself. One last season."

I had watched this exchange with bated breath. My own future hung on the outcome, though I had nothing to contribute. Too bad I didn't come from wealthy American money. My parents had been scholars and had left me nothing but books, journals, and a bottle of perfume. My whole education and training were tied up in archaeology. But more than that, now

TRACY HIGLEY

that I had found my father's letter and my mother's journal page, I suspected my entire life might hinge on my making my own discovery in Egypt that could give my life meaning. I simply had to get back there, to test the theory that had been developing since I'd read my parents' letters.

"I'll take the girl." Howard's thumb jabbed back toward me. "She's smart, and she'll work for free."

The Earl was watching the horses, but his thoughts were clearly in the desert sands. "I can't let you do that, old boy. Fund it yourself." He huffed out a rueful laugh. "You'd go bankrupt." He smoothed his mustache with a thumb and forefinger. "All right. You have your one more season."

Howard's shoulders visibly dropped.

I felt my own relief, loosening the muscles that had gone tight in my neck.

One more season.

CHAPTER SIX

November 4, 1922
Valley of the Kings, Egypt

*O*ne more season.

We attacked it early, in November. Beating the tourists, as Howard promised. Baking in the unavoidable heat that I loved far better than the raw mists of England.

Lord Carnarvon held back at Highclere, along with his wife and daughter, staying cool and waiting for news.

I returned to Egypt with the unacceptable irritant of unanswered questions, a determination to learn the truth about my parents, and a mostly-mad plan to get answers.

I was about a week behind Howard, traveling alone, to the scandalized glances of my countrymen and their wives on the train to Southampton, on the boat across the Channel, on another train to reach the French Riviera, and on yet another boat across the Mediterranean from Marseilles, finally reaching Alexandria on Egypt's northern coast, then taking a train south to Cairo to join Howard. A repetitive and tiresome journey, but I used the time to study and prepare for the season, trying to avoid thinking on questions of hallucinations and trips to the past.

By Wednesday, the first of November, we were staking tents in the Valley and commissioning our foreman Ahmed Gerigar to scrape together as many laborers as he could find. The anti-British sentiment since the end of the war, combined with the lackluster success of Carter's previous digging seasons, had convinced many of our former laborers that digging for the British was either traitorous or fruitless.

Time was running out, not only for our team to make a discovery, but for me to prove myself professionally. Once we were shut down, I'd never get another chance.

And so, perhaps, I had only this one season to test the hypothesis about my parents I'd formed during the summer at Highclere, plus prove myself a legitimate Egyptologist. Two desires, in competition for my attention.

By Saturday, I'd been in Egypt for six days, in the Valley for four, and still unable to steal away to the "research" that occupied my thoughts even more than the dead pharaoh we were chasing—a chance to understand, and even connect, with my dead parents.

Today I arrived late, dressed in my usual tan trousers, white shirt, and wide-brimmed fedora. I joined Howard at the trench.

Howard stood with hands on hips, surveying the start of the day's work. His own hat, a Homburg with a stylishly rolled brim, still sat jauntily on his head, and his shirtsleeves were unstained. A sure sign he hadn't yet yanked a trowel from a laborer to show him a better technique.

Last night we'd finished removing the remains of the workmen's huts, a triangular area never before dug out because it was the entrance to the popular Ramesses VI tomb. Today we would start clearing the site down to bedrock.

Howard half-turned his head at my approach, then went back to his study.

"He's here, Sahara. I know it."

"Then we'll find him."

I felt, rather than saw, his sad smile. We both knew the stakes. And this work was Howard's legacy, his very identity.

We remained there, in an odd moment of camaraderie. Howard and I were two of a kind—independent and not requiring friendship within our work—and we rarely shared feelings.

So when would I be able to get away, to pursue my own agenda? I needed to be on hand for assigning dig teams as we got started, and my free time was severely limited. Even on Friday, when most of our crew was observing their holy day and our work was less vigorous, Howard kept me busy sketching small finds.

The sun already dampened my neck. I should never have cut my hair to shoulder length. My efforts to be fashionable meant I could no longer tie the heavy waves off my neck.

A shadow fell across the work area in front of us. An unusual silhouette, unlike the tunic and turban-wrapped *tarbush* of our laborers. I turned to the man behind us.

He was taller than average and broad in the shoulders. Hatless, with hair the color of coal falling across his forehead and dark-rimmed glasses. A camera dangled from a strap around his neck, silver against an ivory linen jacket and buttoned waist-coat that looked rumpled enough to have been pulled from luggage only minutes ago. A cobalt blue tie was jammed under the waistcoat. The entire effect was jarring, as though another culture had dropped from the sky. I guessed his age to be about the same as mine, early thirties perhaps.

I slipped the masculine fedora from my head.

Howard turned to face the newcomer, hands still braced against his hips, and scowled. "No reporters down here."

"Is it true this will be your last season in the Valley?" His accent was American. He stretched to look past the two of us.

Howard flicked a hand at him. "We're not doing interviews, chap. You need to shove off."

The reporter ducked his head, hiding an odd half-smile.

"Let me watch from a distance, then?" He pointed to a low

rise of sand about twenty meters away. "I'll plant myself over there. Get some wide shots."

Howard shrugged. "Suit yourself. The work's much less exciting than you think."

The stranger thrust out one hand to Howard and lifted a plastic-encased badge on a lanyard with the other. "Jack Moretti, by the way. *Philadelphia Inquirer.*"

Howard shook the hand grudgingly. "Philadelphia."

"Yes, sir. Pennsylvania."

"Hmm. Well, no following us around and getting underfoot. I have work to do." He jutted his chin toward me. "Sahara, you keep an eye on him. Make sure he doesn't get too nosy."

I wanted to comment that our visitor could follow me around any day. I stifled a laugh at the fit Howard would throw.

Howard turned on us both and headed back to his tent, muttering "Americans" under his breath like a curse.

I never took it personally.

Beside me, Jack's hand was now extended my way.

I stepped closer and returned the strong handshake. He smelled of spice, like cinnamon. I breathed it in and doubted I smelled nearly as good.

"Jack Moretti."

I gave him what I hoped was a superior smile. "Sahara Aldridge."

"Miss Aldridge." He bowed his head over my hand. "Nice to see a woman out here."

"Decorating the landscape, you mean?"

He arched his eyebrows. "Actually, I meant it's good to see a woman getting a chance to prove herself in a man's world."

"Ah." I jammed the hat back on my head.

He glanced at the digsite. "Don't suppose I could follow *you* around? Get an exclusive?"

Had he read my mind? "You'd have to trade your camera for a shovel."

He laughed, an oddly musical sound, given his size. Rather like a trombone, perhaps. His eyes were nearly as blue as his tie, unusual for someone with such dark hair. "Sounds like a good deal, if I get to work with you."

I looked askance at his linen suit and brown-and-white wingtips. "I was joking. No reporters inside the perimeter. In fact, you'd better get yourself to that sand mound before Howard takes a shovel to *you*."

His blue eyes held my gaze for an extra beat beyond politeness, then he grinned and shrugged. "Your loss. But just so you know, I was the star of the playground sandbox."

"Hmm, I'm sure you were." I tried to turn away. But those eyes.

"So how about dinner? Give me some background stuff. And maybe the personal interest side—you know, lady archaeologist, and all that."

And all that. I tilted my head and took another look at him. He seemed genuine enough. And he was American, like me. And yet not like me, since I'd lived in England since I was four years old and didn't really belong anywhere. "Sure. Dinner."

"Great! I'll pick you up at the…?"

I forced my attention to the worksite. "The Met's American House. Six o'clock. We could eat there if you like."

"Not a chance. First dates have to be impressive."

I raised my eyebrows at the phrase. "I thought this was an interview."

"Right." He nodded with mock seriousness. "Completely professional."

"Alright, Mr. Professional. Get out of our digsite."

He retreated obediently to the rise of sand beyond our work area.

I returned to the worktable where each of the finds from the past three days were scattered, and started on my assigned sketches. My artistic talent, despite Howard's occasional tutoring, was nothing compared to the director's, whose drawings of finds and tomb walls were published in books. But then, most of my drawings were of a different sort, and for what I felt was a higher purpose—one that fired my blood every day I spent on this site.

I tried to ignore the obvious way Jack Moretti watched me. Why me, and not the center of the digging activity? I was here to work, not flirt. And if I were going to succeed in the unique contribution I intended to give the entire profession, I needed to keep a close eye on both the laborers and their methods.

The sun slid higher in the sky, and though I glanced at Jack frequently from under lowered lids, he never left his position on the mound, only paced, removed his hat every so often to swipe at his forehead, and snapped the occasional photograph. Did he plan to stay the season?

Mid-morning, another man joined Jack on the sand mound. He was hatless, and his orange-red hair blended into the desert sand behind him. The two talked for several minutes, with Jack's hands gesturing expressively, until it seemed Jack chased the red-haired man off.

A few minutes before our dig crew would have quit for lunch, the boy Nadeem, still an eager worker and even taller than last season, ran toward my canopy.

"Alsahra'!"

"Nadeem, did you bring the water to the men as I asked?"

Jack took the opportunity, perhaps of my distraction, to approach my worktable as well.

I eyed the reporter, then held my arm wide and pulled Nadeem to my side. "What is it? Is there a problem with the water?"

Nadeem watched Jack with narrowed eyes and said nothing.

I glanced between them. Howard had trained Nadeem well.

I bent slightly to bring my ear to his mouth, hidden behind his hand.

His breath was hot against my ear. "We have found something."

I nodded. The past few days, as my worktable attested, had yielded a smattering of unimportant finds.

But Nadeem was not finished. He stood on his toes once more and whispered.

"A *step*, my lady. I believe we have found a step."

My stomach dropped, then flipped. My breath caught in my chest.

With laborers spread over the sand, Howard still hoped the section under the huts of workers who'd built the tomb of Ramesses VI would be our best chance. We'd come early to avoid the tourists, hoping against reason to find the tomb of the mysterious pharaoh, hints of whose existence had teased us for years.

And the first sign of an undiscovered tomb was always the same here in the Valley.

A step.

Suddenly, the two competing desires borne out of the past summer at Highclere came roaring at each other, neither willing to be denied.

CHAPTER SEVEN

November 4, 1922
Valley of the Kings, Egypt

I gave Nadeem's shoulder a quick squeeze, then turned on Jack Moretti and pointed.

"Back where you came from."

"Ah, come on. Give a fella a break."

Nadeem had my hand and was tugging.

I scowled at Jack.

He raised his hands in surrender and took a few steps backward.

"Show me," I said to Nadeem.

But there was no need to be led by the boy. A cluster of laborers buzzed around the deep trench, with more appearing every moment.

I knew this last season must be about proving I could make a unique contribution to the field. But I hoped to also learn the truth about my mother's journal page, testing a theory too ludicrous to share with anyone.

The existence of a step changed everything.

This work we were doing, the legacy we could leave and the improvements we could make, this was where I needed to focus.

Howard and I reached the trench at the same moment. He met my glance and his eyes conveyed everything I felt. Four years of futile digging. Tenacious belief in our hunch. Hope and cynicism blended into something almost painful.

I motioned him to the ladder. Forget chivalry. Howard had invested his entire life in Egyptology. If we'd truly found a step, he should be the first one down.

He took a deep breath, turned and descended.

I followed quickly, trying not to step on his hands.

Ahmed was already protecting the area with his body, keeping back the day laborers. He waved to Howard. "Here, *sayidi*. Here. See what it is."

Howard dropped to his knees in the sand.

I joined him, breath suspended, our white-gloved hands brushing at sand, feeling the ledge of uncovered, sun-bleached limestone, scraping wider and wider without finding the end of it.

Howard bent until he was at eye level with the ninety-degree angle. His fingertips traced the edge like a blind man reading Braille.

"Is it natural?" My voice trembled. It was the only question that mattered. Nature often wore stone into sharp edges, or cleaved it into something resembling a ledge, fooling the amateur into believing he'd stumbled onto something hewn by man. Only a close examination would reveal the truth.

Howard, still crouched so low he was nearly lying on the ground, lifted his gaze to me. And shook his head.

His eyes were glassy with emotion. He whispered only one word. "Markings."

I blinked at my own tears and exhaled as though I'd been knocked flat.

The stone bore the marks of the workmen who had chiseled it.

Ahmed heard the whispered word as well. He sprang into action, his voice booming orders in Arabic to the workmen.

All attention would be focused here, in this place.

We had found a step, and a step most likely meant a tomb.

Whether the tomb was intact, that remained to be seen. Neither Howard nor I would even speak of that possibility, though it was, of course, foremost in our thoughts. The tomb of a royal, untouched by ancient or even medieval looters, had never been found in the Valley.

I glanced at the surface, where workmen yelled to each other and appeared like ants running to a picnic. This was their land, after all. Their heritage.

Among the dark, excited faces, another appeared that clearly did not belong. The reporter, Jack Moretti. He lifted his camera from where it hung around his neck.

"Hey!" I stood and pointed. "Get back where you belong!"

The workmen on either side of Jack may not have understood my English, but they understood my intent. Two men yanked him backward by the arms and dragged him from the trench.

He yelled in indignation.

I didn't care.

I turned back to Howard, to the step. This was our find. And it was not to be shared. Not yet.

In what felt like no time, Ahmed organized the men into a line that would have made Henry Ford proud. Except we were not assembling anything. We were deconstructing what millennia had built, the accretion of sand and pebbles over what was clearly being revealed as a series of steps that led deeper into the ground.

Howard and I worked with the men, sometimes directing but mostly on our knees, doing the work ourselves, to ensure it was done right. We scrabbled in the pale sand like children at play and I thought of Jack and his sandbox. Did he still watch from a distance?

We worked in a fevered haze of dust and expectation. Sweat

stung my eyes, plastered my shirt to my skin, and salted my lips. Even protected by gloves, my fingertips grew roughened and scraped.

Howard's sharply-parted hair stuck to his forehead and his hat lay half-buried beside him.

The trench became my entire world, as though nothing above existed and there was only the blossoming of one step, and then another, and another beneath us. The rhythmic sounds of scrape and tumble became hypnotic, as Egyptian, British, and American worked in harmony to cleave away basket after basket of debris. My chest hurt with the tendency to hold my breath through the achingly-slow progress.

The sun sank until it skidded, coral and pink, across the surface of the desert, and our trench was in shadow. Still we worked.

When the sun's light finally died, Howard called for torches.

Ahmed gripped Howard's shoulder and shook his head. The men were exhausted.

We all were.

We had carefully cleared the width of the steps, about two meters wide, and another two meters down the staircase. Our two-by-two hole had revealed five steps thus far. The rest would have to wait.

I climbed out of the trench, legs cramping on each rung of the ladder. I had never felt so tired yet exhilarated in my life.

Howard, Ahmed, and I regrouped in the twilight in front of Howard's tent, collapsed into dusty camp chairs and clinked glasses of amber Scotch Whiskey, poured from the bottle Howard kept stashed in a steamer trunk.

I held the glass in fatigued fingers, swirled the whiskey that smelled of oranges and wood, then leaned my head back, unable to hold myself upright. The stars were just appearing in the river of sky above us. I traced the Egyptians' constellations with my eyes—the Hippopotamus, the Apis Bull. Did the same stars wink down on the night this tomb was sealed?

Eventually, I hailed a horse-pulled carriage back to the American House, drifted half-conscious into the kitchen to pilfer a loaf of crusty bread and a jug of water, then staggered to my room. Within minutes I'd eaten enough to stop my stomach's complaints, peeled off my filthy clothes, and fallen into bed.

All thoughts of my summer discovery at Highclere, of my determination to test my theory, had been eclipsed by the day's find. Today's effort was the work I had come here to do. I was not here to pursue some wishful girl's fancy about her parents as heroes with a secret identity.

It was not until morning that I realized, with only a wisp of regret, I'd missed last night's "interview" with the handsome Jack Moretti.

CHAPTER EIGHT

A story that opens like Aladdin's Cave, and ends like a Greek myth of Nemesis cannot fail to capture the imagination of all men and women, who, in this workaday existence, can still be moved by tales of high endeavor and unrelenting doom.

Lady Winifred Burghclere,
sister of the Earl of Carnarvon

November 5, 1922
Valley of the Kings, Egypt

The sun rose scorching by eight the next morning, and found all of us at the discovered steps, once again digging down, revealing each step with frantic yet painstaking hands.

Howard barked at Ahmed, at me, even at himself.

I brushed at the corner of the latest step, trying to dislodge some stubborn debris.

"Faster!" Howard grunted. Then, "Careful!" in the next breath.

I scowled at him, on behalf of all of us. "Do you want to do this alone?"

He swiped his forehead with the back of his hand. "If that's what it takes to get it done right!"

The little clot of our best workers huddled around us, handing baskets upward to the waiting line of men and boys on the surface. They exchanged worried glances, like children watching their parents argue.

I stepped aside more than once to sketch and take notes on the process, drawing glares from Howard, who had little appreciation for my cause.

We dug downward to uncover each step, widening the trench toward the unseen floor of the staircase, waiting for each basketful of debris to uncover whatever the last step would reveal.

In mid-afternoon I was taking a break for a cool sip of water and moment of shade under one of the canopies, when a *whoop* went up from Ahmed.

I dropped my copper mug onto the table. It clanked and rolled to the sand. I ran for the trench.

We were ten steps down and still going, but the laborers clearing the area horizontally had encountered something more resistant than hard-packed sand and debris.

Howard was kneeling, one precarious knee on the tenth step and another on the intact earth. He grinned and motioned me forward.

I crouched beside him.

Using a brush in one hand, he scraped debris from the bank that buried the staircase. Slowly, his work revealed some kind of a solid wall.

I hardly dared to breathe. Had we reached the top of a door, a door that may block an undiscovered tomb? My mind and body stirred with a swirling mix of academic curiosity, professional excitement, and a feeling that seemed almost spiritual. Connection to the past, tangible enough to touch.

"You're blocking my light, Sahara."

Within minutes we dug deep enough to be certain. The flat surface rising perpendicular to the steps first became a heavy wooden lintel that signaled a door beneath, and then the door itself appeared, bit by bit, and began to reveal symbols. Hieroglyphs carved into the door to provide information and spells of protection by the gods.

I was not what most would consider religious, though I'd spent many Sunday mornings at St. Stephen's with my parents. If there was a God, a creator, I imagined he was largely disinterested in humanity, or at least in my life. But my non-religious tendencies seemed to flee in the face of the carvings.

We worked shoulder-to-shoulder, trusting no one else, brushing debris from the carved reliefs on the door.

At each recognized symbol, one of us breathed out a translation.

And then it was there in full, the official Necropolis Seal—the jackal-headed Anubis, divine protector of the necropolis, looming over nine bound captive enemies—proof it was an important tomb, quite possibly royal.

Howard sat back on his heels and whistled through his teeth. "God Almighty."

More prayer than expletive. While Howard's religious inclinations in England were as mine—mainly confined to the occasional obligatory Sunday service—here in Egypt every temple and mountain felt imbued with a sense of the supernatural, even the divine.

"Well," he sucked in a breath, "time to get destructive, I suppose."

It was the part of archaeology we hated most. To discover whatever treasure lay beyond, we would have to begin damaging the treasure that blocked it.

Using the smallest pick, Howard chipped at the upper left corner of the doorway, under the lintel, avoiding the seals.

Neither of us mentioned the slight difference in the stone at this spot, as though it had been cracked open and replastered. Our actions might be a repeat of long-ago tomb raiders. But the sealed door meant even if looters had gotten in, no one had left with anything larger than a fistful.

Howard kept chipping until a sizable hole opened. He poked the end of a long brush through the hole.

It hit resistance.

"Should we widen it?" We wanted the least destruction possible, but we had to know if the area behind the door was empty.

In answer, Howard began chipping again.

Minutes later, he pushed the end of his brush through the newly-cleared space. Still, resistance.

"Ahmed, have someone bring my electric torch."

A moment later he was lying on his side, training the beam of light through the hole.

"It's filled." He rotated, now lying on the ground, then lifted himself to elbows. "Has to be a passage behind the door, but they've filled it with rubble to prevent looting."

I covered my mouth with the back of a gloved hand.

But Howard was sharing my smile and scrambling to his knees.

"Disappointing, yes, and much more work, but—"

"But the tomb beyond is likely intact."

He slapped me on the back. The most affectionate gesture I'd ever received from the man.

We spent the rest of the afternoon digging out two more steps and further down the door.

And then we had no choice but to stop.

Professional protocols needed to be followed. The Frenchman who served as Director of Egyptian Antiquities, Pierre Lacau, had to be called in. But even more frustrating, Howard's patron, George "Porchy" Herbert, fifth Earl of Carnarvon, had gone back to England in February, and not yet returned for the season. We would have to wait, for him to be present when the door was opened.

We crawled up, out of the trench, to where Ahmed waited at the lip of the digsite.

Howard inhaled deeply, as though trying to draw courage, and nodded to Ahmed. "We'll have to fill it back in." His voice was thick with emotion.

I squeezed his arm, stepping outside my typical reserve in a moment of unusual camaraderie. But I felt like crying myself.

We couldn't take chances on twentieth-century tomb raiders beating us inside. We'd fill in the steps and set a guard, hopefully deterrent enough.

The wait for Porchy would feel like a century. Perhaps two or three weeks, depending on how fast he left England. We would spend the weeks in preparation, but it would be agonizing.

"At least the digging-out will be fairly quick once the Earl arrives." I was trying to encourage myself as much as Howard.

He swiped his forehead and replaced his hat. "Yes, we know what we're dealing with. And they won't pack the debris when they refill it."

"So what's the plan in the meantime?"

"Experts. Supplies. Paperwork. But you don't need to worry about any of it."

In other words, I'd get the grunt jobs while he ran around Cairo, making purchases and hob-nobbing with officials. So much for camaraderie.

I followed him toward his tent to further discuss.

The reporter, Jack Moretti, was waiting in the shade thrown by the canvas.

He wore the same linen suit as yesterday, this time with a grass-green tie stuffed under the waistcoat, a brown fedora perched at an angle on his head, and a pair of high boots more sensible than yesterday's wingtips.

I, of course, was as sweaty, dirt-streaked, and disheveled as ever.

Howard's brows drew together at the sight of him. "I thought I told you to stay clear."

Jack smiled, despite Howard's tone. "Not here to snoop, I

promise. Although by the looks of it, something exciting is happening."

Howard grunted. "What do you want?"

Jack flicked a glance at me. "The lady stood me up last night. Thought I'd convince her to give it another try."

I lifted my chin. "Sorry about that. The work went on longer than expected, and then I simply forgot." Never a bad idea to play hard-to-get.

Howard looked between both of us as though the idea confused him entirely. "We don't need any press, printing stories about our work. Not yet."

"I assure you, Mr. Carter, I will ask no inappropriate questions. Just general stuff, human interest kind of thing." His hand tapped a rhythm on his thigh, as if he could hear music we didn't.

Howard shrugged at me. "Do what you want."

I nodded to Jack. "Same time, same place?"

"Sounds great." He dipped his head toward Howard. "Appreciate it."

When Jack had headed back toward his waiting driver, Howard took a deep breath. "First things first, I guess. Need to telegraph Carnarvon and let him know what's going on."

He ducked into his tent, invited me to follow, and sat at the makeshift desk. He grabbed a fountain pen and scratched a few lines on a piece of lined yellow paper, then handed the page to me. "Too late to send it today, by the time I get into town. I'll do it it first thing tomorrow."

Breath held, I read the words both of us had dreamed for years we would one day send. I could almost hear the *tap-tap-tap* of the message being received across the ocean.

AT LAST HAVE MADE WONDERFUL DISCOVERY IN THE VALLEY. A MAGNIFICENT TOMB WITH SEALS INTACT. RE-COVERED SAME FOR YOUR ARRIVAL. CONGRATULATIONS. CARTER.

I exhaled, feeling a sense of peace and purpose come over me that I had not felt in all my life.

We would wait out the days in preparation, making certain everything was done in order, for the preservation of future generations.

But before that, I had an interview.

Definitely not a date.

CHAPTER NINE

November 5, 1922
Valley of the Kings, Egypt

What did one wear for an interview? If Eve had been here, she would have known exactly the right thing. But then, all my pretty things were Eve's castoffs, so something in the wooden wardrobe tucked into the corner of my room must be appropriate.

Why did I care? I knew better than to get distracted from my work. The last time I let myself be romanced, it had ended quite badly.

And the other distraction—my plans to test my theory about my parents here in Egypt—that one needed to be set aside as well.

Today's discovery must be my only focus.

Decked in a gauzy layered dress in shell pinks and sunset purples, I grabbed my hat and headed for the lamplit verandah of the American House. My shoulder felt light without my usual tanned satchel of books and journal, which I'd forced myself to leave behind.

I typically avoided the verandah at popular times of day, when the house residents, often led by Minnie Burton, socialized over chit chat about nothing.

No avoiding tonight, however.

Minnie perched in one of the oversized wicker chairs, ever-present pearls luminous at her throat, and tiny leather diary in hand. How many comings-and-goings were noted in that diary?

I smoothed my hair, arranged the straw hat with pink roses atop my head and smiled, then waited at the edge of the verandah that ran the length of the boarding house. Its series of stone arches looked out over a view toward the Valley, but tonight, only the barest hint of the hills traced a line across the dark sky.

A wood-bladed fan rotated in lazy circles over our heads, teasing the wisps of my hair that refused to cooperate with the Marcel-wave style I was going for.

Behind me, Minnie's voice bounced against the stones. "You look pretty this evening, my dear."

I half-turned and tried for a polite smile. "Thank you."

"That sun-kissed skin and those adorable freckles. You're like that pretty actress, Mary Pickford."

The rumble of a car and bounce of headlights in the distance promised rescue soon.

But Minnie wasn't finished. "So you're taking a break then, finally? Going out with the young people?"

I suppressed a laugh. There were no young people here. Certainly Minnie had noticed. The American House held about a dozen folks, mostly British and American archaeologists employed by the Met Museum in New York, none of them close to my age. And I wasn't sure I even qualified as "young people" anymore.

Jack saved me from an answer by arriving with the car and driver.

I gave Minnie a little wave and ran lightly down the few steps.

She was already cracking open her diary.

Jack wore a different suit this evening, a little more formal than the one I'd seen, this one looking more like it had been purchased this afternoon. Had he made an effort to look this good for my sake?

"Wow." He tipped his hat. "Miss Aldridge, you look smashing."

I smoothed my dress and shrugged. "Just wanted you to see I don't always look like the hired labor."

"Well then, success."

I fought the flush creeping up my neck.

He opened the car door, helped me climb up into the seat behind our driver, and joined me.

We exchanged a few general comments about Egypt as we wound through shadowy, fertile fields of sugarcane. I was conscious of the driver's listening ear. And of the warmth of Jack's arm against mine.

His leg bounced in his habit of never-ending motion.

Our driver dropped us at the ferry, and we crossed the Nile in about ten minutes. Neither of us spoke at the rail, but it was a comfortable, even companionable silence.

Careful, Sahara.

On the east bank, in the shelter of the Luxor Temple, another driver waited, smiling and bowing, this one with a horse-drawn carriage, the traditional *caliche*.

I raised my eyebrows.

Jack waved away my amusement. "I arranged with Lateef before I came to pick you up."

We traveled another fifteen minutes northward along the Nile, until it became clear our destination was the Winter Palace Hotel.

"I know you probably come here often. But I'm still getting to know the area, and it seemed the safest place to get a good meal." Jack hopped out, circled the *caliche* and opened my door.

"No apologies needed. I eat most meals in a tent. This will be a treat."

I waited on the sidewalk, turning my head toward a breeze that lifted the hair from my neck.

Jack circled the carriage, pressed some bills into the hand of the driver, then leaned in, to say something I could not hear.

The driver glanced at the money, then lifted wide eyes.

"*Sayidi!*" He threw his arms around Jack's neck, and actually kissed him.

Jack punched the man's arm lightly and returned to me.

"Jack, you clearly paid him too much. You need to be careful. Some drivers might take advantage—"

"I heard from another driver Lateef is going through a rough patch. Sick kid needs treatment." He shrugged. "If the money will do him more good than it'll do me, then he should have it."

I said nothing. The smoldering admiration for Jack's generosity was dangerous.

He held an arm toward the hotel entrance. "Shall we?"

The lobby buzzed with hotel guests leaving for the evening, wealthy Europeans and Americans waiting for tour guides to escort them to torchlit temples. High-heeled women on the arms of men in suits tapped their way across marble floors and tapestried rugs, some heading for the dining room.

Jack ushered me into the sumptuous dining room as well. During the day we would have seen a gorgeous view of the Nile through the floor-to-ceiling windows. Tonight, the low-hung chandeliers glowed warm, and the glass windows and gilded mirrors reflected a hundred tiny flickers. The room hummed with private conversations.

I caught a glimpse of myself in one of the tall mirrors as we were seated by a waiter in a red fez. Dark eyes looking a bit shadowed. But I looked like a girl on a proper date. For some reason, the thought made me queasy. Thankfully the windows were open, allowing that cool Nile breeze to flow through the dining room.

Jack had made a friend of the waiter by the time we were seated, sharing some kind of joke I didn't hear. But once we were settled, his attention quickly shifted to me.

"So," he leaned across the table, voice low, "I suppose it's too much to hope that you'll tell me about all the excitement the past few days?"

I pulled back, frowning. "You said you wouldn't—"

"Come on." He winked. "You can't blame a fella for trying. But, I promise, we'll make it general."

I said nothing, only narrowed my eyes at him. Secrecy was paramount at this stage of our discovery. Howard would kill me if I spilled too much. And he'd taught me the press was never to be trusted.

Jack laughed. "Fine. Tell me about yourself."

The waiter appeared again, filled glasses with water and handed us menus.

I studied the food choices.

When the lamb kebabs and rice pilaf had been ordered, a bottle of wine had been decanted, and an awkward silence had fallen across the table, Jack looked at me, head tilted. "Well?"

"Well, what?"

He sighed. "I feel like an archaeologist myself, here. You're making me dig for everything."

"Good joke."

He glanced at my serious face and grinned. "You're pretty intriguing, Sahara Aldridge, you know that?"

"I'm not. Really." I fidgeted with the heavy linen napkin on my lap. "Fine. Here you go... Born in America, sailed for England when I was four years old with my parents. My father was an archaeologist, wanting to work in Egypt."

"Your parents are here as well?" Jack took a sip of his water.

"No. They died when I was fifteen."

"Oh, I'm so sorry."

"Thank you."

"So, no family? Not even in America?"

"They didn't speak much of our life there. My grandparents are no longer with us." Change of subject, please.

"So, how did you come to be here in the Valley?"

"My mother and father were friends of Lord Carnarvon, who has been funding Howard's digs for years."

"Ah, yes, I've heard about him. Loves racehorses and race cars, doesn't he?"

"Among other things. After my parents died, Lord Carnarvon and his wife took pity on my sad state, and footed the bill for me to study Egyptology at Oxford. They also invited me to spend most summers at the family estate in England."

"Highclere Castle?"

I raised my eyebrows. "You are well-informed. Yes."

"I've seen photographs of Lady Evelyn. She seems lovely."

He pronounced her name in the American way—Ev-a-lynn— rather than the British Eve-lynn. A flicker of longing sparked in me, to be more American somehow. To belong there, perhaps.

"She is lovely. I grew quite fond of her. And during those summers when Howard Carter would visit, I tended to follow him around and pester him with a million questions. Eventually Lord Carnarvon convinced Howard to let me dig with him."

"Lucky girl."

I straightened, blood rising. "Luck had little to do with it. I graduated top of my class—"

"Whoa," Jack held up his hands. "Apologies. I didn't mean to imply—"

"No, it's fine." I slouched backward. "I'm a little sensitive, I guess. I take a bit of teasing at the American House. Most of the old boys think I should be back in England, attached to a husband and providing him with a house full of babies."

"And?"

I tasted the wine. "And what?"

"How do you feel about that? It sounds more like insulting than teasing."

I studied the table setting, the polished flatware and bone china plates. Noticed the clink of knives and forks against china around the room. Despite the high ceilings, the room seemed close and intimate and I suddenly felt overheated.

I didn't intend to talk about the details of my life with a

reporter. Was I so starved for attention that I'd started sharing personal information with the first interested stranger? Why the longing to tell him everything—the step, my mother's journal, my days in the war?

Inhaling a breath, I shrugged one shoulder and smiled. "I'm fine on my own. How about you? Is there a girl back in Philadelphia with a house full of your babies?"

Oh my stars, Sahara. Could you be more awkward?

"No girl. No babies. I don't stay in one place long enough for all that. I guess I'm having way too much fun. Following my curiosity."

"Hmm. Curiosity, I do understand."

"Yes?" He grinned. "How about fun?"

I felt my smile slip. "Don't meet many people interested in fun around here."

Our meal arrived, and Jack immediately sprinkled pepper over the lamb and rice, and the garlicky stew of tomatoes and spinach. He replaced the pepper, caught me staring, and lifted a forkful of rice in my direction. "I like to spice things up."

"I see that."

Over dinner I asked about Philadelphia, about America, about anything far-removed from the twelve steps and the door that lay across the Nile, waiting for us in the Valley.

Dessert arrived, a delicious almond tart with apricot preserves, along with strong coffee. I made a mental note to try to duplicate the recipe in one of my late night pastry sessions alone in the American House kitchen. I moaned in delight over the first taste, to Jack's amusement and my embarrassment.

"Sweets are kind of my weakness."

"I see that."

"So, how long have you been a reporter?"

He scratched at his jaw and looked away. "I guess I should come clean. I'm really more of a photographer than a reporter."

"Write a story about your pictures, or take pictures of your story. Doesn't seem like it makes much difference." I watched his eyes for a reaction.

His smile was sad and distant. "I suppose it wouldn't seem to make a difference. But one is a wordsmith and the other is more of... an artist."

The last word emerged quietly. Almost painfully. And I felt like Jack Moretti had just given me a little glimpse into his soul.

"So then, why the story? Why not just document the work here with photographs?"

"For one thing, it's not about documenting as much as... illuminating. Giving people a glimpse at beauty. At something *true*."

"Sounds like you should be focused on taking pictures, and forget the reporting, if that's the thing that makes you feel valuable." I spoke the words carefully, aware we had gotten personal.

The brightness in his eyes dimmed. "Not much luck being taken seriously in that regard."

"I do some drawing myself."

"Not surprised, with those elegant fingers."

I gave him an eye-roll and slid my hands under the table.

"I'm determined to continue the work my parents were passionate about—documenting the *process* of archaeological work, not just the finds themselves, so we can make improvements. So much has already been lost to methods that were anything but meticulous, and even destructive." My fists tightened in my lap, and I fought to keep my voice quiet in describing the cause that fueled me. "Archaeologists are so eager to uncover treasures, they neglect what can be learned along the way. But there is so much more. If I can document and show the process by which we work—" I closed my lips and shook my head. "I'm sorry, I'm rambling."

"No, I admire that." Jack lifted his coffee cup in a toast. "And I admire you, honestly. I've never met anyone so intensely committed to their work. Your father taught you this love of Egyptology, but even without him, you're out here all on your own, in this challenging place, living an adventure. And you're making a contribution, so you're one of the lucky ones."

I glanced toward the windows, inhaling cool air in hopes of

staving off a ridiculous blush. I was unaccustomed to taking compliments from very attractive men.

"But what about you? You came to Egypt to take photographs. Of the Nile? The Valley? Or of a digsite?" I reached for my own coffee.

"Yes." He smiled. "All of it. And of you."

I swallowed the coffee too hot, too soon, and coughed. "Of me?"

He reddened slightly and looked away. "Of... the unusual archaeologist here..."

I set the cup down with a coffee-sloshing clank. "Are you saying you came from Philadelphia to Luxor specifically to take pictures—or write a story—about *me*?"

He sighed. "More coming clean, I suppose. Yes, I knew about you before I came."

I forced myself to breathe. Had I let myself hope his interest was of a personal sort? Stupid.

"I highly doubt news of my unremarkable career has found its way to America!"

"No, not like that." He ran a hand through his dark hair, sighed, and studied the far wall. "It was my aunt. She told me about you. She met you once. Thought you were interesting. She —checked up—on you from time to time, to see what you were doing."

I didn't know whether to be flattered, terrified, or angry. I settled for questions.

"Your aunt? She met me?"

He brought his focus back to my face. "At Highclere. When you were about fifteen, I believe."

I felt my brow furrowing, my memory casting back to that time. The year my parents died.

June 8, 1905.

"What was her name?"

"Giada. Giada Moretti."

The name hit me like a jug of ice water. I hadn't thought

about that woman in more than a decade. Not even when Jack Moretti introduced himself.

But now, with Jack in Egypt, and with what I'd recently uncovered about my parents...

It was too strange. Too coincidental.

And I needed to get out of here.

CHAPTER TEN

August, 1905
Highclere Caste, Hampshire, England

Giada Moretti showed up one afternoon at Highclere during my summer break from boarding school.

To a fifteen-year-old, her name sounded as mysteriously elegant as any I'd heard.

Albert Streatfield, Highclere's butler, brought her ivory calling card on a silver platter to the Library where I was reading Flinders Petrie's memoir, *Tanis,* about his excavations in the Nile Delta.

With more than fifty rooms on its second and third floors, and over sixty staff members to tend to all of it, Highclere Castle was a place where one could get lost forever, and yet never seemed to be quite alone.

I preferred the Library. Lord Carnarvon told me it held nearly six thousand books. The idea both overwhelmed and fascinated me. So much knowledge and creativity in one beautiful room. Each afternoon I loved to curl up on one of the tufted couches near the massive fireplace under the watchful eye of Henry Herbert, First Earl of Carnarvon, framed in oil. Beside me, a stack of whatever volumes struck my fancy would provide the entertainment for the oft-dreary English afternoon.

"She wants to see me?" I frowned at Streatfield. "About what?"

"She didn't say, miss. Only that she'd come from America to see your parents, and in their absence would like to speak with you." He cleared his throat. "I have already spoken to the Countess, and she has given her approval. Shall I show Miss Moretti to the Drawing Room, perhaps?"

Streatfield's deferential question was accompanied by an amused twitch of the lips. It was an unspoken game we played, the two of us. He pretended, usually with a straight face, that I belonged in the Drawing Room, ringing bells for maids to hurry to my assistance. We both knew I should probably be downstairs, waiting to answer those same bells. Streatfield had undoubtedly intercepted the calling card, bringing it himself rather than Roberts, whose attitude toward me was less congenial.

I lifted my chin and adopted my snootiest tone. "Yes, Streatfield. Show her to the Drawing Room, and tell her I shall join her presently."

He bowed slightly from the waist. "Very good, miss."

His approving smile did not escape my notice.

I slipped quickly to my room, to change my morning dress into a lavender muslin and lace more acceptable for afternoon tea, and then headed for the Drawing Room.

The money Almina brought to her marriage to the Earl was lavished everywhere, and nowhere more than the Drawing Room. It was rarely mentioned, and then only in whispers, that Almina was Alfred de Rothschild's illegitimate daughter, born out of longstanding affair between her mother Marie and the fantastically wealthy banker. Instead, everyone happily accepted the money and the gifts, including the bolts and bolts of flamboyant green silk damask that covered the walls of the Drawing Room and hung in heavy folds from each window.

With the pale afternoon light filtering through the south-facing windows, the entire room, including Miss Giada Moretti, had an almost sickly-green glow.

She stood near the window, absently touching the heavy drapes that pooled on the floor. She turned as I entered.

Lady Almina sat at her piano, straight-backed and frowning. She rose when she saw me.

"Sahara, this woman has come to see your parents. From America." The Countess emphasized the final word with clear disdain. Her visit to New York City two years ago provoked nothing good to say. Everything American "moved too quickly and spoke too casually."

Somehow, I had always sensed a comparison to me.

I crossed the room, held out a hand, and spoke in my most Countess-like tone. "Miss Moretti, I am so sorry my parents are not here to greet you. Were you acquaintances when we lived in America? I'm afraid I do not remember—"

"No, no, of course you wouldn't." She was gripping my hand with both of hers, with a smile that seemed to swallow me up rather than greet me. She was about forty, I guessed, with long, dark hair flowing in waves down her back, a stark contrast to Lady Almina's hair styled high on her head, elegant and conservative.

"I will leave you two to visit, then." The Countess dipped her head slightly to the guest and retreated from the room.

"Please," I extended a hand, "make yourself comfortable."

Miss Moretti glanced over her shoulder, to the window where she had been standing. "I thought perhaps we could take a turn outdoors, go for a walk."

"Oh." I glanced at my tea dress. "I'm afraid I'm not dressed for—"

She laughed, a silky sound, condescending and mocking. "Don't be ridiculous. We won't be climbing mountains."

The Countess wouldn't like the breach of etiquette. But this woman was quite… commanding.

I drew my shoulders back, trying to match her presence. "Very well."

We crossed through the Saloon, with its soaring ceilings and atrium balcony running around the perimeter. The rich, oiled wood served as a backdrop to the huge portraits lit by yellow lamps. We passed through to the entrance hall. A footman was on hand to open the iron-studded walnut door for us, and I followed Miss Moretti out to the gravel forecourt, still studying that gorgeous hair.

A jaunty two-seater Studebaker Roadster in red waited in the courtyard, its driver leaning against it. He wore a smart, gray double-breasted jacket with gold buttons, with matching black boots and gloves. At the sight of Miss Moretti, he straightened and reached to open the back door.

She waved him off and walked past.

We circled the castle, strolled beyond the East Lawns, and headed for the gardens. The gravel crunched underfoot. I should have insisted on at least changing my footwear.

"Tell me what you remember of America, Sahara."

I frowned at the familiar use of my first name. "Nothing, really. I was only four years old when we came to England. The same age as Lady Evelyn is now, in fact." Little Lady Eve was already a favorite of mine, and Nanny Moss often let me bring her outdoors to play. Most days, I spent more time with Eve than her parents did.

"So, no memories of life before that? No memories at all, memories that don't seem to belong in England?"

I inhaled deeply before answering. The green odor of newly-cut grass hung heavy in the air, with the humid sense of impending rain. "Why do you ask?"

She glanced sideways at me, with what seemed like a forced smile. "Oh, no reason. Just the self-centeredness of an American, I suppose. Hard to believe you were born there, yet don't consider it home."

"It's hard to consider anywhere home." The words slipped out before I had a chance to stifle them.

She slowed and faced me. "And why is that?"

I shrugged and continued along the path, unwilling to have a heart-to-heart conversation with this slightly odd stranger. "We've moved around a bit. London. Boarding school. Summers here at Highclere."

"Fascinating."

Not really. But she was odd. And it did feel like she was studying me.

"How did you meet my parents?"

"Oh, we belonged to the same club." She waved away the question. "But I lost track of them years ago."

"I am sorry they weren't here to reconnect with you."

"Yes. They are traveling to...?" She let the question hang.

I answered without thinking. "Venice."

"Venice." She nearly hissed the word, an undercurrent of anger in her voice. "Whatever are they doing in Venice?"

"What brings you to England, Miss Moretti?"

"Oh, please, call me Giada."

I had never in my life called a woman of her age by her first name, and I didn't intend to start. Although the name *Giada* was so wonderful, I felt an almost irresistible urge to speak it.

Instead I said nothing. But neither did she, and we walked in silence for some moments.

"So," I finally repeated. "What brings you to England?"

"Just some business dealings. Nothing that would interest a young girl like you."

Again, the condescension. I was beginning to dislike Giada Moretti.

"I'm surprised your parents didn't have you accompany them on such a long voyage, my dear. When will they return, do you expect?"

"I'm not sure. The end of the summer, perhaps. They promised it would be before I return to school."

"Of course, of course. So tell me what I've missed of their lives. What work have they been doing these past ten years?"

We had reached the Monk's Garden now, and passed under a stone arch into the walled enclosure, its walkways lined with topiaries and pear trees, with the glass Peach House in the center. I strolled toward the Peach House, a favorite haunt of mine this time of year.

"They study Egyptology, as I'm sure you know. My father has been teaching at Oxford for the past three years, usually summer and fall terms, so they can be free in the winter term to travel."

"Yes, they must have been part of many extraordinary finds by now, I should think."

We entered the glass-paneled house, and were nearly overcome with the scent of ripening peaches and the fragrant roses grown for the vases in the Castle. I reached for a yellow Floribunda, and immediately pricked my finger on a thorn.

"Oh, be careful, dear," Giada said at the sight of the pinprick of blood on my forefinger. "I wouldn't like to see you injured while you are orphaned here."

Orphaned here. The phrase cut more deeply than the thorn. It poked at the thought I kept most hidden. The awareness that my parents had chosen, once again, to travel without me. To leave me behind. To leave me in a place where I didn't belong, had no family.

I took a handkerchief from my pocket and dabbed at the red droplet.

"So, you were saying?" Giada led the way forward through the mass of yellow roses. "About your parents' archaeological finds?"

No, I wasn't saying, actually. My parents had done exemplary work in Mentuhotep's tomb, getting to know Édouard Naville, and all the scholars working there. But why the questions?

"And Lord Carnarvon? Did they meet him there, in Egypt?"

My father had met Lord Carnarvon years earlier, in the dusty library at Oxford when the Earl was indulging his passion for research into ancient Egypt. A few years later, after the Earl's automobile accident, when he began wintering in that warm climate, my father had connected him with some of the Egyptologists there.

"No, before that. You certainly seem interested in archaeology. Are you a scholar as well?"

She plucked a peach from a low-hanging branch. "More of a —researcher—I would say."

"Oh?" Now that interested me. There were not enough women in academic circles. "What is your area of research?"

She shrugged. "The past."

So, more willing to ask questions than answer them. I eyed the safety of the Castle, which felt far-off now, through the glass walls. "Perhaps we should be heading back. It's nearly time for tea. You are welcome to join us."

She still clutched the peach, and gripped my wrist with her other hand. "But we have so much more to talk about." Her dark eyes glittered.

Again, I sensed a current of anger behind those eyes.

I twisted my arm to free it from her grip. "Do we? I'm certain we'll have plenty of time as we walk back, and perhaps over tea."

She said nothing.

I turned my back to her, and sensed she followed. A small *thud* on the ground near our feet drew my attention.

She had thrown the peach to the ground.

On the way back to the Castle, she asked again about my parents' trip to Venice.

"I would have thought Venice too medieval for their interest. Isn't their focus solely on ancient history?"

"Everyone needs a holiday."

"Ah, yes. A holiday. And Venice is very beautiful."

"You've been there?"

"Yes, several—I've seen several photographs, of course."

I studied her profile. Everything about her seemed duplicitous.

In truth, I wasn't certain why my parents had gone to Venice, but I had no desire to share any work they might be doing.

"Yes, I'm sure they are enjoying their sightseeing." I kept my voice light. "I believe they were even going to visit a circus."

"The circus? In Venice? Surely not that Barnum and Bailey show?"

"I—I don't know. Perhaps not a circus. My mother mentioned meeting a strongman…"

Giada had stopped walking. "A strongman, you say?"

What was I doing, babbling on? In my desire to give this woman no information, I was doing the opposite. I bit my lip, hard, and continued on.

"It must be tea-time by now. Perhaps we should hurry—"

But Giada was already hurrying. She strode across the gravel path as though a race had begun.

I struggled to keep up with her.

When we reached the Castle door, she turned and took my hand in her cool fingers. "It was lovely to meet you, my dear. Do give your parents my regrets at missing them. When you see them again."

"But— you won't stay for tea? I'm sure Her Ladyship—"

"No, no, I'm afraid I must dash off. So nice to have met you."

She said the words, but there was an hollowness behind them.

Her driver opened the door, she disappeared into the interior of the Studebaker, and it soon pulled away. She didn't wave, or even glance at me, as it did.

I stood with my back to the Castle door, a cold feeling in my belly.

The feeling something very, very wrong had just occurred.

CHAPTER ELEVEN

November 5, 1922
Luxor, Egypt

*T*his *interview* with a stranger was a huge mistake.

I escaped the Winter Palace Hotel dining room, with full awareness that Jack Moretti followed me.

Jack Moretti. Nephew of the enigmatic Giada Moretti, who spent an afternoon asking me questions seventeen years ago.

I reached the verandah and kept moving, down the white steps to the line of shops at street level under the hotel.

"Sahara, wait!" Jack grabbed at my sleeve.

I yanked my arm from his grasp and kept walking. I needed to think. And he felt unsafe. Even dangerous.

He fell into step beside me.

"Sahara—"

"Not now, Jack." I tried to outpace him, then tried to ignore him.

In 1905, when his aunt had visited me at Highclere, my parents were on holiday in Venice.

Except they never returned. The boat they took from Venice to Alexandria sank, all lives lost. End of their story.

And yet... Part of me had always wondered about Giada Moretti and her questions.

Now, now with the new information from my mother's journal, pieces fell into place like broken pottery reassembling itself.

My mother mentioned seeing a strongman in Venice. A circus, I believed at the time.

But Giovanni Battista Belzoni, the man who had found KV17, the tomb of Seti I—the man whom my mother, in her journal page, said she intended to meet in Venice...

Before Belzoni discovered tombs, before he even arrived in Egypt, he had been known for years as The Great Belzoni. Fantastically tall and incredibly powerful, he had made his living as a strongman in a traveling circus.

A wash of questions and dread swept me. What did it all mean?

Certainly, now that I had recalled this decades-old bit of memory, I could only believe my mother had gone to Venice to visit the strongman Belzoni, "before his impressive, yet destructive, work begins," her journal said.

But not gone to Venice in 1905. She might have *left* 1905 but she could only have *visited* Belzoni in the early 1800s.

And that day at Highclere, Giada Moretti had seemed to know something of the strongman I mentioned.

Had she followed them to Venice after I gave her that information? Was she somehow responsible for their deaths?

And if she was, what about me? I had given her the information she sought.

My knees buckled, throwing me off balance.

Jack moved to catch me.

I shoved him away.

Was it my fault they died?

How to fit these pieces together? Oddly, thoughts intruded of a book I'd read, by the wildly-popular new author, Agatha Christie. *The Secret Adversary*, it was titled. Who was my secret adversary? It was like a mystery to be solved, all this information about my parents and Venice, about Giada Moretti and my own experience back in 1914 in the tomb of Seti I.

"Sahara, please, tell me what is wrong." Jack's voice was quiet but insistent.

I slowed my frenzied walk along the Luxor street and looked up. We had left the Winter Palace in a golden glow behind us. With a glance up and down the street, I crossed to the *corniche*, the promenade that ran between the street and the Nile.

Jack followed.

I gripped the railing and gazed over the darkened Nile, the burnt-orange outline of the Theban hills a sharp crease against the night sky.

Why should I tell Jack anything? He was as much a stranger as his aunt had been all those years ago. Not to be trusted. Not to be befriended.

I studied my white-knuckled grip. "You surprised me, that's all. Brought back memories of the summer I met your aunt. The summer my parents died."

He rested his wrists, hands clasped, on the railing. Too close to my own.

I dropped my hands to my sides.

"Sahara, I'm sorry. I—I know I acted as though I didn't know your parents had died, but I did. And it was thoughtless of me to bring up that time so casually."

"I think it's time you took me home, Mr. Moretti."

He sighed. "I've mucked it up now, haven't I?"

I said nothing. His dishonesty, coupled with the strange family connection, left me chiding myself for allowing my loneliness to overtake my good sense. The building warmth through our dinner conversation fooled me into forgetting I was not someone people connected with, but rather someone people left behind.

I fought the desire to question him, to learn more of his aunt and her interest in my parents.

We said little on the way back to the American House.

Minnie Burton was still on the verandah when Jack opened the door of our car and helped me out.

I turned to say my goodbyes.

"Can I see you again? I'd still love to write that story—"

I shook his hand. "I'm too private of a person for newspaper stories, I'm afraid. But thanks for your interest."

I left him there at the automobile, nodded briefly to Minnie on my way past, and escaped to my room, where I sank with relief into the overstuffed window chair where I spent most evenings with a book.

Hopefully, Jack Moretti had gotten the message. I wasn't interested in more questions from anyone in his family.

Right now all I wanted was answers.

I had let the startling events of the past two days dilute my desire for answers about my parents. Now each piece of information was like another puzzle handed to me, another unfinished drawing begging for completion—the brief conversation with Jack, the memory of his aunt's visit. My mother's journal about visiting Belzoni. My own freakish experience in the tomb of Seti I, and even my father's letter to my mother about Hatshepsut, which I discovered at Highclere a few months ago. The answers must be pursued, answers that might shed light on the deaths of my parents.

Could Howard spare me while I chased the truth?

It didn't matter.

Regardless of what it cost me professionally, or if it delayed the achievements I hoped to make here, it was time to test my theory at the Temple of Hatshepsut.

CHAPTER TWELVE

November 6, 1922
Mortuary Temple of Hatshepsut
Theban Necropolis, Egypt

his entire thing was simply crazy.

The morning after Jack's revelations, I awoke with a headache, a result of tossing on my bed all night, plagued with questions, with fears of what I was about to do, and with fears it would not work and I'd be left with only more questions.

Yesterday, the most provocative find of my career had been unearthed. I should be helping Howard prepare for the project ahead. We had only this one last season of Lord Carnarvon's funds, and had to make it count.

Instead I stood at the Mortuary Temple of Hatshepsut, breathing in courage at the head of a forty meter causeway that had once been lined with sphinxes. The causeway terminated at an ascending ramp of steps that climbed to the immense first courtyard, and on either side of the ramped steps, a colonnade with a dozen or more wide-ranging stone columns supported the terraced courtyard above them like a grove of granite trees under a limestone sky.

I strode down the causeway, across the first wide enclosure, toward the first set of steps. My presence went unnoticed as I crossed the courtyard.

In the distance above, far across the elevated courtyard, another line of stone columns rose, with another long ramp, leading to a second lofty terrace. And looming behind it all, the Theban cliffs, orange and craggy, lit afire by the rising sun at my back.

The Mortuary Temple of Hatshepsut lay carved into the cliffs about a half-kilometer from where Howard and I were digging under the workmen's huts near the tomb of Ramesses VI. As Egypt's first and most famous female pharaoh, Hatshepsut had built monuments, commissioned art, and restored architecture all over Egypt.

It was here I would conduct my experiment. I didn't know the exact method necessary to make the magic happen, but I had to give it a shot.

Hundreds of laborers crawled the site, raising puffs of dust where they worked. Herbert Winlock had been excavating and restoring this temple for more than ten years, picking up where Naville had left off, but the work would continue, perhaps for another hundred.

In a rectangular roped area to my left, thousands of stone fragments tumbled over themselves. Bas-reliefs, statues, broken columns, waiting to be sorted and identified. All pulled from the site as time was scraped away, layer by layer, from the most magnificent ancient temple the world had ever seen.

But I wasn't here to see the remains of the past. I was here to step into it.

But, really? Did I actually think this was going to work? And if it did, was I prepared?

My head still ached. Perhaps even a bit of fever coming on?

The site teemed with too much frenzied activity to notice one wandering girl. I stepped across metal tracks, laid recently to transport the small mine trolleys that carried random pieces to the sorting area.

Up the first long set of steps, until I was above the first colonnade.

Where did I have the nerve to try it?

From my experience eight years ago in the tomb of Seti, it would seem I needed to be touching something. And then what?

The first courtyard was so huge it took nearly five minutes to cross to the second ramp with inset steps. I glanced left and right. Hopefully Winlock would be too busy to recognize me.

The strap of the leather satchel I'd slung over my shoulder cut into my neck. I adjusted it to ease the pain. Would it "travel" with me? I'd packed a canteen of water, my journal, and a pen, just in case. I would have packed a map of the temple, or a book that might help me with details once there, but I had nothing of the sort in my small bedroom library and actually knew of nothing that had been written on the temple as yet.

I skirted the second long ramp, rather than climb it, and crossed the platform to the grid of stone columns at the rear. Nearly a hundred of them, soaring over my head, in two sections of double rows. I slipped into the shadows, to the rear of the columned hall. Larger-than-lifesize paintings, in that characteristic deep gold and bright red, graced the walls. Paintings of snakes and birds, people and gods, vertical lines of hieroglyphic symbols. I ran my fingertips over a carved relief of a raven and closed my eyes at the familiar tingle of connection.

Here? Was this as good a place as any?

I half-hid myself behind one of the columns, took a deep breath...

And was hit with a wave of self-doubt.

What did I know about any of this?

A torn journal page that hinted my mother might visit a man who'd been dead more than eighty years. A remembered visit from a beautiful yet creepy American woman who seemed to know about Belzoni. A letter that alluded to my parents visiting Hatshepsut in her own time. And my own experience, eight years ago, when I supposedly found myself in the middle of an ancient funeral.

So much supposition. Was I mad, stretching these few disparate details into a theory that defied everything known about the universe?

"Surprised to see Howard gave you a minute off."

The voice at my back spun me around.

"Mr. Winlock!" I pressed a hand to my throat. "You startled me."

He laughed. "Called your name twice, but you were off somewhere else, I guess." He tapped his egg-headed temple and grinned.

"Yes," I exhaled, still jittery, "Imagining this magnificent scene, as it once was."

We surveyed the platform side-by-side, but my gaze strayed to my right, to the adjoining temple of Mentuhotep II, built some five hundred years earlier than this one.

"Your parents worked on Mentuhotep, didn't they? With Naville?"

I nodded, wordless.

"Before my time, I'm afraid."

There was that familiar ache, that blank place in my heart, at the mention of them. I blinked away the emotion.

The silence lengthened.

Winlock was an odd duck. Everyone said he was extraordinarily imaginative and a great storyteller in the evenings at the American House. From my room I could often hear him in the sitting room, regaling the other residents with anecdotes of his years in Egypt. But he had little to say one-on-one.

But then, I supposed, we were all a bit odd out here, weren't we?

"Well," I finally said, "I think I'll spend a little time exploring the Hathor Chapel."

"Right. Right-o. Enjoy."

He wandered off, but glanced back at me.

I strolled to the smaller shrine to Hathor at the southern end of the colonnade. No one worked here, and an eerie hush reigned over the twelve-columned hall, decorated with scenes of Hatshepsut's life and the goddess Hathor.

I returned in a few minutes to the colonnade to find Winlock gone.

I stepped to my previous column, then peered out over the colossal second terrace, to the first one far below and stretching so far the laborers there were indistinguishable.

Yes, this was crazy. Questioning my sanity made sense. But another question seemed even better...

What do I have to lose?

Well, perhaps there was a danger I would actually do it. Truly travel in time, and then not be able to return. Or maybe even die trying.

But there was something here, something that connected me to my parents in a way I had never experienced.

I was doing this.

A few more deep breaths. A pounding in my head and chest that reached to my fingertips. Determination was doing nothing to erase my terror.

I braced both hands against a carved bull, symbol of power and regeneration to the ancient Egyptians, and focused my mind on where I wanted to be. On *when* I wanted to be—here at this temple, on the day of Hatshepsut's official commemoration after her death.

It seemed like there should be a few special words, didn't it? Had I said anything, eight years ago in Seti's tomb?

No, Howard was talking.

I had noticed a small stone on the floor of the tomb.

What if I needed that stone?

I closed my eyes and chided my stupidity. Why didn't I retrieve it back then? Save it?

Because you thought you were insane.

Well, yes. There was that.

Focus, Sahara. What exactly happened eight years ago?

I was touching the painted wall mural. I flattened both palms now against the column.

Wishing I could experience seeing the mummy of Seti I for its final time. I thought again of this temple as it once was, built to commemorate a great pharaoh who had just died. Tried to imagine it. Wanted to see it.

I bent to pick up the stone. I kept one hand cupped around the column, but closed my eyes and bent at the waist, slid my hand down the column as I skimmed my fingertips along the ground, mind still focused on the past.

The vertigo swept me at once.

I stayed bent, waited for it to pass, unsure if meant anything, or was simply the result of turning my excited brain upside down.

But I knew. Before I straightened, eyes still closed, I could feel it and smell it and hear it.

The year 1922 had disappeared. And Hatshepsut's Temple had blossomed to life.

The noise! There was so much noise! I'd heard hundreds of digsite laborers make a racket, but that was nothing compared to the din in the temple courts below. Chanting people, bleating and braying animals, merchants calling and children crying. Smells of unwashed people blended with animal dung and incense, watering my eyes.

I leaned beyond the column, far enough to glimpse the courts. Thousands, perhaps tens of thousands, of people crammed the enclosures. A sea of black and white, the occasional glint of sunlight on gold jewelry, tan arms and chests and legs.

And *trees!* So many trees, planted in stately rows on either side of the enclosures, with gnarly trunks and glossy green leaves, vaguely familiar. Did Winlock know there had been groves of trees thriving here?

In the portico where I stood, a number of people moved, criss-crossing between the columns. They passed me to enter the chapel, the temple of Hathor, behind me. From their clothing they seemed to be priests and priestesses. My eyes strayed upward to the newly-appeared and gleaming white pyramid atop the Hathor Chapel.

And my clothing? I looked down to find myself dressed in a tight-fitting white sheath dress, as I had been eight years ago. My leather pouch was gone.

I exhaled carefully, tried to steady myself without drawing attention.

Proceed with logic, Sahara.

First... *Is this my body?*

I looked at my hands and arms.

Yes, the clothes were unfamiliar but all else was the same. I smoothed a hand over my hair, and the length seemed unchanged but it was now braided into dozens of thin plaits, each end wrapped with gold bands. There was an odd feeling at my forehead. I reached up and found a beaded headband wrapped low around my head, with a medallion of some kind in the center. I pulled it off to examine it. It was woven with fine metal, strung with tiny red beads and droplets of jewels. The metal-worked medallion in the center had a tiny gold scarab hanging from it. I replaced it carefully.

Okay. Same body, different clothes and hairstyle.

A surge of panic gripped me. Could I get back? I wanted nothing more than to reverse the trip, to see if the strategy from Seti's tomb, simply *wishing* myself back again, would work. What if it didn't?

But my father had said "once in a lifetime."

I would not leave this place until I explored my questions, until I discovered the connection with my parents. Until I understood exactly how this time travel thing worked.

Time travel.

The words pounded in my head, crazy and foreign and impossible.

Enough. I could think about the impossibility later, after I was safely back in 1922.

For now, I needed to get my bearings before I got myself in trouble.

CHAPTER THIRTEEN

1458 B.C.
Mortuary Temple of Hatshepsut
Theban Necropolis, Egypt

𝒥 pushed out of the portico and threaded my way through the crowds on this upper terrace.

Bare-chested men, women with kohl-lined eyes, and near-naked children jostled me, most of them moving in the opposite direction, toward the temple.

When it seemed I was about halfway across the upper terrace, I turned to get my first look at the temple, as it once was.

Oh my stars.

My breath huffed from my chest, jaw dropped.

I had no idea.

Herbert Winlock had no idea.

The temple was so much...*more.* So much grander than anyone knew.

What we had believed was the upper platform, above the second set of columns, was in truth only the middle. An entire third set of columns lay above me, with another platform atop them, and a facade rising behind all of it, against the craggy cliff-face.

It was massive. It was glorious.

A magnificent statue of a pharaoh or a god graced every single column. Stony faces stared across the desert behind me, arms crossed against chests, the traditional crook and flail in each hand.

How fragmentary was our knowledge of the past! Was what we called "history" simply the merest breath of what truly was? With one step into the reality of the past, all I'd learned in class-rooms and books mocked me with its simplicity and lack of substance.

The crowd surged and receded, faces alight with celebration. Was it the day of the pharaoh's death? Had I controlled my "arrival time" as I had expected? Could I ask someone?

The thought jolted me. I never considered the language barrier! The Arabic spoken here in the twentieth century had little in common with Late New Kingdom Egyptian.

I stood in one place, let the crowd flow around me, and focused on listening to any snatches of conversation I could grasp.

You should have brought the lentils.

I swung my head toward the speaker, which seemed to be a woman about my age pushing past me. Was—was she from my time?

She returned my glance, scowled, and kept moving.

Mama, wait!

This from a small child, grabbing at the wrist of another woman. Though I hadn't actually seen the child say the words.

I turned to face the oncoming crowd now, searching faces, waiting for someone to speak.

"Step aside, woman!"

The words were spoken directly to me. By a man blocked by my unmoving position. I heard the words come from his lips. Except his lips were saying something different.

Was it possible? Could people speaking Late Egyptian sound like English to me?

My head pounded—a drumbeat that was more than the overwhelming stimuli, more than the incomprehensible idea of time travel. A headache that blurred my vision, left me dizzy and nauseated, palms clammy.

And the smell didn't help. That mixture of body odor and some kind of aromatic smoke—was it frankincense? Yes, that's what the trees were. Frankincense and myrrh.

I pushed to the edge of the crowd. I needed air.

Was there no end to this mob?

Finally, I reached the wall that enclosed the platform, but instead of offering breathing room, I was more likely to be crushed.

I had to get out of here. What was I thinking? To come here with so little preparation, so little knowledge of the layout, the period, the people. My ignorance was colossal and entirely foolish. And yet...

I am here.

What better way to learn? And I had so many questions. I shoved further into the press of people, moving against the flow, down the stepped ramp, then toward the side of the next platform.

A sharp cry drew my attention to the ground ahead.

A child, perhaps five years old and naked, kneeled with his forehead to the ground, hands protecting his head.

"Worthless child!" A large man in a white skirt with gold earrings in each ear kicked the boy. "Get out of the way!"

"Hey!" I surged forward, stepped between him and the boy, and drove my elbow into the man's ribs. "What are you doing?"

He raised one muscled arm over my head.

Instinctively, I blocked the threat with my forearm, while reaching for the frightened boy. "He's a child!"

But the man's expression had shifted from anger to surprise. His arm lowered.

"Ra-Ne-Hannu!"

I glanced beside me, then back to him. Was he speaking to me? The out-of-sync words and lips were confusing.

His chin lowered to his chest. "Forgive me, priestess. I did not know the boy was yours."

Uh, priestess?

The child was behind me now. He clutched my dress and hid his face against my hip.

"Yes. Well." What did one say in this situation? "Keep moving yourself, then."

It wasn't until he nodded and moved on that I realized the language-thing seemed to work both ways, and he understood what I said.

I bent to the child. "Where is your mother?"

But the question was immediately answered by a woman much younger than I who cried out and reached past me for the boy. She smiled briefly at me, and they moved on.

As soon as they were out of sight, the headache flared again.

I couldn't shake it off. Better to keep moving.

But the spectacle was too engrossing. I kept my spot against the wall and scanned the faces, the clothes, the fabulous looming architecture.

How many laborers had it taken to construct such a thing? Did they work willingly or were they forced? How many years?

Scholars debated the date of the exodus of the fledgling Israelite nation enslaved in Egypt, dividing into two camps around an early and a late date. If the early date was correct, the exodus would happen about ten years from now. I swept a glance across the crowd. Were some of them here, even now? Or did they mainly reside in Lower Egypt, closer to the Delta?

Lost in the wonder of it all, I didn't see the approach of a small-boned and wiry man until he was pressed against me.

"What—?" I shoved against him, heat surging to my chest.

He was my height, with a few missing teeth and a ragged scar that ran under his left eye. The stench of his breath hit me as he pushed back.

He jutted a chin toward my forehead. "Give it here."

The aggressive stranger had me trapped against the wall. I flattened my palms against his emaciated chest and shoved.

A memory surfaced, of a cricket match I'd attended at Bramall Lane in Sheffield as a child, with a crowd that surged and swelled. My mother kept one firm hand gripping mine, and with the other clutched her handbag against her chest, muttering about sneaky pickpockets.

But there was nothing sneaky about this attacker.

He reached claw-like fingers for my head and yanked the headband off. Sharp nails scraped my skin.

"Give that back!" I reached for the headband, feeling an odd sense of protectiveness despite having only owned it for a few minutes.

He held it just out of my reach, drove his other fist into my stomach, then disappeared into the mob.

I gasped at the pain of the blow and put a hand to the bruise.

A warm wetness against my fingers tripped my pulse into double-time.

Did he—? He stabbed me!

I peeled my hand away from my side.

Blood was already spilling down the white sheath dress, soaking the flimsy fabric.

I staggered, returned the pressure against the wound, and instinctively started for the upper terrace, pushing through the crowd.

Every jolt of every stranger brought a fresh wave of pain.

I'd been a fool, to come here so ill-prepared. No research, little planning, only a few stray bits of knowledge. My curiosity and my inattention had cost me.

I lurched with one arm extended in front of me, as though I could clear a path just by wishing it, my fingers tight against the seeping blood.

My breath exhaled in short puffs and dried my throat and lips.

Could I die in the past? The possibility that had seemed remote an hour ago now seemed likely.

The first set of steps, finally.

I careened upward, grabbed at indignant worshippers to haul myself forward.

I didn't want to leave, not yet, not before I'd seen everything, learned all I could. But I'd witnessed enough blood loss during the war. This injury could kill me.

Eyes focused on that row of columns where I'd emerged from 1922.

I'm not going to make it.

Second set of steps. My vision blurred.

Could I just do what I needed to do, right here? Return to my time by touching these steps instead of the column?

Would I "materialize" in front of Herbert Winlock? Would he have sense enough to get medical help?

Doesn't matter.

It took little effort to bend, to brush the step with my free hand. I focused on my own time, wished myself back there.

Stop.

That's what I'd said to myself eight years ago, in Seti's tomb.

Stop. I want to go back.

Nothing. Nothing but the searing pain and a lightheadedness that threatened to topple me.

I must keep going. It must only work if I was touching the same place as when I arrived. If it worked at all.

Up the steps, across the platform. The next set of columns—my columns—in sight.

The underlying fear that I couldn't leave, even if I wanted to, began to harden in my belly.

God help me.

An illogical, presumptuous prayer, to a God I didn't know, demanding help I had no right to request.

I let the crowd carry me forward, toward the front of the temple. People knelt briefly in worship and left small gifts. Perhaps it was a funeral after all.

Finally back at the columns. I slipped into the shadows.

Which column was right? They all looked alike.

"Ra-Ne-Hannu, why are you not inside?"

Not again.

I couldn't play the role of priestess, not now. And where was the real woman? Would she show up and wonder why I was impersonating her? Or—even more unbelievable—had I somehow taken her place?

"Ra-Ne-Hannu! You are hurt!"

I took my best guess at the right column. Braced my one free hand. Closed my eyes, controlled my breathing. Imagined the temple in its partially-excavated state. Imagined the workers hauling out bits and pieces in their mine carts. Imagined my leather satchel and my khaki trousers.

The transition was slower this time. More like a fading, that I could feel even with eyes closed. The headache remained. And then those same flashes as before—a mix of searing light and fragmented memory—of amber flames and black smoke, thick and clogging my nose.

The flaring switched off, along with the sounds, the odors, and most blessedly, the pain.

I blinked open my eyes, pulled my hand from my buttoned-down shirt, and found myself whole and home.

The wound was gone.

Deep breaths.

Swallowing against the tightness in my throat.

I rested my head against the column, then jerked away. Not taking any chances.

Ra-Ne-Hannu. The woman I'd been mistaken for. Who was she?

My memory spun to the picture I still had of my mother in the trunk of Highclere, taken just before she'd left for Venice. Only a few years older than I was now, so similar to what I saw in the mirror. Her name penned at the bottom of the picture.

Renae Hannah Aldridge.

Renae Hannah... Ra-Ne-Hannu. Another jolt to my sanity. I would have to think about that later.

I inhaled once more and stepped out from behind the

column, to what now seemed like a pitiful representation of a place that had once been so much more.

A single figure moved toward me, across what I now realized was only the middle platform.

Oh my stars. Not now.

But there was no mistaking the cocky swagger of the ever-present Jack Moretti.

CHAPTER FOURTEEN

November 6, 1922
Mortuary Temple of Hatshepsut
Theban Necropolis, Egypt

I emerged from the colonnade into the sun-bright courtyard, blinking and trembling.

"Sahara?" Jack strode toward me. He removed his brown fedora, tilting his head and squinting.

We met near the base of the long ramp of steps. He wore no suit today, looking more casual in an open-collared dark blue shirt fit close across his chest, khaki trousers, and black and white wingtips. His camera still dangled from his neck.

"Hello, Jack."

"Are you well?"

I removed my hand from where I'd unconsciously pressed it against my side. "I'm fine. What are you doing here?"

The sun seemed no higher than before my excursion, but it felt hotter and brighter somehow. I wiped the back of my hand across my forehead.

Jack replaced the hat, leaned back against the steps and

crossed his feet at the ankles. The dark shirt stretched across his chest, giving a hint of the muscles beneath.

"Just following you."

I took an involuntary step backward.

He laughed. "Sorry. Didn't mean to sound so... shifty."

My mouth felt like I'd been licking the desert. I pulled the canteen from my leather satchel, unscrewed the cap, and gulped. The water tasted stale and bitter.

"Going on a long journey?" Jack nodded toward my satchel, then up at the temple.

I glanced back at the columns. "No. Just... sightseeing."

He nodded. "Minnie Burton told me you hired a driver to bring you here."

"So you really were following me?"

"I figured sightseeing's always more fun with a partner."

My head was dizzy. Too tired to deal with Jack's banter.

"I don't need a chaperone, if that's what you're thinking."

He laughed again. "I think if anyone was the chaperone here, it would be you."

I wanted to walk away. Just to process the thousand thoughts crowding my mind. But I didn't.

"Seriously, Sahara, I wanted to apologize again for last night."

"No need." I took a step away.

"Sahara." He reached for me, touched my elbow with light fingertips.

The touch brought a shiver, despite the heat. I breathed deeply, and caught the scent of his cologne.

"I know I brought up painful memories. And I'm sorry."

"It's not the memories that disturb me."

He raised his eyebrows, inviting more.

Why couldn't I just walk away?

"I—I'm uncomfortable with deception. Of any kind. Your aunt seemed like a person with something to hide—enough that I still remember her, all these years later. And when I realized you hadn't been entirely honest, about who you are, or about your reasons for wanting to have dinner—"

"You assumed I was up to no good."

I shrugged. "I'm not interested in being put on display. And I have work to do."

"Fair enough. How about we compromise?"

I sighed. I didn't want to make any deals with this stranger. And I very much wanted to be alone, to think about the unbelievable thing that just happened.

"What kind of compromise?"

"How about I agree to keep you out of the papers, if you agree to show me the sights, keep me out of trouble while I shoot some photographs."

Keep him out of trouble? The idea sounded impossible. Jack Moretti clearly liked to get himself into places he didn't belong.

Just like you.

Well, yes, but for different reasons. I followed my curiosity. Pursued the research. Jack seemed like the kind of man who fell into adventures simply for the fun of it.

"Come on, Sahara. Don't think. Just say yes. You could stand to have a little more recreation in your life, I'm guessing."

"Archaeology is serious business, Jack."

"Absolutely."

I made a face, an attempt at a scowl which ended up a smile I tried to cover with my hand.

"There we go." Jack pointed. "That's the Sahara I'm looking for."

My heart skipped a little at the phrase.

Jack lifted his camera and snapped the shutter.

"Fine. I'll be your tour guide. But only in my free time."

I could take the opportunity to ask a few more questions about the mysterious Giada Moretti. Who was she? How well did she know my parents? And had she followed them to Venice?

"So... " Jack grinned. "Starting now?"

No, not starting now. I had to *think.* I was going to lose my sanity if I didn't get a chance to evaluate this whole crazy traveling-through-time impossibility.

"Sunset," I said. "I'll meet you at the American House an hour before sunset. I'll show you the best Egypt has to offer, and you can take some photographs while the light is warm."

He lifted an eyebrow. "Sound's like you've got an artist's eye."

I shrugged. "There's a lot you don't know about me."

Indeed.

Jack insisted on accompanying me back to the house, but left me at the verandah with promises to be back in a few hours.

I had to cross the sitting room, and was immediately accosted by Frances Breasted. She and her husband James, an Egyptologist from Chicago, had been here only a week, but Frances and Minnie Burton had made short work of getting to know each other.

"Oh, my dear!" Frances clutched my sleeve. "You look positively peaked!"

"Yes, thank you. I mean—just a headache. Excuse me, please."

I escaped to my room, finally alone with my thoughts, and secured the door behind me.

I shoved aside the worn copy of *Jane Eyre* that lay face down, pages spread, on my bed. I'd read myself to sleep last night after the botched evening with Jack, finding solace in my favorite novel of the orphaned misfit Jane. Had it only been last night? Today's events could fill a journal.

Now, propped against my bed's headboard, pencil and notebook in hand, I stepped through the entire experience again.

Had I truly been mistaken for my mother?

I chewed the end of my pencil, already gnawed down from previous musings.

And if so, when had she been there?

My father's letter, referring to the possibility of traveling back to Hatshepsut's time, was dated 1904.

I doodled "1904?" in my journal with the word "Hatshepsut" beside it.

But did it matter when they had *left*?

A sudden realization pulled me upright, heart pounding.

Could I somehow intersect with my parents in the past, before they died?

The thought propelled me from my bed, started me pacing across my room.

I would have to know where, and *when*, to find them. And how could I possibly know?

Another thought washed over me, weakening my knees and dropping me into a chair.

Could they have been there *today*? Even if they had traveled back to ancient Egypt from, say, '04, did they travel to *that* day—the same day I had visited—and somehow we were all there together? Had I missed them? Missed my opportunity to see them again?

My stomach rolled at the thought, and I blinked back tears.

I was a grown woman. But somehow when I thought of my parents, I still felt like the lonely fifteen-year-old girl they left behind in England.

I dropped my head into my hands.

Think, Sahara.

If it were truly possible to intersect with them—somewhere, sometime—how would I do it?

The Valley of the Kings was littered with tombs, many of which had been uncovered before '05 when they died. What if they had visited some of them? All of them?

I could systematically work my way through each possibility, traveling from funeral to funeral—odd thought—looking for traces of them.

Jack's smile flashed in my thoughts. And the man thought my life was boring!

I had at least a fortnight before Lord Carnarvon arrived and we would open the tomb. Howard needed me to make preparations. Could I take the time to... But no, perhaps that didn't matter. Would any time pass while I was gone? Could I travel back in time right now, stay for a month, and return to this spot in my room as if it never happened?

My mind twisted and threatened to splinter at this, so I pushed the idea away. In fact, if I were going to keep going down this path, I needed to push away all ideas of logic, and of cause-and-effect.

I returned to pacing, following the knife's edge line of sunlight that crept across my floor.

I stopped at my bookshelf and scanned the volumes. Which tomb first? Where would they have been most likely to go?

But then a brief flash of common sense. Who was I becoming? I never did anything half-prepared. Did I really want a repeat of today? Look what had happened when I didn't have all the answers before launching into a crazy adventure. I'd been stabbed today, for glory's sake.

And there were still so many questions... My father's letter with its odd warning of "dangers to mind and body." Were things happening to me without my knowledge? And I couldn't be certain I'd return with no time lost. What if I got stuck in the past for too long, and missed the opening of the tomb we'd found? My career would be over, along with my dream of being part of the reform the profession badly needed.

But didn't I have to find them?

Three black holes had consumed my heart for the past seventeen years. A deep sense of being unmoored from the love and belonging of a family, a vague guilt over the death of my parents, and an illogical but desperate wish to change the past. How could I walk away from a chance to understand the truth of the past, not simply the history I remembered and had interpreted into meaning? Refuse a chance to heal everything that hurt?

But I needed a plan.

If it were true I could only visit each place one time, I didn't want to ruin my chances of intersecting them again by blundering into a time and place before I was ready.

No, better to first visit a place where I knew they could *not* possibly be. A place that had not yet been discovered when they were in Egypt. A place that had already driven me nearly mad with curiosity...

The newly-discovered, still-sealed tomb that might just be the lost burial chamber of Tut-Ankh-Amun.

CHAPTER FIFTEEN

1458 B.C.
Mortuary Temple of Hatshepsut
Theban Necropolis, Egypt

"What are you doing in here? No men allowed!"

Renae looked up at the senior priestess's barking shout toward the doorway of the columned Hathor Chapel on the west side of the temple. Then grinned at the sight of Alexander under the lintel of the door.

It still gave her a thrill, even after fifteen years, to see him looking at her with those dark eyes.

He lifted his hands in defense against the priestess Nashim's ire.

Renae dropped the basketry she was weaving and slid out from behind the stone worktable.

With a quick glance at Nashim, she slipped past the group of chattering young girls, grabbed Alexander's upper arm and pulled him through the doorway, out to the portico.

"Yes." She tried to mimic Nashim's stern tone. "What *are* you doing here?"

"I came to see my favorite priestess, hard at work."

"Well, you're going to get me in trouble." She glanced back into the chapel. "Nashim is very strict about our work hours. And you know today is a big day."

"You're the only woman I know who would keep strict work hours during her holiday."

Renae laughed. "Hmm, yes, why didn't my holiday include sunbathing on the beach?"

"You have no one to blame but yourself, and you know it." Alexander poked her side gently.

"But it's the trip of a lifetime, that's for sure."

Renae looked down across the terraces of the mortuary temple, to the crowd building in anticipation of today's events. How amazing she and Alexander could be here for this moment. To honor the strongest female Egyptian pharaoh to ever rule this kingdom.

Alex circled her waist with his arm. "I know you would've liked to have met her."

She shrugged. "Of course. But it would have taken too long. Hard enough to talk my way into the priestess role."

"Oh, you could talk your way into anything you set your mind to, my dear."

"Well, being here to witness this spectacle has always been the dream."

Besides, we can't stay much longer, or else...

Did Alex notice her sharp intake of breath at the sudden thought?

A burly man bumped against her as he passed. Then glanced at her. His face flickered in surprise.

"Ra-Ne-Hannu?" He glanced back down to the second terrace, his brow furrowed. "I thought –" He shook his head.

Renae gave him a half smile. The man was a brute, one of Nashim's heavy lifters employed to corral the bulls for sacrifices. "If you are looking for Nashim, she is inside the chapel."

Alexander gave a little snort. "Be careful though, she's not taking favorably to men today."

Renae elbowed him in the ribs.

Alexander turned her to face him, and locked his arms behind the small of her back. "Can you get away? I thought maybe we could get something to eat, and just absorb all of the excitement. I feel like we probably shouldn't stay much longer. I want to make sure you see everything you wanted to see."

Renae tossed her head back, shaking the oddly-straight hair that still felt like a wig, even though it was attached to her head.

"Sure, what's the worst that can happen? Nashim will fire me?"

Alex kissed the top of her head.

She hooked her arm through his and lifted her chin toward the platform. "Let's see what we can see."

They walked with linked arms down the steps, ready for a new adventure.

She loved that it had always been this way, since they found each other in their university days. More than fifteen years of jumping through history had not dulled the excitement every time they walked side-by-side into something new. Into the unknown.

The crowd parted slightly to give them space. Perhaps sensing she had some official capacity here. A little bubble of pride surged. She had been here only a week, and had managed to find a place and gain respect. Knowing the history, knowing where to go and whom to talk to certainly helped. But still, she could take a little credit, couldn't she?

They were descending against the flow of people crowding forward, toward the festivities that would soon begin in the colonnade above. The air hung heavy with ritual incense and earthy animal smells.

"Alexander?"

They slowed to a stop at the odd sound of his name being hissed through the crowd.

Renae searched for the speaker.

There—that woman—giving a little wave, and an uncertain half-smile.

"Alexander Aldridge! It is you! And Renae, right?"

Renae glanced at Alex in question.

He seemed briefly confused as well, but then his face cleared, and he smiled.

"Joanne?"

The woman moved toward them, circling a tightly-clustered family, her lips parted in surprise.

"Wow, how long has it been?" He turned to Renae. "Renae, you remember Joanne Walters. From Canterbury?"

The memory clicked. Renae smiled, then held out her arms for a quick embrace.

"Joanne! Of course! How funny to run into you here!"

Unbelievable, even.

"I know! What are the odds?"

The three stared at each other for a moment, as if no one knew how to begin explaining what had brought them all to this moment.

"Are you living here now?" Joanne was looking at Renae's priestess garb, and Alex's more common knee-length, belted shirt.

Alex shook his head. "No, we're actually working on the start of the Mentuhotep project." He thumbed in the direction of the temple to their east.

Her eyebrows lifted. "With Carter?"

Renae shook her head. "No, he's still in Cairo fighting those ridiculous Saqqara accusations. We're working with Naville."

Alexander reached a hand out and squeezed Joanne's forearm, as if they were such good, old friends. "But how about you? What have you been up to, and why are you here?"

Joanne's eyes shifted sideways. "Oh, I've always wanted to. You know, see this place in all its glory. Experience this festival day." She brought her eyes back to Alexander's. Smiled, but only with her lips. "Just like you, I suppose."

Renae tried to keep her face impassive. Why the oddly evasive answer?

Alexander smiled in agreement, as if he sensed nothing of the strangeness.

Not too surprising.

"It's been what, ten years? Since we've seen you? Are you still living in London, working at the Petrie?"

"No, no, I left the museum years ago. I'm at a nonprofit in the States now. The Moretti Foundation. Have you heard of it?"

Renae's stomach clenched in a sudden surge of nausea. Had she kept her face expressionless again? She slowly turned her head toward Alexander. Would he be able to contain his reaction?

"Moretti?"

That was all he said. Just that one word. Certainly Joanne would not be able to pick up on all the emotion behind it. The fear. The anger. Even confusion.

"Yes. My boss, the director of the foundation, Giada Moretti —she's doing great work, funding conservation and retrieval. Do you—wait—I think you all went to the same university. Back in Philadelphia, right? University of Pennsylvania?"

Renae kept her breath steady. Their alma mater, across the ocean in the States, boasted Ben Franklin as its founder. She and Alex hadn't been there in years.

"You must know Giada," Joanne was gushing, "she would've been there around the same time as you."

Alexander turned to Renae, as though searching his recollection.

Renae swallowed, fighting the nausea down. "Hmm... Moretti... Yes, the name seems familiar. Perhaps we did know her."

"Well, I'm certain she would remember you! She has that kind of memory, and besides, you two were... Well, you know." She laughed.

Renae forced a smile in return, and hoped it didn't look as much like a grimace of pain as it seemed from the inside of her head.

"Well," Alexander said, "we should probably keep moving. Renae has responsibilities, believe it or not."

Did he just wink at Joanne, as if they shared a secret? How was he able to keep his cool?

"Of course, of course." Joanne was shaking her head, smiling, reaching out for a quick embrace and a kiss on the cheek for Alex, then for her.

"I'm sure Giada will be tickled to hear I ran into someone in this place, at this time, that she knew so long ago. People say it's a small world, but they really have no idea, do they?"

Renae was pushing her shoulder against Alexander's shoulder. *Start walking.*

She tried to laugh. "Yes, they have no idea. So good to see you, Joanne. I hope your stay here is everything you hoped for."

They all waved small goodbyes to each other. As she and Alex walked down the steps, Renae kept her spine straight and her chin lifted, trying to negate the way everything inside her was turning to water.

"Alex, if she—"

Alexander tightened her arm against his side. "Not yet. Not yet."

They waited until they were halfway across the first terrace.

Renae dared to turn her head, to see if Joanne were following them.

If perhaps she and Alex were the real reason Joanne was here.

Had Joanne brought others? Others who would suddenly appear out of the crowd, grab them both, and undo eleven years of hiding?

"I don't see her." She studied the crowd around them. "I don't see anyone looking at us."

Alexander's breath released audibly.

They faced each other, and she felt their faces reflecting equal measures of horror over the absurdly coincidental meeting.

"Alex, if Joanne tells her—"

"Joanne doesn't know where we're staying. She only knows we're here in '04."

"No, we were stupid enough to tell her we were at Mentuhotep with Naville."

Alexander's face darkened.

"She will find us, Alexander. She will find us and she will kill us."

Renae took his hands in hers and pulled them to her chest. To her heart. Her throat tightened. "There's something else."

He looked into her eyes, his expression like marble, face taut.

She hadn't wanted to make this announcement, not like this.

"I'm pregnant."

He pulled his hands from her grip and took a shaky step backward.

"I know." She reached for him and blinked away tears. "Obviously I didn't mean for it to happen. Not again."

"You jumped while pregnant? How could you do that? Were you trying to—"

"I don't know." She covered her face with her hands. "I don't know. Don't ask me that."

Alexander regained his composure, took another deep breath. "We have to go home. Home to America. To fix this."

Renae placed her hands over her belly and looked back across the terraced platform toward where Joanne had disappeared.

"You're right." Her hands were cold, despite the Egyptian sun.

"But first we have to find a way to stop Giada Moretti."

CHAPTER SIXTEEN

November 6, 1922
Luxor, Egypt

$\mathcal{I}$ was ready early, and waiting on the verandah well before Jack would arrive for our sunset photographs. The sun slanted, hazy and hot, across the desert and through the arches, lighting the dusty stone tiles and wicker chairs. I placed my satchel against the leg of a chair.

Minnie was absent from her vigil, probably seated around a meal in the dining room with the other tenants.

I tugged at the fit of my sapphire and white plaid double-breasted jacket with gold buttons and tailored trousers. Did I look too manly? The style was nothing like the taffeta and lace concoction Eve would have forced on me.

Why had I arranged a sunset dinner for myself and Jack, when everything in me screamed to run the other direction from his questions and his family?

Secrets of discovered steps needed to be kept secret, especially from the press.

And secrets of dead parents visiting long ago places should

especially be kept from men whose aunts may have had a role in their deaths.

What was I doing, playing tour guide?

Besides all that, Jack was simply too distracting.

I pressed a hand against my side, a reflex that was becoming habit.

Distraction could be deadly.

I sank into one of the verandah's wicker chairs, my good sense colliding with something more visceral. I knew better than to allow my focus to be divided, to allow myself to trust people.

But Jack's blue American eyes, flashing with humor and daring me to like him, made me forget. Made me long for connection, belonging. For something more than even my passion for archaeological reform.

A fat fly droned a lethargic circle around my head. I swatted it into the distance.

Enough.

I would take tonight's opportunity to further my goals, not forget them in a haze of attraction for blue eyes and a lovable smile.

If Giada Moretti somehow knew of my parents' plans to visit Belzoni in the early nineteenth century, perhaps Jack did, too. I needed to find out.

Jack arrived moments later, with the familiar face of the driver Chefren and his Fiat. He jumped out before Chefren could, and signaled to the Egyptian to stay behind the wheel.

"Where to, my lady?" Jack opened the door of the car and held out a hand.

I half-smiled but ignored his question, and brushed past him to speak into the Fiat. "The Vista Restaurant in Kurna, Chefren."

"Oh, very good, *sayida.*"

We drove down the Wadi Al Melok Road toward the village of Kurna, past the house Howard had built for himself years ago. The domed mud-brick house on the hill above the tombs allowed Howard to stay close to the work and remain undistracted by social demands.

I'd taken the afternoon to make a plan for my next trip through time and to study. By tomorrow, Howard would have the stairwell refilled, to await Porchy's arrival. If I was going to travel back to the ancient time of the tomb's creation, and if touching the sealed doorway was required to make it happen, then my excursion would have to be tonight, before the doorway was reburied.

But first, I would get to the bottom of what Jack knew. I gripped the satchel on my lap.

Jack had brought something as well, some kind of padded, leather folder.

I pointed to the folder. "What's in there?"

He slid the binder between himself and the door, blocking my view of it, and shrugged. "Show you later." Instead, he pointed to my bag. "You've got something to share as well?"

"No, just brought some books in case there were any facts I couldn't remember."

"Facts about what?"

"Whatever we might talk about. Sites in the area."

His forehead crinkled. "You brought books to answer questions I haven't yet asked, just in case those questions came up?"

Now that he put it that way, it seemed ridiculous. I spread a flat palm across the satchel. "I don't like not knowing the answers to things that make me curious."

On the way to Kurna we passed the sprawling Mortuary Temple Complex of Seti I. The same Seti whose tomb, a few kilometers away in the Valley, had been the site of my first trip through time, the tomb made famous by Belzoni.

I pointed out the temple. "This pharaoh's tomb is near where we're currently digging, but his funerary rites and memorial cult were celebrated here at this temple."

Much of the complex was in ruins, but nine massive columns still stood.

"A pit near Seti's tomb gave us one of the first clues of the pharaoh we're searching for. Theodore Davis found a bunch of large storage jars, filled with embalming supplies—bags of natron salt, animal bones, linen collars. And a piece of linen with the name of the pharaoh the supplies were likely used to embalm, Tut-ankh-amun. That was back in 1907. He thought he'd found the pharaoh's tomb, but Howard doesn't believe it was. That's why we're still looking. And since things were different then, Davis simply donated all of it to the Met a couple of years later."

"Different, how?"

"Archaeology. It started more as a rich man's hobby—romanticizing the past by collecting beautiful things. That's still the motivation of many. Lord Carnarvon, even the aristocracy whose collections Howard helps build in the off-season. But these days, we want to study the artifacts, even the social organization of past cultures."

"But the collectors still bring the money?"

"Some. More and more it's educational institutions, though. Their history departments. Though I hope for more."

"Why does that not surprise me?"

"My parents believed we could glean understanding beyond the history, all the way into anthropology—the ideology and group identity of a people, their cultural development. If we removed and studied the material artifacts more carefully, with an eye on what might be lost in the process of digging."

He was grinning.

"Is something funny?"

"How often do you actually need those books? Something tells me you already have every fact you need inside your brain."

I looked out the window, fingers tightening. "Yeah, it's a bad habit. You should've heard the names they called me in boarding school."

He elbowed me.

I turned to him.

"What names?"

"Smart-a-hara." I tucked a stray hair behind my ear. "Know-it-All-dridge."

He was smiling. "I love it."

I frowned.

"No, I'm sorry. I hate that they called you names. But I love your ability to remember so many things." He inhaled and shrugged, as though confessing. "I'm endlessly curious myself, but I have no patience for looking things up in books. I wish I had your powers of recall."

Could I ask him to teach me to spend time living, rather than reading about others' lives?

Get back on track, Sahara.

"So, I still don't understand why you came all this way to meet me. Or why your aunt 'kept track of me,' as you said."

"My turn to be embarrassed." He studied the view through the windscreen of the car.

"I was mostly by myself, growing up. My aunt raised me, and didn't let me socialize much. Private tutors, and all that. Her mentions of you always fascinated me. You seemed—I don't know—larger than life or something."

"You were raised by your aunt?" The shared experience of not having parents connected us, yet worried me. I did not trust his aunt. "Did something happen to your parents as well?"

"A topic for another day." His smile seemed forced. "We're out to have fun tonight, right?"

"So, you were a lonely kid growing up, hearing about another lonely kid across the ocean. I think perhaps you romanticized me a little bit."

"Hmm."

"You didn't spend any time with other kids?" Just how attached was he to his aunt?

"She let me play baseball in the city league. Which I loved. Much better than the stupid riding and fencing lessons. What about you? Any hobbies?"

The restaurant appeared ahead of us, and I drummed my fingers across the satchel. "I love studying history. Drawing artifacts."

"That's not a hobby. That's work."

I bit my lip. "Then I guess I don't have any hobbies."

"Wow. I don't think I can relate. I jump from hobby to hobby like a grasshopper."

"So what did your aunt tell you about my parents? Did she tell you about their trip to Venice after she met me?"

"That was a long time ago. Hard to remember that far back, right?"

No, not really.

But we had arrived at the Vista Restaurant. I let him open my door, then led him into the tiny local establishment that boasted the best views in the area.

The owner, Farik Sapar, motioned us up the stairs, requiring no special request for seating on the rooftop at this time of day.

We emerged onto the rooftop, facing the scooped out valley, with the dusty cliffs looming like ancient sentinels and the sun warm and heavy.

Jack sucked in a breath.

My guess had been correct. A sideways glance at his face, transfixed by the golden blush in the west, was all I needed to see.

I hung my satchel over the back of a chair and led him forward to the edge of the rooftop, where a stone wall came only to my thighs.

He snapped a photograph immediately, then another. And one catching me in the periphery, though I shook my head and looked away.

"There," I pointed across the road we entered, "you can better see the steps to the Seti temple, and the work they've been doing there. And down that way," I pointed the other direction, toward the east. "Well, I guess you have to lean a bit, to see around to the left more." I pushed the upper part of my body forward, "You can just make out the Nile—"

"Careful!" Jack grabbed at my arms with both hands and pulled back. "Do you have any fear at all?"

He kept one arm circled around me, still holding me to his side, as if I might pitch over the wall.

I caught my breath. *I guess I was a little off balance.*

Or perhaps it was Jack, and his attentive arm, that had me off balance.

"Sorry, yes. Sometimes I get excited. Forget what I'm doing."

"I've noticed. I feel like you might need somebody to follow you around, just to make sure your curiosity doesn't lead you into a ditch."

The glow in my belly at the protective words didn't stop the indignant reply. "I don't need anyone watching over me, Jack."

His arm still circled me, as if we were a couple looking over the romantic scene.

But he pulled back and held his hands upward, shaking his head. "Message received. You're good on your own, you don't need anyone."

His aggravated tone was a reproach.

Why had I been so annoyed? He was only trying to watch out for me. Something no one ever did.

A smooth voice behind us asked, "May I bring you some tea?"

We turned back to the tables, to the proprietor.

"Yes, please, Farik. Thank you."

Farik served pale-pink hibiscus tea in delicate china cups with a plate of *eish baladi,* warm flatbread accompanied by a cumin-rich hummus and some locally made cheese.

We nibbled on the starters and talked lightly of my work, of archaeology in general. I was still reticent to share details, and didn't want to say too much.

Jack's eyes drank in the horizon, squinting slightly at rays chasing across the desert floor to spread over our table. "I can see how much you love it."

I studied the fine lines at the corners of his eyes, lines that deepened when he squinted. But they were always there, weren't they? A clear indication of a lifetime of smiles. He seemed the kind of chap who found joy in everything.

"I can see why it brings you to life." His eyes were still on the scenery, and the words quiet.

An odd phrase. "Brings me to life?"

"I just mean when you're looking at it, when you're talking

about it—even facts that would seem bookish and dry to most people—it's like you come alive."

He turned back to me, unusually somber. "I don't think I've ever been that passionate about anything. Well, except maybe collecting baseball cards when I was a kid." His mouth turned up on one side. "You should see that collection."

"Well, it is alive to me, I guess. It's hard to explain, but it's like I can see it. As though when I'm looking at what's left behind, at the ruins, the details of the past fill themselves in."

" As though your mind is sketching it?"

"Yes, exactly." He'd put it into words, what I'd always felt.

"Ever wish you could truly see it? Go back and see it all, like it was? Originally?"

I slid my glance back to his eyes, eyes that had seemed warm and laughing a moment ago. Was there deception there? The question was innocent, but too targeted, considering my suspicions.

"Your binder," I jutted my chin toward the leather-bound piece on the table beside him. "Is that your baseball card collection?"

"No." He laughed and leaned back. "I just brought some photographs I've taken since I've been here."

"Since you've been here? Hasn't it only been a few days? How do you have them developed already?"

He put a finger to his lips as if to quiet me. "Don't tell the hotel staff. I may, or may not, be using my washroom as a dark-room." That twinkle was back in his eye.

I laughed, despite trying to stay on my guard.

He was watching me, studying me.

I looked away first.

"Why do you do that?" He reached across the table, and pulled my hand away from my mouth, his touch light but electric on my wrist. "You cover your smile whenever you laugh. Why do you do that?"

I shrugged. "Wasn't aware that I did."

"Well, you do. And you shouldn't."

"So let's see the photographs."

He slid the portfolio toward me, but didn't open it.

With a glance for permission, I opened the cover.

A banded strap held a handful of photographs. I pulled them out one by one.

They were unlike anything I expected.

CHAPTER SEVENTEEN

ourists by the thousands came to Egypt to take photographs. They photographed the tombs, the hills, the temples.

Jack had come to Egypt to photograph the people.

Here, a small child, dirty and ragged and perched on the curb of a Luxor street, studying Jack with expectant eyes, perhaps waiting for *baksheesh* after allowing the photo.

And here a young mother, poverty etched into her face and the hunch of her shoulders, pulling water from a village well, a cluster of children circling her skirts.

My breath shallowed. I blinked away sudden tears.

They were all like this. The impoverished, the disabled. Children toiling in fields alongside father in backbreaking work.

"Jack." It was only a whisper. I didn't trust my voice. "These are… astonishing. I had no idea."

I pulled out the final photo, a close-up of Lateef, the *caliche* driver whom Jack had paid too much money for our short trip to the Winter Palace Hotel two nights ago. Eyes closed and smiling, with a chubby-faced boy of perhaps only two years old, cradled against his bearded cheek.

I couldn't take my eyes from it.

This is what he sees, when he looks at people.

"I went back to visit him, after we met him the other night."

My heart felt like it was breaking.

"Jack, when I talked about photographs being useful only for documenting the archaeological process, for chronicling the historical finds we make, I—I think I was being a fool."

I lifted my eyes to his, and swiped at tears. "This is so much more. So much more important. These are things people need to see, need to understand."

He pulled the portfolio toward him and closed it, shrugging and smiling. "Just a few candid shots, nothing more."

It occurred to me that in the same way Jack Moretti didn't seem to take life too seriously, he didn't take himself seriously enough.

As if by mutual agreement we kept the conversation light for the rest of the meal. I couldn't find a way into the questions I meant to ask. Or perhaps I didn't want to. Must I always be so suspicious? Why couldn't I simply enjoy myself, open up a little?

Jack jumped from the table a dozen times to snap pictures of the sun as it descended, and long before darkness fully fell Farik came and lit torches on the rooftop. We had been joined by several other clusters of diners, but had spoken to no one, and the evening seemed to belong to us alone.

"My favorite color," I said, as the sun flamed behind a stretch of low-slung clouds.

"Which one?"

"Inky ribbons of clouds across the terra-cotta canvas of a Luxor sunset."

At his silence, I sought his eyes, expecting amusement at my overblown description.

Instead, his expression spoke of something else. A longing wistfulness that broke something free in me. Did he feel it, too? Did a sunset like this whisper to him also that the world might be more than a mechanism set in perpetual motion? That it might be a place of mystery and wildness, a place to long for in the way we long for fairy tales to be true?

Jack severed the connection first, clearing his throat and drumming fingers against the table.

Farik brought plates of flaky *feteer*.

I reached for the plate first. "And now my favorite dessert."

"What is it?"

I picked up a piece and held it to Jack's eye level. "See all those thin layers of dough, with the chocolate between? Ancient Egyptians would leave it at temples as an offering for the gods. Probably with honey, now chocolate." I took a bite and smiled, eyes closed for a moment around the flavor. "It can be sweet, like this one, or savory, with meat or cheese. I make this all the time —the chocolate version—in the dighouse kitchen, after everyone's asleep."

Jack tilted his head to take in my body, head to toe. "Clearly, you don't eat it all the time, or you wouldn't look that good."

I laughed. "I discipline myself to one piece. Leave the rest as a treat for the other residents."

When the *feteer* was gone, I reached for my satchel. "We should be getting back. I'm sure Chefren is waiting by now." And I did have much more planned for tonight, after all.

On the way back in Chefren's Fiat, a velvety silence covered us until Jack broke the quiet mood.

"I'm really sorry about your parents."

An odd thing to say, and yet I felt more connection to him than I had when we had talked about my parents at the Winter Palace two nights ago.

"It's fine. People leave, people die. It happens."

He frowned. "You've lost more than just your parents, haven't you?"

"So many died in the war," I said generally. "How about you? Did you fight in the war?"

"No. In the States the draft didn't start until about eighteen months before the end. I registered of course, but never got called up. I guess I was in the "old man" end of the pool." He half-smiled and blinked, looking away. "About twenty-seven. Probably would've needed a cane to get across the fields. Did you lose someone you cared about in the war?"

The American House was in view, and the answer was far too painful to share in the remaining moments we had together.

"A topic for another day," I said, repeating the answer he'd given me when we started out.

"Hmm." The reference clearly was not lost on him. "And your parents? Did they ever tell you anything about the reason they went to Venice?"

After the warmth of the evening, the oddly-specific question left me cold.

"Vacation. That's all."

Just before we rolled to a stop, I tucked my scarf between the seat cushions, nearly out of sight. When Jack opened my door, I slipped out quickly, shielding the interior with my body.

He walked me to the steps and up to the verandah, the car and driver idling in the road.

"Oh!" I placed a hand on Jack's chest. "Just a minute!"

I trotted back down to the automobile, leaned into the back and pulled my scarf from the cushions.

At the same time, I whispered to Chefren. "Come back for me in thirty minutes, and say nothing to the gentleman."

Chefren raised an eyebrow, but nodded.

I turned back to Jack, who was already descending the steps, and held up my scarf. "Almost forgot it!"

Back on the verandah, under the ever-watchful eye of Minnie Burton, Jack took my hand. "Thank you for a lovely sunset. When will my next tour take place?"

I tensed. "Next?"

"You didn't think one photo shoot of a sunset was going to hold up your end of the bargain, did you?"

"Tell me again what we're bargaining for?"

"Your tour services, in exchange for my not writing a story about you."

"Hmm. It's starting to sound more like blackmail."

Jack glanced at Minnie and winked. "Call it what you wish."

I wanted to say, "Maybe I'll see you when I get back from the Eighteenth Dynasty." Part of me wished I could come clean, bring Jack into the adventure I was planning. And yet another part of me wanted to say, "I think it's best we don't see each other. Because I think your aunt killed my parents."

"Perhaps tomorrow. If Howard doesn't need me."

He lifted and kissed my hand. "Tomorrow, then."

I pulled my fingers from his grasp and retreated into the house.

Jack's last question echoed. Why ask about my parents and Venice?

I had let my guard down again, but Jack was not a trusted friend. I was on my own here, and it was up to me to carve out my own place, my own destiny.

I spent the half hour mentally preparing for what was ahead.

When I emerged onto the darkened verandah, I found Chefren smoking against his car, waiting for what would come next.

"To the King's Valley, Chefren. All the way to the digsite."

He frowned. "In the dark, *sayida*? That is no place for a lady."

I jumped into the back and pulled the door closed.

When Chefren was back behind the wheel, I patted his shoulder. "Don't worry, you'll be there with me. And I'll only be a moment. I just need to check on something."

Chefren shook his head, but drove on.

I'll only be a moment.

I was still awed by the idea it might be possible to travel backward into the ancient past, spend as much time as I liked exploring and researching, and then return to find Chefren and his Fiat waiting where I left them moments before. If it was true. Still not sure about that.

What other answers was I a fool to move forward without? I studied the back of Chefren's red skull cap and ran through the list.

Whose tomb will it be? King or noble? What dynasty?
Has it already been plundered?

Can I bring anything with me? Bring anything back?

Will it be the same time of day there?

That last question brought a series of other, more foreboding speculations.

What if it's night in the desert, and a jackal tears me to pieces before I can find civilization?

What if I end up on the other side of the sealed door and can't get out?

Will there be expectations put on me?

And then there was still the risk to my career, if I didn't return immediately.

And Jack, with his ready laugh and his secrets. Was I leaving behind a threat?

Or perhaps ... a possibility?

Get ahold of yourself, girl.

The only way to get answers was to go after them.

I distilled my questions into three goals.

One, learn the identity of our tomb's owner.

Two, understand how my ability to travel in time worked and make sure I could control it, before beginning to search for my parents in tombs and times they may have visited.

And *three*, to survive.

Then, of course, a million other smaller curiosities.

I brought nothing with me except a bit of money to pay Chefren upon my return, and a new handheld electric torch purchased in England before coming to Egypt this season.

I left Chefren idling in the auto on the narrow access road to the digsite, and descended, breath held, to Howard's tent. The automobile's headlights disappeared behind me. No lantern illuminated the tent. Thankfully, Howard must be spending the night in his house, rather than the digsite.

Past the tent, I flicked on the electric torch and swept a shaky beam of light across the sand to the entrance of the tomb.

The chilled desert air felt sharp against my tongue and in my lungs. Above me the stars banded across a moonless sky. I was glad for the torch.

A rustling sound near the stair stopped me short.

"Who's there?" The voice was deep, threatening.

The guard Howard posted. I'd forgotten.

"It's only me. Alsahra'. I—I needed to get some—a sketch—"

I needn't have bothered. The guard stepped aside with a disinterested yawn.

I hastened to the unearthed stairs and descended, one hand scraping the side of the new trench. The light swept the steps beneath me, and I counted.

One, two, three... Twelve steps down. There was the top of the dug-out door at my feet, with its carved Necropolis Seal. I ran my fingers over the indentations, closed my eyes for a brief moment. Steadied my nerves.

It was time.

"*Sayida?* You are well?

Oh, for glory's sake. Chefren. Somewhere in the dark above.

I ignored him, quickly tried to summon up an image of the tomb, see the door in my mind's eye, recreate the sights and sounds and smells, the moment and the time in which it had all happened. To see myself there, in that ancient place.

I bent to the carved door, flattened a palm against it, and turned the top of my head toward my feet.

The vertigo came, a welcome feeling.

I could control this wild thing I had discovered!

And then I fell.

125

CHAPTER EIGHTEEN

One's ideas wander beyond their usual sphere—
everything around is calm and motionless—
the sense of magnitude, time, both past and future, and everlasting
space, creeps in through all this stationary, fixed, immutable
illustration.

~Howard Carter, *The Tomb of Tut-ankh-amun*

1325 B.C.
Thebes, Egypt

I fell hard.

Plunged downward, stomach flipping, head still bent. Hand scraping stone.

Jolted against the ground, lost my footing. Slammed to my knees.

Wha-a-t?

I flung myself upright in the darkness, blinked and breathed. My palm stung like a burn, but was still braced against the door. The lower part of the door.

Of course! I began my trip on a mound of sand with only the top of the sealed doorway revealed. Once I arrived, that mound of sand was gone. I had fallen nearly two meters to the bottom of the doorway.

My knees throbbed. I hobbled to my feet and brushed the grit of sand from linen-covered knees. A jeweled collar felt heavy on my throat and chest.

Already I felt the difference in the air, in my clothes, in my*self*. My willful cropped hair now fell, sleek and blunt-edged, to my shoulders.

The night was still cold and starry, the air still clear and sharp. My torch had disappeared, but even in the darkness it was obvious the steps leading upward were newly cut, and the hieroglyphs in the door were unsoftened by millennia.

I crept up the stairs—sixteen of them now—and reached the surface to find myself face-to-face with three surprised men.

They were bald and bare-chested, with skin as dark as the night sky, and each held a tool resembling a shovel. All three converged on me with shovels raised, as though Kek, god of primordial darkness, had suddenly appeared.

I shot my arms into the air and stumbled backward, nearly pitching down the stairs.

"Get to work, you lazy Nubians!"

The command pierced the night air from behind the three laborers.

I squinted to locate the arrogant voice.

Another man, feet spread wide on the floor of a two-wheeled chariot glared down at me. His skin was a few shades lighter than the three and he wore a gold pectoral neck piece on a bare chest. Two horses harnessed to the chariot stood in silent submission.

He raised a whip. "Where did you come from?"

Again, the odd mismatch of words and lips I noted at Hatshepsut's temple this morning.

This morning. Or a hundred thirty years ago, depending on how you looked at it.

I forced down a hysterical laugh. The idea of being in ancient Egypt, in the middle of the desert, at night, with four strange men, was beyond even my usual tolerance for risky behavior.

"I need to return to the palace." It was the first thing that came to mind. If this tomb was indeed the tomb of Tut-ankh-amun, the most likely location for the royal palace would have been at the site now called Malqata, built by Tut-ankh-amun's grandfather, Amenhotep III, which he called "The House of Rejoicing." The sprawling palace complex lay about three miles away, if I remembered correctly, still here on the West Bank of the Nile, outside the ancient floodplain. The Met had been excavating the thirty thousand square meter site for about ten years.

"You should not be out here. It is no place for a woman at night."

No kidding.

"Which is why the Great Royal Wife would want me returned at once."

Again, a strange bluff, and the first excuse I could think of.

The supervisor chuckled, a mocking sound that chilled me. "Great Royal Wife? She is not wife anymore. Or perhaps she is not wife yet."

I lifted my chin at the nonsensical answer. In my experience, haughtiness always got better results than deference. "Will you take me or not?"

He hesitated, then inclined his head toward the seat of his chariot. "I will take you. But be assured you will not go unpunished when we arrive."

I wasted no time getting on board the obsidian black chariot with its metallic gold edges. The night air had me shivering.

My driver clucked his tongue at the horses and turned the chariot on its wheels, then scowled at the laborers. "See that you have the stairs filled in by my return!"

I thought of Howard and his barked orders to the Egyptian men who helped at the dig. Some things never changed.

He questioned me relentlessly in the twenty minutes we rolled toward the palace.

Where was I from? What was I doing in the tomb? Where was my husband? A dozen more.

I bluffed through some, remained stonily silent at others.

Watched the empty spot slide by where the American House would one day stand.

Once again, the impossibility swept me. But in its wake, excitement pounded a rhythm in time with the horses' hooves.

I was here! In ancient Egypt. Able to explore, to experience, to research the questions that had puzzled me for years. To take in the sights and smells and tastes of a period that had fascinated me since childhood. It was amazing and terrifying, wonderful and exhilarating and unbelievable. And yet somehow a mystery some part of me had always known to be true.

When the chariot rolled into the walled courtyard of what was most certainly the palace at the site of Malqata, I nearly cried.

In the darkness, the torchlit palace complex spread like a sparkling city toward the man-made harbor that connected The House of Rejoicing to the Nile by a long canal.

But there was no time to indulge in sentimentality. My driver had mentioned "punishment." Before he reined the horses to a stop, I leaped from the chariot, bolted for the side of the courtyard, and ducked into the darkness of the colonnade.

My rescuer yelled something.

I was too far to hear.

I slipped into an empty hallway that ran parallel to the courtyard and slumped against a wall to catch my breath and steady my nerves.

The hall stretched out into darkness, with infrequent torchlight flickering against wall murals of flowers and reeds. From the perspective when we had approached, this hall might be one of dozens.

So. My goals...

Learn.

Control my ability.

Survive.

Right now objective three seemed most important.

This palace was enormous. Could I disappear into it? Find a place to sleep, food to eat, without being noticed and tossed into an ancient dungeon?

A heavy clomp of sandals cut my thoughts short.

I turned to face a large man, weighted with jewelry from gold arm bands to earrings. He approached with a now-familiar Egyptian scowl.

"It is late. Why are you not in your bedchamber?"

Gladly. A private bedchamber sounded great right now.

I chewed my lip. Was there a map to this place?

He jutted his chin forward. "Go."

I walked in the direction his chin pointed. Sporadic torches burning in wall sockets lit a shadowy hall. It branched repeatedly, with other corridors disappearing into darkness. Was I supposed to take one of them?

The big man lumbered behind me still, so I must not be too far off track.

"To your bedchamber, woman!"

I stopped and turned.

He was pushing open a door.

Perfect. A night of solitude to catch my breath, make a plan, and get some sleep.

Behind my escort, another man approached. Hopefully not my chariot driver.

I turned to enter the room.

Not so perfect.

Solitude did not appear to be in my future. Nearly a dozen women roamed the room, most occupied and ignoring my arrival. One or two glanced my way with narrowed eyes and tight lips.

A surge of anxiety hit me. Was I part of a harem?

I spun back to the door. Too late to disappear again?

But my escort was sliding the door closed.

A moment before it swung shut, the other man in the hall walked past and glanced into the bedchamber.

My breath stopped and my head swam.

Impossible as it was, I would swear the man passing by was Jack Moretti.

CHAPTER NINETEEN

1325 B.C.
The House of Rejoicing
Thebes, Egypt

The door slammed shut and blocked my view of the hall. Jack's lookalike glanced at me as he passed. No sign of recognition.

I clenched my teeth, breathing heavily.

He'd been dressed in the standard Egyptian garb, bare-chested down to the white two-pointed kilt wrapped and tied at his waist, and his head shaved bald. Black pencil outlined his eyes in the traditional *wadjet,* the Eye of Horus, with its elongated almond shape and looped scroll beneath the eye.

And yet, with all the ancient accoutrements, it was Jack. It had to be.

Unless some freakish force was drawing me to a man who was his ancient double, as though we were destined to find each other in any time.

I shook off the melodrama. Not possible. It had to be Jack.

But that was also impossible.

Giada Moretti's sharp eyes flitted across my memory.

My jaw ached with tightness. The anger coursing through me took in Giada, and Jack, and even myself.

If Jack was here, then everything he'd said was a lie. Nothing I felt was true. I allowed myself to open up and trust, and I was a fool.

And something very dangerous was happening to me.

I reached for the door, then let my hand drop. Not yet.

But a fourth objective for my list.

Figure out if I was crazy, or if Jack Moretti had followed me to ancient Egypt.

"Ra-Ne-Hannu?"

I turned instinctively to the name.

But, what? Was I again being called by the name given to me at Hatshepsut's Mortuary Temple? How could that be?

I tried to smile at the woman who had called the name, but disappointment floated behind my smile. It could not have been my mother's name, then. Just an ordinary priestess.

But still, someone by that name at Hatshepsut's temple would have been dead by this time. It made no sense.

The woman, a girl really, squared off against me. Her skin was lighter than most in the room, but her eyes were intensely dark. "I thought it was you, but you seem different. You *look* different. What are you doing here?"

I surveyed the chamber. Women lounged on cushions borne by wooden bed frames while others brushed or oiled their hair. Some were removing jewelry or stripping off their dresses.

Several of them had nasty looks for me.

I looked back to my interrogator. What to say?

"Tovah," the girl said, touching her chest. "I've seen you around the palace. But I thought you left."

I couldn't take my eyes from her lips. At the start of her sentence, the words and mouth didn't match, as I'd come to expect. By the time she finished, they seemed to line up, as though she spoke English. The effect was like looking through a dirty window. At first, you saw only smudges, with everything beyond a blur. But then a shift would come, the smudges would disappear, and the outdoors would come into focus.

"Tovah. Yes, I'm sorry."

"So? Didn't I hear you were leaving? Returning north?"

"I—I changed my mind. I am going to stay."

Most of the women were circling now, eying me up and down.

One of them lifted my jeweled collar in pinched fingers. "We don't need any more women here."

A few others snickered. "We could use that collar, though," one of them said.

Tovah stepped between me and the group with a raised hand. "Leave her alone. She has more breeding than the rest of you combined."

"Ha! This from a slave girl? What do you know of breeding?"

Tovah shrugged. "Ignore all of them. Everyone's suspicious since the king's mur... death."

Interesting.

She jutted a thumb toward the side of the room. "You can take Ramla's bed. She has... left."

The word was ominous. I didn't ask questions.

I crossed to the bed Tovah indicated and lay across it. I had no other clothes, and didn't intend to strip under the scornful eyes of the room.

Exhaustion caught up with me. I had traveled in time twice today, and both my eyesight and my brain were getting fuzzy.

Within minutes, the torches were extinguished and I was left to think about my extraordinary circumstances.

The thoughts lasted only a few seconds before sleep overtook me.

But rest only seemed to last a few minutes.

The strangeness of my surroundings prodded me awake, and the night ticked past in anxiety-lengthened hours. I lost all sense of time.

And then someone was clapping and calling out instructions in a sharp voice.

Torches flared. Was it still the middle of the night?

No, the women were all rising, stretching, yawning. The bedchamber was an interior room, with no windows to let in the dawn. But it must be morning.

The woman calling out instructions was about fifty with a matronly figure wrapped in soft robes and pastel-hued sashes, but her eyes were not kindly.

She eyed me briefly, still in my bed, as she passed. "It is time to get ready!"

I found my protector Tovah and copied her actions. Water from a basin, splashed onto my face. She handed me a kohl pencil and a blurry bronze mirror, and I tried to copy the eye-lining they all wore.

"Where are your things?" she grunted. "Your dresses and jewels?"

No quick lie surfaced.

But Tovah saved me. "Did your people take your belongings when they left? Even though you stayed behind?"

"Yes," I breathed. "Yes, they left me with nothing, I'm afraid."

She shook her head, as though disgusted on my behalf. "We all have more than enough."

From the sideways looks I'd gotten from some of the other women, I doubted anyone but my new friend intended to share.

"Thank you, Tovah."

"Hurry, ladies. It is time for the morning meal." More clapping from the woman in charge.

Again, the fear that I was part of some sort of king's harem tickled at me. I needed to be careful.

But then again, hadn't the king just died?

It was too soon to be making assumptions. I'd brought myself back to the funeral site of *someone*, but all I really knew was the tomb's door was carved with royal seals. It could be anyone in the royal family. Though Tovah had said the king was dead. Murdered?

I rehearsed my goals. *Learn. Control it. Survive.*

Jack?

That last one still felt like a hot, angry welt across my chest.

I filed out of the bedchamber and positioned myself in the middle of the line of women, head down.

We walked, escorted, down a stunning corridor, now lit by clerestory-style gridded windows high above our heads. Wooden columns supported the lofty ceiling, the pillars painted a fire red along their lengths, then carved and painted at the capitals to resemble lilies. The floors and walls sported bright blues and yellows, scenes of animals in marshes, the flora and fauna of ancient Egypt. I resisted the urge to run my fingertips along each glossy column I passed.

The corridor led to a chamber just as richly decorated, with a high ceiling and a series of long tables set at the perimeter. My stomach rumbled at the overflowing trays of food crowding the tables—green vegetables and lentils, some kind of meat—pigeon, perhaps?—and mounds of dates and figs set beside tan flatbread and pots of golden honey.

Tovah shoved me toward a position near the center of the middle table.

Did the seating arrangement matter? Was I making some kind of statement with my choice of seats?

Openly hostile stares shot in my direction from some of the other women.

Tovah sat on my left, but the seat to my right remained empty.

A few minutes later a young woman in a white flowing tunic with winged sleeves and a wide, jeweled collar, swept into the dining hall with several sword-armed men trailing.

She crossed to our table, circled it, and sat in the center, directly beside me.

My stomach clenched. This was the Great Royal Wife, no doubt. Or princess, perhaps. She seemed to be barely twenty years old.

She turned a regal eye on me.

"Who are you?"

Tovah spoke from my left. "Ra-Ne-Hannu, your majesty.

From lands in the far north, left behind when her party departed. She wishes to serve as one of your royal court."

My tight shoulders let go a small pinch of tension. Not a harem, then. More like a lady-in-waiting to whomever this girl was.

But my relief didn't last.

The girl beside me gripped my arm and stared into my eyes. "You were with Ahmose?"

I swallowed. "Uh, yes?"

Her voice dropped to a whisper. "I must speak with you as soon as the meal has ended." She glanced up at the guards who had brought her in. "Tell no one but Xonsu. She will bring you to me."

Oh gravy.

I forced myself to nibble on some grilled meat and hunks of flavorful cheese, rather than dig into the bread and honey, but my thoughts were only half-there.

The royal girl beside me spoke exclusively to the women on her right, as though she were purposely ignoring me.

"Ankhe-sen-amun is much distraught since the death of her husband." Tovah's voice was low and grave on my left. "Do not be offended at her strange ways. She is not herself."

Ankhe-sen-amun. I rolled the unfamiliar name around in my mind.

I ripped a piece of flatbread and dipped it into honey. "Tell me about her husband. What was he like?"

"Tut-ankh-amun was a good ruler, young as he was."

My heart surged. So the tomb was his!

Howard and I had truly found the lost tomb of Tut-ankh-amun!

Tovah's voice turned reverent. "He was Tut-ankh-amun, Horus Pleasing of Birth, One of Perfect Laws who Pacifies the Two Lands, Elevated of Appearance Who Satisfies the Gods, Lord of the Forms of Ra, Living Image of Amun."

Wow.

"He restored the worship of Ra, as was right, and brought us back from his father's heresy. Brought us from Amarna, back here to The House of Rejoicing where we belong." Her voice lowered to a whisper and she leaned closer, shoulder pressed against mine. "Now that he is gone, without an heir, the palace is filled with rumors and no one feels safe."

Oh, how I wished for my satchel with pen and journal! The information I could glean here! But nothing to write it down. I was repeating everything twice in my head, desperate to retain every drop.

The meal was winding down. Bowls of water were brought by deferential servants, and I followed the lead of others who dipped their fingers to wash.

"Tell me, Tovah, how do I find Xonsu?"

Tovah's scowled. She glanced to the end of the table, where the older woman who seemed to be our supervisor was finishing her meal and wiping her mouth. "She is there, where she always sits."

"Of course." I smiled. "Forgetful of me."

Xonsu stood just then, and all the women of the table besides the royal widow immediately stood with her. I scrambled to my feet. Did anyone notice I was late to rise?

I glanced down at Ankhe-sen-amun and she nodded once, her eyes intense. Clearly, she still expected me to meet her.

The ladies filed out, past Xonsu, and I stepped aside, until I was last in line.

When I reached Xonsu at the arched doorway of the dining hall, I paused. "The Great Royal Wife wishes me to be brought to her."

Did I sound... authentic? The ancient Egyptians had no word for "queen" since most pharaohs had a retinue of wives, referenced by their position in the lineup.

Xonsus' eyes widened for an unguarded moment and then her lips formed a hard line. "Very well."

She exited the dining hall and turned the opposite direction of the departing line of ladies.

I followed.

We marched through a honeycomb of hallways, until I was so disoriented I could never find my way back. All the way, I kept my eyes open for any sign of Jack, impossible as it seemed. But everything was impossible here.

Finally, at the end of a wide hall, I saw a wooden double door guarded on either side by sword-holding sentries.

Xonsu flicked a hand toward the door as we approached, and the two lurched to swing the doors open.

Inside what could only be the royal bedchamber, Xonsu turned to me and lifted her chin.

"The Great Royal Wife will join you shortly, I assume. Touch nothing."

And then she disappeared and the double doors trapped me in.

I scanned the chamber. More accurately, the cluster of rooms. To the right opened an alcove with a raised platform bed, but also another small dressing area. This central space felt like a small audience chamber, with low couches and a raised, ornate chair.

Ankhe-sen-amun arrived a few minutes later, escorted by guards, whom she dismissed at the door.

She turned to me, then crossed and gripped both my hands, her fingers nearly white against my own.

"You must help me, Ra-Ne-Hannu. You are the only one who can."

CHAPTER TWENTY

*T*hree objectives here in the ancient past.
Learn whose tomb we had discovered. Done.
Figure how to control my travels through time. So far, so good, but no way to be certain until I tried to get home.
Survive. Choppy waters, but not dead yet.
Jack. Don't want to think about that now.
What was *not* on my list of priorities was helping a young, widowed queen in crisis.
I extricated my fingers from Ankhe-sen-amun's grip.
"I am not certain how I could help—"
"You can move freely through the palace and learn what is happening. You can get word to your people about my plight. Perhaps you can even find me another husband who will not see me as simply a tool in his rise to power!"
So she had her own list.
"Your majesty—"
Ankhe-sen-amun shook her head, pulling me to a wooden, linen-draped couch at the side of the room. "We will be friends. Please. Call me Senamun."
Nicknames in Ancient Egypt. Amazing.
Tut-ankh-amun's wife had dropped the *ankh*, meaning "life"

and kept the female prefix before the god-name *Amun*. Her nickname sounded like "sen-a-moon," or even "cinnamon," which matched the beautiful color of her skin.

I rubbed at my forehead. "Senamun, thank you for your offer of friendship. But..." I slowed my refusal. Wouldn't I love to hear more about the inner workings of the political life here in this time and place before I left?

She interpreted my pause as agreement. "Listen, we have little time before I am expected in the throne room, and Ay cannot find you here. I must tell you, I believe my life is in danger!"

"In danger from whom?"

"From that wretched commoner, Ay!"

My mind spun through facts. A tomb in the West Valley, WV23, was another of The Great Belzoni's discoveries. It had been plundered completely in ancient times, retaining only the sarcophagus, smashed to pieces. Though clearly built as a royal tomb, it had been used for the mummy of the vizier Ay, who was believed to have assumed power after Tut-ankh-amun.

So. The vizier Ay, now that Senamun's husband was dead, was threatening the life of the young widow?

"Why would he want to kill you?"

She closed her eyes and sucked in a breath. "Because I refuse to marry him."

Glorious murals of Ay and his chief royal wife, Tey, had graced the tomb walls, but at some point the faces were horribly scratched out, presumably by a successor wanting to erase the memory of the former ruler. Not hard to imagine this girl's life could be in danger.

"Only fourteen days since my husband's seventy days were completed, and already Ay expects to be crowned Lord of the Two Lands, King of Upper and Lower Egypt, Son of Ra, and thinks a marriage to me will assure him the throne."

"And you do not wish to marry him?"

She looked at me as though I'd asked her to eat dirt.

"He is old, and fat, and cruel. I would sooner marry my pet baboon."

I stifled a laugh. Could I tell her that history would put Tey as the Royal Wife on the wall of Ay's tomb, so she had nothing to worry about? Of course, I couldn't know for certain. Ay might have married this girl first, then Tey after Senamun was... dead.

Senamun dabbed at tears with delicate fingers. "But I do not think only of my preferences, Ra-Ne-Hannu. I think of this land I love, and what is best for my people. Horemheb, as Chief Commander of the Army, has been Hereditary Prince of Upper and Lower Egypt and Deputy of the King in the Entire Land for nearly ten years!"

Another jolt. Theodore Davis found Horemheb's tomb in the Valley in 1908.

The sudden *realness* of all the dusty facts my brain possessed was like having fairy tale characters walk into my life and introduce themselves.

"It is Horemheb who is to claim the throne, should Tut-ankh-amun die childless." Her face blanched.

I sensed unspoken pain in the simple word, and more of a story.

"Horemheb would probably be king already, if he were not fighting in Asia. Not that I would agree to marry Horemheb either, commoner that he is."

I was having trouble keeping up. "So whom do you wish to marry?"

Senamun jumped from the couch and paced before me, one hand clutching at her throat.

"A royal, of course! My family has ruled the Two Lands for more than one hundred fifty Inundations of the Nile. We do not put commoners on the throne!"

"So who is the royal man you can marry?" Did Senamun have a brother? Marrying your brother was quite the norm in ancient Egypt, keeping it all in the family.

"Did Ahmose tell you nothing? He himself took the letter."

This Ahmose character was causing a problem.

"Letter?"

"How can you not know this?"

"I, I was not—"

She stopped her pacing, hands to her hips. "A month after my husband's death, the letter to the Hittite king, Suppululiuma. When I asked him to send me his son to marry."

Hittite king, with a royal prince for Senamun. Got it.

"But you must know, the king sent Ahmose back with an envoy. He suspected my motives and wished to see if my request was genuine. I assured the messengers I did indeed wish to marry the Hittite prince, and sent them back with my entreaty. If I am successful, the prince should be arriving very soon. We must sign the marriage contracts in secret, and quickly, before Ay discovers what I have done."

Whew. How had I fallen directly into court intrigue? It was a bit much.

"It sounds like a good plan, Senamun—"

"But I need help! I need to make Ay believe I will marry him, but not until after a delay of at least ten days. I need to bring the prince into the palace without discovery. And I need to stay alive!"

"If Ay wishes to marry you, why would he kill you?"

She sank to the couch beside me once more. "I—I think he may have killed my husband."

So, more than court intrigue. Quite possibly I'd involved myself in a murder plot.

"He was always sick, it is true. Ever since we were children together. His bones were not strong. But the accident—I cannot believe the chariot wheels both failed together!"

"You think Ay sabotaged his chariot, in order to kill him and claim the throne?"

"Yes, and if that is true, he will not stop at killing only my husband. He will kill me as well, to keep the power he had as vizier and regent since Tut-ankh-amun's coronation as a child."

My crash course in late Eighteenth Dynasty politics was making my head swim.

"Please, Ra-Ne-Hannu, find out what you can about what Ay is planning. And try to learn of the Hittite prince's arrival." She gestured toward her lavish bedchamber. "I am as good as a prisoner here. Nothing I do goes unnoticed by those who are loyal to Ay."

"Senamun, I do not think I can—"

"But you must!" The words were sharp, delivered not in the tone of a friend but of a woman accustomed to being royalty all her life.

I sighed and nodded, since there was not much else I could do. But I had little intention of embroiling myself in any of this.

"Good." She smiled sadly. "You will save me, my new friend. But listen, this is what you must do. Go to Bek, a servant in the quarters for foreign guests. You can trust Bek. Ask him to alert you as soon as the Prince's emissary is sent ahead to prepare us for his arrival. Tell him to keep it secret, then come to me at once."

Sounded complicated, and I really didn't want to be involved.

"I must go." I needed to escape before anything else was asked of me.

She gripped my hands a final time, her dark eyes wide and desperate, but said nothing.

Outside the royal bedchamber, I was immediately picked up by a two-person escort, not the door-sentries nor Senamun's bodyguards. There was no shortage of staff, it appeared. They walked on either side down the long corridor, matching my pace. Were they following along with me, or was I following them? Impossible to tell.

But only a few steps from Senamun's bedchamber, a cluster of men appeared from a left-branching hall.

Four armed guards flanked a central figure, an imposing presence with his heavily-jeweled robes, pectoral collar, and intricate eye makeup.

A servant woman approached from the right and hunched her shoulders downward before him.

His voice thundered down on her. "Where is Ankhe-sen-amun?"

I'd seen John Barrymore play Sherlock Holmes at the cinema before leaving England a few months ago. The Vizier Ay had his squared-off chin, his thin lips, the dark brows that gave him a sinister look. The Egyptian version of a brooding Englishman.

I stood motionless.

The woman shook her head. "Vizier, I do not—"

A sharp slap across her face cut the answer short. She went down without a sound.

I gasped at the cruelty.

Ay's attention shifted.

"Ra-Ne-Hannu? I thought I had taken care of you."

CHAPTER TWENTY-ONE

*A*t Ay's mistaken identity, I braced damp palms against my thighs.

The vizier stepped closer, squinted.

I swallowed and lifted my chin to meet his gaze.

"No, you are not her."

"No."

"Who are you?" He loomed over me, eyes roaming me from top to bottom.

I felt a distinct chill at the appraisal.

He grabbed my upper arm, digging his fingers into the flesh. "You are clearly foreign. Have you come from Mitanni to spy on our kingdom? You are too pale to be one of those wretched Nehesyw, worming your way into palace life."

I tried to wrestle free, but he tightened his grip, then wrenched my arm behind my back, his face inches from mine.

"Where have you come from?" The question was a hiss in my face. "Answer me, woman!"

One of my escorts stepped forward. "She has been with the Great Royal Wife."

I tossed him a look like a slap of my own.

"Ah, one of the child's little friends, then?" Ay still sputtered into my face. "And tell me, what is her latest scheme?"

"I am a friend of Ahmose only, my lord."

He frowned as though the claim were ludicrous.

"Anyone can claim connection to an ally. If you are truly a friend of Ahmose, then bring him to me. To explain your presence. Or find yourself treated like any Mitanni spy."

He released my arm and thrust me backward.

"I—I do not know where he is—"

"Present yourself in the throne room with Ahmose two days hence, when I return from Karnak."

He nodded to my escorts. "Watch her until then."

The vizier glided away, smarmy and revolting.

I escaped to the courtyard and trailed trembling fingers along ferns and yellow lilies as I tried to get lost in the leafy center, well aware of the watching eyes of the vizier's guards in the colonnade.

A murder plot. A queen's life in danger. Suspected of spying. Was it time to return home? Ancient Egypt was once again more than I bargained for. Could I stay out of sight long enough to explore, to watch for the Egyptian Jack?

Sadly, since I'd used the already-sealed tomb door as my touchstone to travel here, there was no getting inside Tut-ankh-amun's tomb until I returned home and watched it opened with Howard. Did I have a duty to learn more about the young king before returning home? Or should I cut my losses and escape to safety?

The encounter with Ay had shaken me more than I cared to admit.

Really, Sahara? After being stabbed yesterday?

But there was something different about Ay. Something very unlike the common thief who'd hurt me yesterday. Something... evil.

A movement at the edge of the courtyard caught my eye, and I stepped farther back into the green shadow of a lush palm tree.

A man idled at the other side, under a doorway lintel, his eyes scanning the courtyard. He hadn't seen me.

A frond slapped my face. I batted it away to get a better look. Jack.

My stomach twisted. I started forward, his name on my lips, but then stopped.

Too late. He had seen me.

I stepped from the plant and motioned him toward me.

His brow furrowed briefly, and he looked left and right, as though uncertain I was indicating him.

Really? Who else would I be waving to in this place?

Seemingly satisfied I intended to signal him, he ambled across the courtyard. That familiar shoulders-back swagger, minus the crumpled suit and tie. Minus a shirt, in fact.

And I hadn't been wrong about the muscles.

We were alone, but I kept my voice at a whisper, albeit an angry one. "What are you doing here?"

He tilted his head. "I beg your pardon, my lady?"

"Knock it off, Jack. How did you get here? Are you able to—do what I do?"

"I am sorry, but I believe you have mistaken me for someone else."

Not possible. Even his height—everything about him was Jack Moretti. Except for the shaved head. And the white kilt. And the eye makeup.

I couldn't be wrong, could I?

"You're trying to tell me you are not Jack, the man I met in 1922?"

He smiled briefly, and the smile was Jack's. "I am Ramesses. And I have never visited this Nineteen Twenty-Two. Is it far from here?"

Yeah, about as far as you can get.

Speechless. But mind spinning.

I was being taken for this Ra-Ne-Hannu, whoever she was. And now I was confusing this poor ancient Egyptian man with a twentieth century Italian guy. Were the two mistakes connected? Did everyone have a *doppelgänger* in ancient Egypt?

"I—I'm sorry. My mistake." I performed an awkward little bow-curtsy combination.

But he slid toward me, touched a hand to my upper arm.

"You should be careful. The palace is awash with rumors and suspicion since the death of the king. No place for a stranger."

My skin sparked under the touch of his warm fingers.

He lingered before he dropped his hand. His eyes looked into mine with an intensity that heated my face.

"Thank you." I took a step away.

He studied me a moment longer, with that look that already seemed familiar, from across the table at the Vista Restaurant in Kurna. But then the look changed, the warmth snuffed out like cold water thrown on an ember.

He bowed at the waist, and then retreated from the courtyard.

Beyond him, an unknown woman bustled toward me, extraordinarily thin, with the flesh hollowed out beneath sharp cheekbones and a nose that hooked over tight lips.

Her eyebrows traveled upward and her lips parted. "Ra-Ne-Hannu, you are still here?"

I sure am.

But then as she drew closer, she frowned. "You are not Ra-Ne-Hannu."

I'm sure not.

She pinched my chin and turned my face to the left, then back. "You look much like her. The skin, the build. But you are younger. Younger than Ra-Ne-Hannu, who had the white streaks in her hair. And you resemble the daughter as well. But older than she."

Right.

"Who are you?"

So, the Ra-Ne-Hannu ruse wasn't going to work with everyone, it seemed. And claiming a connection with the mysterious Ahmose had backfired.

"I am Alsahra'." I fell back on my Arabic name. "I am Ra-Ne-Hannu's older daughter."

Her frown deepened. "I met no older daughter before she left."

I shrugged. "I was not feeling well. I kept to my bedchamber."

"And now?" She pursed disapproving lips. "You have stayed behind when your parents and sister have returned to Ven-usur?"

"Yes. I wished to see more of your beautiful country."

Wait—where? Ven-usur?

My vision tunneled, and that single word seemed to bounce from the courtyard walls.

"Have you been to my homeland?" I asked her. "To Ven-usur?"

She waved away the question. "I have been nowhere but the Two Lands of Egypt, and would not step off its beautiful black soil for all the silver in the treasury. I know nothing of this foreign Ven-usur."

I studied the painted tiles, unmoving. Green and yellow geometrics blurred.

She sniffed, as though even *my* otherness were distasteful. "You should return to the foreigners' quarters, where you stayed with your parents. It is not fitting for a visitor to be roaming the palace alone."

The foreigners' quarters. Where Senamun had asked me to watch for the incoming Hittite prince. The temporary home of a woman older than me, who looked like me, who left Egypt not long ago.

Left Egypt for a place that sounded suspiciously like *Venice.*

CHAPTER TWENTY-TWO

*T*he bony woman who'd chastised me for wandering the palace abandoned me to the empty courtyard.

I ran tense fingers through my hair, but they snagged against my beaded braids. My mouth tasted like paste.

The foreigners' quarters. I had to get there.

A moment later a young boy dashed across the garden. He balanced a tray full of purple grapes and a pile of pomegranates cut open to reveal their red seeds.

I stepped in his path and resisted the urge to snatch a cluster of grapes off the tray, just to blunt the awful dryness of my tongue.

"Tell me where to find the quarters for foreigners." I kept my voice low.

He lifted his eyebrows. Surprise at being spoken to, or surprise at my stupidity?

"I am going there, lady. You can follow me."

The boy wore nothing but a triangular loincloth and a little sling hung to a belt tied around his waist, and even his head was shaved. But he reminded me of Nadeem, back on the digsite. Had it only been two days ago I had seen Nadeem, joyfully carrying water to the older men on the site?

I trotted after him, through dim corridors and across sunny courtyards, until we reached a high wall with a narrow reed gate. The guards Ay had tasked to watch me still followed.

At the gate, I stepped ahead of the boy and opened it for him.

His eyes turned to saucers, at what was likely inappropriate helpfulness.

The foreigners' quarters were more than a chamber. The gate opened to a warren of small villas, assumedly for the use of visiting foreign dignitaries. Like my mother?

I scanned the circle of mud-brick houses with flat roofs and high open windows that hugged a central courtyard. In the garden, lemons hung heavy on trees and red poppies bent in the breeze. Small pools nestled among the greenery, blue lotus flowers floating.

A tranquil scene at odds with the chaos in my brain.

The boy scuttled away.

I waited for the guards to follow us in, but perhaps they were content to block my exit outside the gate.

Servants roamed the courtyard, clipping trees and scrubbing flagstones. A woman spotted me and crossed, head bent long before she reached me. She wore a dark wig in the chopped-off style, but wisps of gray hair curled at her temples. "Ra-Ne-Hannu, I was told your family had gone to Kush." She lifted her head, then frowned when she took me in, with what was becoming a familiar response. "Oh—"

"I am her older daughter, and will be staying longer."

Confusion crossed her face. She dipped her head, then bowed and extended a hand toward the nearest villa. "Please, your home has been scrubbed clean."

I made my way to the tiny dwelling she indicated and paused at the door to thank her.

Before I could, the gate I'd entered across the enclosure creaked open.

Jack's Egyptian double, Ramesses, entered.

He caught me staring and stopped short.

He was so much like Jack. It was mind-bending.

I half-smiled.

He didn't move.

Alright, then.

I ducked my head under the villa's doorframe.

The house was small, furnished with only the basics. The walls were unadorned, but the floor was laid with polished tiles.

"Wait—" I called to the woman. "Come in, please. I would like to speak with you."

She hesitated, then followed me into the villa.

Was it appropriate to close the door behind her? I left it open.

"What is your name?"

"Ranpu, my lady."

"Ranpu, I am Alsahra'."

She bent her head, eyes trained on the tiles.

"Can you tell me, when did my—mother—leave?"

"I do not know. They left in the night, after Her Majesty, the Great Royal Wife, Blessed of Hathor, sent word by messenger."

"They—all three of them, then?"

"Yes, my lady. Your mother, and her husband, and her daughter." She lifted her head. "They did not tell you?"

I waved away the question. "I knew they planned to leave. I will catch up with them on the road soon."

Ranpu bit her lip and looked to the open door.

The boy I'd followed rounded the door, tray still in his hands.

The grapes and pomegranate seeds remained, but the tray was now heavy with bread, cheese, and chunks of charred meat.

He entered without speaking, crossed to a table behind me, set the tray down, and turned to leave.

"Tell me, Ranpu, where can I find Bek?"

The boy spun, glanced at Ranpu with fear in his eyes, then stared at me.

Ranpu scowled. "This is Bek. Nothing more than a serving-boy. What do you want with him?"

Senamun's trusted contact in the foreigners' quarters was a child?

I smiled at them both. "Ankhe-sen-amun mentioned he is a good boy, one who can help me with anything I need."

They both were staring now.

"That will be all, Ranpu." I nodded toward the door in what was hopefully a dismissive attitude.

She bowed and backed out of the house.

I waited until I was certain she was out of earshot. "Now, Bek. Ankhe-sen-amun tells me you are trustworthy, yes?"

He smiled shyly. "I can get you juicy cooked sparrows. Good beer, whatever you want."

"Thank you. I may take you up on that later. For now, however, I am looking for some information."

He glanced toward the open door.

"First, did you know Ra-Ne-Hannu and her family?"

"Oh, yes, my lady. You are very like her. You have the same kindly eyes. But you are not her daughter."

"How can you be so sure?"

"Because I watch. And I listen. And I have never seen you before."

"Well, that will be our first secret, then." I plucked a few pomegranate seeds off the tray he had brought and handed them to him. "You like these?"

He hesitated, then grabbed them, grinning, and popped them into his mouth.

It would seem young boys could be bribed with food in any millennia.

"Do you know where they went?"

He shook his head, but mumbled "not far" around the tart seeds.

"How do you know they did not go back to—Ven-usur?"

"They were not prepared for a long journey."

"And is Ven-usur far from here? Do you know where it is?"

"Ahmose showed me a picture."

A picture?

Wait—Ahmose?

"Who—who is Ahmose?"

He huffed and rolled his eyes. "Ra-Ne-Hannu's husband!"

Unbidden, my father's face appeared in my mind's eye. I chased it back, along with the emotion swelling my throat.

Ra-Ne-Hannu and Ahmose.

Of course.

Ay's threat surfaced. Bring Ahmose to prove I was not a spy.

"Where is this picture Ahmose showed you?"

He laughed again. "The wind has blown it away by now. But I can draw it again." He waved me out of the house, grabbed a dried palm frond from the ground, and proceeded to scratch in the dirt at our feet.

"This is Kemet, the Black Lands of Upper and Lower Egypt. The whole world that is our land." He drew a rough oval above what I assumed was Egypt. "And this is the Great Green, where our Mother, the Nile, sends her waters."

The Great Green. The Mediterranean.

He continued to trace lines in the sandy soil. "And here, in the middle of the Great Green, there is more land, but not Egypt. It is land like the leg of a man, with a sandal."

Oh, good golly. Bek was drawing the boot of Italy.

"And at the top of the leg, here." He poked a sharp hole in the dirt, in northern Italy. "This is Ven-usur, where Ahmose and his family come from."

Venice. My stomach fluttered and my palms were instantly clammy. It had to be them.

Could it possibly be true my parents were *here*, even *now* in this time? Had I unknowingly succeeded in intersecting with them before their deaths? How would they have arrived here, years before the tomb of the young pharaoh had been opened? I had barely begun to understand how all of this worked. Perhaps I had gotten lucky on my first try!

"But it takes many months to get there," Bek was saying. "And many boats." He traced a line through the squiggle of the Nile. "A boat to the mouth of the river, then another boat across the

Great Green, and a long journey up the man's leg. Ahmose and Ra-Ne-Hannu did not have provisions for this long journey. And they did not go toward the harbor. No, the Great Royal Wife sent a message they were to go into the desert."

I scratched out his drawing with my sandaled foot, and pulled him back into the villa.

"Why did she send them into the desert?"

He shook his head and shrugged. Then eyed the pomegranate seeds.

I bent and gave him another handful.

"You have done well, Bek. I have one more question for you."

His head bobbed, still eyeing the tray.

"Have you heard anything about the arrival of some Hittittes?"

"They came, and left again, many days ago, my lady."

That must have been the envoy Senamun mentioned, sent to scope out the situation.

"Yes, but since then? Perhaps in the past day?"

He swallowed and shook his head. "They will come again?"

"Yes. Maybe not so many this time. And maybe in secret. But you must keep the secret, if you hear. Can you do that?"

"Yes, of course."

"And you must hurry to find me, or find Ankhe-sen-amun, to tell us of their arrival."

Reluctant as I was to get involved, returning to Senamun to grill her about the possibility of my dead parents being in Egypt, without bringing her assurances I was spying for her as requested, might not be effective.

"Yes, yes, I will find you."

"Good." I tossed him a cluster of grapes.

He caught it in one hand, smiled, and ran out the door.

I took a moment to scan the interior of the villa with more care. Ranpu indicated this was *my* villa, assumedly where Ra-Ne-Hannu and her husband Ahmose had lived.

And perhaps their daughter.

I was still unable to wrap my mind around that detail.

The villa was modest, by palace standards. I stepped across tan reed mats covering most of the floor, to a low table braced against the back wall, with a three-legged acacia-wood stool beside it. On the other side of a narrow doorway, a large bed frame with leather bindings and carved legs dominated the tiny room.

A few items on the table drew my attention.

A yellow rolled papyrus tied with a leather thong. A small hinged chest, empty. A polished-bronze handheld mirror.

I ran my fingers over each item. Had my father tied the leather around this papyrus? Had my mother held this mirror?

I sank into the stool beside the table, papyrus in hand.

The reality that had been pressing on me since I'd encountered the skeletal woman in the courtyard could no longer be denied.

I had entertained the hope that I'd miraculously converged on my parents' location here in ancient Egypt, where they traveled before their deaths.

But the existence of a daughter here with them changed everything.

The woman's comment about my resemblance to the daughter, after so many had mistaken me for the mother, tempted me to believe something my heart had been whispering since I heard that Ra-Ne-Hannu had a daughter.

We should be back long before the birth. We've told no one here at Highclere about the baby, since they would likely try to convince us to stay.

My mother's lost journal entry, brought to me by Eve.

The idea that my mother might have been expecting a child when she died had been too horrible for me to contemplate.

But now... Had they been here in Egypt, with a daughter? How could that be possible? Or was the daughter somehow... me? A younger, earlier version of me, who had somehow traveled to this time?

Younger than Ra-Ne-Hannu, who had the white streaks in her hair. But older than her daughter.

My mother's hair, when she left for Venice seventeen years ago at the age of thirty-seven, had been as dark as my own.

If it was true, if they had been here, I could only conclude they did not drown off the coast of Italy when I was fifteen. That in fact they survived, that my mother gave birth to my sister, that they still traveled through history with this child, nearly a woman now.

And that they had abandoned me in a way much different, much more painful, than what I had always believed.

The thought stabbed me with an anguish that outmatched the injury at Hatshepsut's Temple.

It could not be true.

The papyrus was crumpling in my tight fingers. I untied the leather, unrolled it with my customary great care. Every papyrus I'd ever unrolled was in danger of cracking due to age. Again, an odd jolt of the mismatch of facts—this papyrus was supple and strong.

But my fingers weakened at what was written there.

I spread the piece on the table, flattened it with my fingertips.

A series of symbols covered the page. Written at different times, it appeared, with varying pressure and ink and by two different hands.

But I recognized every symbol. Not from my Oxford study of languages. These were not the hieroglyphs of ancient Egypt, nor the more cursive hieratic script used by priests.

They were the sun and moon, the fish and bird, of the secret father-daughter language of my youth, the coded cypher my father and I created together.

Had he left me a message? Had he known somehow I would be here, and left me word of how to find him?

I searched the villa for a reed and ink, but there was nothing. I would have to decode each symbol of our substitution cypher and translate the words in my mind.

Thirty minutes later, I dropped the papyrus to the table and buried my head in my hands.

It was not a message from my father to me.

It was the back-and-forth scrawling between my father and someone else.

His other daughter.

CHAPTER TWENTY-THREE

I breathed against the pain, trying to force it down, wish it away, smother it with strength.

It remained, searing hot.

The gaping hole left by their supposed deaths mocked. My recent attempts to be more open, more trusting, were beaten down with the hammer of reality.

And beneath it all, tenacious fingers of jealousy coiling around my heart.

The coded messages on papyrus were nothing more than comments on daily happenings—quantities of fruits eaten, the appearance of a partridge near the villa. As though they were simply practicing.

But it did not belong to her. It was *our* code.

I reached for the hand mirror, held it in front of my face.

I knew my hair was different, but the sight was still a shock. My usual waved bob, trapped into submission by a crop of pins and half-covered under my fedora, had straightened itself into a blunt cut with overlaying gold-wrapped braids. I barely recognized myself.

How much did she look like me? Was she a good replacement?

I must find them.

Young Bek said Senamun sent Ahmose and his family into the desert. If I wanted answers, I'd need to get them from the queen.

But did I want answers? Did I want to know about the family of three, drifting through history without a care for the one they'd left behind?

Still studying myself in the mirror, I swiped at the tears that threatened to trace a line of black kohl down my cheeks, then laid the mirror beside the untouched tray of food.

I'd imagined myself in the role of hero, of savior, warning them to avoid Venice in 1905 and preventing their deaths.

Clearly, my intervention was not needed.

But yes, I wanted answers. If for no other reason than to understand why they had given me up. Why I hadn't been worth staying and fighting for.

I had a deadline, though. I needed to be back in 1922 before Ay returned and demanded proof of my loyalty.

I managed to escape the foreigner's quarters without being stopped, with no sign of the men tasked with watching me. I retraced my steps through the palace, toward the hall that held the royal bedchamber.

The two guards at the end of the hall scowled at me with steely eyes.

Staring at Senamun's chamber door, a thought struck me that twisted everything I'd learned on its head.

If the Great Royal Wife had sent Ra-Ne-Hannu and her husband Ahmose away in the night to some secret desert location, then why hadn't she questioned Tovah at breakfast when I was introduced as Ra-Ne-Hannu? And why hadn't Senamun made the same mistake in identification, or at least mentioned how much I looked like Ahmose's wife?

Had I gotten everything wrong?

I lifted my chin toward the guards.

"The Great Royal Wife has requested to see me."

They wore only linen kilts and sandals, but the javelin-like spears held in a tight grip and pointed upward looked deadly. They remained immobile, like the guards I'd once seen outside King George's Buckingham Palace.

"She gave me specific instructions to return when I had the information she wanted."

Not that I actually *had* the information, but it wasn't technically a lie.

Still no response.

I stood on my toes and hollered through the door. "Your majesty!"

Both guards whipped their spears from vertical to crossed in front of the door, with an aggressive set of their bare shoulders.

The door swung open.

Senamun's eyes were red-rimmed with purplish shadows. But her expression brightened when she saw me.

"Ra-Ne-Hannu! You have news?"

I eyed the guards. Should I speak in front of them?

She answered my question by reaching a hand through the crossed spears, grabbing my wrist, and pulling me toward her.

The spears lifted.

Inside the bedchamber, she shoved the door closed and escorted me to her reclining couch.

"Tell me! Is the prince arrived?"

"I have found Bek, as you said. He's been instructed to bring any news of arriving Hittites to either me or to you."

Her shoulders slumped. "So, there is no news, then?"

"Not yet. But there is other talk you should perhaps know about."

She narrowed her eyes, lips pursed.

How to approach this? I needed to be careful.

"It is about the—family—you apparently sent away in the night. People are talking. Ranpu in the foreigners' quarters says they have gone to Kush. Another servant tells me they left for their home in Ven-usur. And the girl Tovah said they returned somewhere north. But Bek says you sent a mysterious messenger in the night, telling them to leave for the desert."

I watched her eyes, waiting for any sign she knew of my ruse, calling myself by another woman's name.

But she had closed her eyes, and now rubbed at her temples.

"Aahh, I am going mad here, waiting for whatever is next." She stood and pulled the draped linen cape from her shoulders, then unwound a long rectangle of fabric from her waist and threw it to the floor. Dressed only in a narrow white shift, she looked so young.

She paced the floor, fingers twisted. "The entire palace has their eyes on me. They wait to see what the widow will do, what she will say. Whom she will marry. I was raised from birth to be a royal wife. I have let them define every moment of my life."

She pounded a fist against her thigh. "Why did he have to die? We could have reigned for years, had many more children."

None of this seemed connected to the family I was tracking, but her pain was palpable. "I am sorry for your loss, Senamun. It must be difficult to be pressured so soon to marry again, before your grief has had a chance to subside."

"Grief! Pah!" She spit the word out. "I have known nothing but grief, for all my twenty-one Inundations. First my parents, then my two precious little baby girls who died still in my womb, their tiny bodies secreted away from me in stone vessels. Now my husband." She sucked in a ragged breath. "No one cares about the grief of Ankhe-sen-amun, I can assure you!"

"I care."

She brought her eyes back to me, and they glistened with tears.

"Yes, you are kind, I can see that, Ra-Ne-Hannu." She slid to the couch beside me again, and held my hands. "Perhaps I am a fool, but I trust you. Or perhaps I only trust you because you are not Egyptian."

"The family you sent away—they were also not Egyptian. Did you also trust them? Were they helping you?"

She gazed through the rough-cut window, as though remembering. Then brought her attention back to me, brow furrowed.

"I do not understand. Tovah, she said you were part of Ahmose's party, from the north."

"She misspoke. I did not know them."

Hopefully all the people I'd given conflicting stories would never end up in the same room.

"Hmm. The husband and daughter, yes, they helped me. I do not believe I ever met Ahmose's wife."

She looked me up and down, eyes squinting. "You remind me of her—the daughter. But she was much younger than you. Even younger than I." She frowned. "You say you did not know them?"

"I—I am not sure. Why did you send them away?"

She returned her gaze to the window. The sun had climbed overhead and the gardens beyond tormented me with a cool respite.

"I did not. He took them."

This was new information. "Who took them? Where?"

"Ahmose. He was a friend to me, but said he and his family had important business in their home country and must return. So he took them away."

"To Ven-usur?" Despite Bek's crude drawing in the sand, I wanted confirmation.

"He did not say. I offered to send them on a ship from the harbor here at The House of Rejoicing, but he declined."

All of it was so confusing. "So, why does Bek say you sent them by night into the desert?"

She crossed to the open window and touched her fingertips to the edge. "That was many weeks ago, when I sent the letter to the Hittite king, Suppiluliuma. It was Ahmose and his family who took the letter, made certain it arrived. I sent instructions they were to be given safe passage, an armed Hittite escort, to wherever they required. But instead, a month later, they were escorted back by Hittite soldiers who disbelieved my petition."

I scrambled to do the math. Senamun's letter was sent a month after her husband's death. Then perhaps another month for Ahmose and his family to make the round trip to the land of the Hittites, most likely in the desert of Anatolia. Oddly, only a week ago in my time of 1922, that region officially abolished Ottoman rule to become the Republic of Turkey. I shoved aside the intrusion of my other life. Senamun's details brought me to eight weeks after Pharaoh Tut-ankh-amun's death, and about four weeks ago.

"Did they leave for Ven-usur immediately after returning?"

She shook her head. "They stayed. Ahmose said he wanted to be a support to me until the seventy days were completed, until the Opening of the Mouth ceremony could take place before his burial." She half-smiled at me. "Ahmose was very kind. It was good to have someone like a father again, if only for a short while."

So, they were here a fortnight ago. "And after the funerary rituals? Did they leave then?"

She tilted her head, forehead creased. "Not long after, I believe. A day or so, perhaps."

"And why did I hear they had left for both Kush and Ven-usur?"

She shrugged. "You see what I must contend with? Everyone is always talking, and rarely do they know the truth."

I tried to hide my disappointment. They were truly gone, whoever they were. And with almost two weeks of a head start and no idea of their destination, how could I hope to catch them? "Who would know where they went, or how they traveled?"

"Perhaps the Hittite prince. Surely they would have requested passage from him when they took my letter. Before they were forced to return here to the palace."

The prince.

"Do you know a man called Ramesses, Senamun?"

She lifted one shoulder. "Half the men in Egypt are called Ramesses."

"Broad-shouldered, with an easy smile and blue eyes?"

"Blue eyes? No, that I have not seen."

I sighed. "And Ahmose's daughter—what was her name?"

She smiled. "Her full gods-name, I do not know. But her father called her *Per-Sia*."

Per-Sia. *Persia*.

My parents had loved my unusual name. Growing up in England, Sahara had been an oddity.

And if I had a sister, it seemed more than believable she would have a name like Persia.

A deep longing swept away the earlier twinges of jealousy. I would give anything for a sister.

"Ra-Ne-Hannu, what is it?" Senamun was peering into my eyes. "What has grieved you?"

I shook my head. "I only wish I could be of more help."

She patted my hands. "It is good, sometimes, to simply have a friend."

"Tell me, Senamun, what is done with foreign spies in this palace?"

A flicker of confusion crossed her face. "Treason against the pharaoh is the most serious offense in the kingdom. Spies are burned alive, to cause great suffering and also to prevent their *ka* from crossing to the west and eternal life."

Right.

So, my only hope of finding Ahmose and proving my innocence to the vizier lay in the hands of the Hittite prince. Would he arrive before Ay's deadline?

I cast aside all thoughts of returning to 1922. My parents, perhaps my sister, might be here in this land, in this time. I was not leaving until I had answers.

Astonishingly, the Great Royal Wife insisted I remain her guest in her chamber for the day, as we waited for the Hittite prince to come to her rescue. It felt like something out of Grimm's tales, as though she should let down her hair from the window, or beseech an old hag for a magic potion.

Senamun gave me water for bathing and a new linen dress of much finer quality, both of which were a relief but did little to calm me.

The day stretched interminably. She tried to teach me Senet, a board game with pawns that challenged me to beat her to the afterlife. We ate flatbread, cheese, and melons brought by deferential servants and I numbed my anxiety and boredom with too many sugary dates. Senamun coaxed me into telling her about my homeland, so I spoke of England, which sounded like *Ankhland* in her mouth. And then she insisted I sleep on her couch like we were university chums.

I spent another tortuous night, pawing through every memory I had of my parents, imagining a sister traveling through time, puzzling over what I would say to them if I ever found them. Even sending up another tentative prayer or two for clarity, to any God who might be listening.

At long last, the morning light began to creep across the chamber floor. Before it touched the low couch where I lay, neck stiff and heart exhausted, a shout at the door startled me to my feet.

CHAPTER TWENTY-FOUR

*T*he yelling from the hall had Senamun flying across the sitting room from her bed as my feet hit the floor.

"Your majesty!"

She glanced at me, eyes narrowed.

"Is it Bek?" The voice sounded young.

Senamun grabbed her robes and began wrapping the fabric around her waist and across her shoulder in a complicated pattern. "Open it," she said to me, indicating the door.

I crossed to the door and flung it open.

Senamun tucked the final fold under her arm. "Let the boy in!"

Bek strolled between the two guards with a smirk for each. No doubt enjoying his favored-servant status.

Senamun scowled at the guards and slammed the door shut. "The Vizier Ay claims his guards remain to protect me, but we all know I am a prisoner in my own palace."

I put my hands on the boy's shoulders. "What is it, Bek? Is there news?"

His head bobbed. "Yes, lady. Yes, majesty. There is a caravan that will soon arrive. They are saying many camels, armed men —not traders."

This was it, then. My pulse fluttered. Surely the Hittite prince would remember those who brought him Senamun's proposal. Would he know what happened to my parents?

Senamun circled Bek, hand on her chest. "Who is saying? Where did you hear this?"

"At the guard house, my lady." He dipped his head. "Vizier Ay, Mighty of Strength, had runners in the desert who brought news. Ay has extra men posted, and many of them prepare to ride out."

Senamun met my look of hope with one of horror. "We cannot allow Ay's men to reach the prince first!"

She grabbed a headpiece from a side table and strapped the beaded band tight across her forehead, its rearing cobra at the center.

Then with a determined set of her chin, she opened the doors and addressed the guards.

"My friends and I will be spending some time in the courtyards." She led the way out of the chamber. "We have no need for accompaniment."

Bek and I followed her, but when I glanced back it was clear the guards were also following.

Senamun must have sensed them, because she stopped in her tracks and spun slowly. "I have instructed you to remain."

Her tone was as icy and regal as any queen's could be.

"You will continue to guard my chamber, to ensure no one enters while I am away and lies in wait for my return."

The two guards glanced at each other. Probably weighing the option of disobeying the queen-who-wasn't-really-a-queen any longer, and the vizier who wasn't yet a king. After a moment, they each took a step backward.

Senamun spun and continued to sail through the palace hall, with Bek and me in tow.

We passed through the courtyard where I had seen Jack's lookalike, but didn't stop.

Bek peered up at me and shrugged.

Through another long hall, across a dusty open courtyard, to what looked like a hut, but turned out to be a horse stable.

I stooped to enter under the low doorway, then hesitated while my eyes adjusted.

Bek sped past me toward a pair of horses standing side-by-side near a small, two-wheeled chariot like the one that brought me to Malaqat. He seemed to know Senamun's mind, for as he strapped the chariot to the horses, she climbed aboard.

"Come, Ra-Ne-Hannu." She waved me over. "You will be my excuse. We will say we are on a pleasure trip to the Nile."

Was I crazy? Riding out to the possibility of an armed conflict?

But I must learn more of the family that recently left Egypt. I climbed into the chariot and perched beside Senamun.

Bek stepped in front of us both, grabbed at the reins, and clucked to the horses.

It was clear why Senamun trusted the boy. He was smart, intuitive, and not afraid to get involved.

We wheeled out of the stable, and I gripped the side of the chariot. "How will we reach the prince before Ay's soldiers?"

Senamun's face was set like stone, eyes boring into the desert. "His soldiers will be on foot. But we will have to move quickly."

At that, Bek flicked the reins over the backs of the horses, and the chariot rolled faster.

We moved past the administrative complex and kitchens, gleaming white in the sun, out through the gated wall of the massive palace enclosure, flanked by two statues of a seated pharaoh, perhaps Amen-hotep, grandfather to Tut-ankh-amun.

What would Jack say, if he could snap photographs of this scenery? I could almost see him, jumping from our chariot to aim his camera in every direction.

The life-giving Nile and its farmland lay green in the distance to the east, beyond the harbor and connecting canal.

The House of Rejoicing lay outside the flood plain, safe from the yearly Inundations, the waters roaring down from Aswan, overflowing the banks of the Nile and bringing needed water and rich silt deposits to both sides of the river. Deep-dug canals funneled precious water to irrigation basins, where farmers carefully released it to keep the farmland fertile. The "gift of the Nile" propelled Egypt into a major ancient power, supplying other nations with grain for more than two thousand years. Even in Roman times, still a thousand years away, Egypt would be called the "breadbasket of the world."

But here in our chariot, we traveled over desert, toward a plain shimmering with deadly heat.

On the narrow path ahead, a dust cloud bloomed from the desert floor.

"The Hittites?" I asked Senamun.

She shook her head. "More likely, Ay's soldiers, sent to kill the prince. Hurry, Bek." She muttered what sounded like a curse. "How did he find out? I was so careful to keep my plans quiet."

"Could Ahmose have betrayed you?"

"Not a chance. I trusted him with my life, though I knew him only a short time."

"Why so much trust?"

"He was a seer. He knew things. Of the future, and the past. And he saved my life."

I lifted my eyebrows, inviting more.

"Just after Tut-ankh-amun's death, when I was still foolish enough to ask questions about what had happened, I nearly met the same fate. I was intent on accusing Ay before the priests. Ahmose made me see sense and recommended a more strategic approach."

Did that sound like my father? All I had were memories of childhood. It had been so long. *Ahmose* and *Alexander* had little in common, other than the initial letter. But there would have been nothing in the Egyptian language that sounded like his given name.

Senamun was right. The cloud of dust, as we approached it from behind, was a contingent of soldiers, marching out into the desert. Bare-chested with sandals, they bore little resemblance to the photographs I had seen of British soldiers in the Great War.

They carried leather shields and spears, each with a short dagger strapped to their waist.

Bek yelled to them as though he were a general.

They turned to see the Great Royal Wife behind, and parted ranks to the soft sand on either side of the packed road, allowing us to pass without sinking a chariot wheel.

I glanced behind as we passed.

They re-formed ranks, no doubt wondering if they should have allowed Ankhe-sen-amun to outpace them.

And now we were ahead.

Beside me, Senamun exhaled and leaned back, flattening palms across her thighs.

With the disturbance behind us, we could now see farther, to where the Hittite prince's retinue approached.

Bek barked an urgent command to the horses.

The scuffle of the soldiers' sandals at our backs increased.

It was impossible to judge the pace of the Hittites ahead, but it didn't take long to reach them.

About a dozen men riding on horses met us. The forerunner wore metal plating across his chest and a head covering in a dark red that streamed down to his shoulders.

Greetings were quickly exchanged. The prince nudged his horse forward until it nosed the edge of our chariot.

Senamun put a hand to the horse's head, her eyes trained on the prince. "You are Zananza?"

No shyness, nothing that indicated an impending arranged marriage, with all it entailed. Instead, Senamun's lifted chin spoke only a challenge.

"I am he."

The prince was perhaps thirty years old, and not bad-looking. He had a pleasant smile, and seemed amused by the young royal petting his horse.

"You are ready to join your kingdom to the mighty Egypt? To stand beside me to rule?"

No awkward small-talk, then. Perhaps arranged marriages

had something to recommend them, if they avoided the need for all that dancing around and evaluating each other.

He bowed his head. "As your letter stated. To you, I will be a husband. To Egypt I will be a king."

Senamun glanced to where I sat in the chariot, as though contemplating giving the soon-to-be-pharaoh my seat.

I wouldn't refuse a chance to ride horseback into the palace surrounded by Hittite soldiers. But I needed a moment to speak to this prince.

Senamun flicked a hand. "You will follow us. There are soldiers on the road, unfriendly to my rule. They seek to put a commoner on the throne—my husband's vizier. Stay behind and you will be safe."

Bek expertly turned the horses and our chariot.

But when we pivoted, we faced the oncoming warriors of Ay in our path.

Ay's contingent of soldiers drew up and stopped. There were more of Ay's Egyptian guards than Hittites, perhaps forty soldiers to the Hittite dozen.

Senamun's assertion that Zananza and his men would be safe behind a two-wheeled chariot carrying two unarmed women and a boy seemed rash.

"Stand aside," Senamun called out. "These men are accompanying your Royal Wife back to the palace. They will pass unharmed."

The Egyptian at the head of the pack twitched his head only slightly, but enough that the group of soldiers parted to let our vehicle pass.

I exhaled the breath I'd been holding.

But it was too soon to feel relief.

As soon as we were through the soldiers, they closed ranks behind us, cutting off the Hittites.

The first ring of sword-on-sword reverberated in my chest.

"No!" Senamun stood and spun in the chariot, hands gripped along the backrest. "Let them pass!"

But there was no stopping it now.

The Egyptians soldiers were on foot, rather than horses, but they outnumbered the mounted men. The clash had every man engaged.

Cries and grunts split the desert air. Sand and blood flew.

Bek tried to step off the chariot platform.

I blocked him and shook my head, heart pounding. My eyes stung and bitterness rose in my throat.

Bodies fell with oddly-gentle thuds into the sand, eyes open and staring.

Senamun flung her headpiece to the sand and stood in the chariot with hands clutched to her head.

I had seen gruesome injuries, when Lady Almina had turned Highclere into a hospital during the Great War and I had worked beside her to tend the wounded soldiers.

But I had never seen a battle.

Despite the stories the men at Highclere had whispered like confessions or moaned in their sleep, I was unprepared to watch men cut down before my eyes.

The heat and the blood made my head sway, but my training took over. Where would I do the most good?

The Hittite numbers dwindled. Three Egyptians to every one made it only a matter of time. Was the prince still fighting?

Senamun jumped out of the chariot, heedless of the danger, and ran toward the fight.

I blew out a breath. Courage prompted me to follow her, to protect her, but this was not my fight, not even my *time*.

But Bek made my decision when he dashed after his sovereign.

I could not leave them both out there. I jumped into the sand.

"Bek! Senamun!" My voice disappeared into the battle-screams and the clash of iron.

What did she hope to accomplish? To shield the Hittite prince with her own body? Did she think Ay's soldiers would not cut her down?

I had nearly reached Bek when the world spun and dimmed.

A blow to the back of my head.

I was going down.

Slowly, slowly, with the blue desert sky rotating above me and the golden sand rising up to graze my cheek.

In that hazy moment, I saw the face of Oliver, a soldier I had cared for during the war. I thought of his stories of battle at Artois, on the Western Front. Stories of how it felt to be shot from behind.

And then, darkness.

CHAPTER TWENTY-FIVE

July, 1915
Highclere Castle, Hampshire, England

"Sahara, pull down those blinds before this room gets any hotter."

Lady Almina stood with hands on hips, frowning at the afternoon sun streaming through the French windows of the Library. Dust particles hovered in the sunlight and danced above the groupings of chairs forming the men's day room, where they could spend the day reading or playing cards as they convalesced.

I did as bidden, and watched the sharp crease dividing light from dark slide down the far wall.

Did I imagine a sigh of relief from some soldiers, as the room seemed instantly cooler?

It was high summer at Highclere, and after a year of war, we were all ready for some relief.

With nearly all the men given their own guest room, and maids doubling up to leave extra quarters for the thirty or so nurses, everyone at Highclere was busy creating a retreat for wounded soldiers that was also a top-notch hospital.

"Sahara…" A whispered word from across the room, from the handsome Oliver Bainbridge, reclining on an overstuffed sofa, leather-bound book in his hand.

I circled one of the lofty gilt-edged wood columns that graced the room and bent to him.

He was finally gaining some strength after weeks of touch-and-go.

"What can I get you, Oliver?"

He sighed and grasped my hand. He was my age, with light hair and a stubbly beard and a smile that left me feeling warm and safe.

"You can get me out of here. Perhaps a picnic on the lawns with my favorite nurse."

I returned his grip and his smile. "There will be time for picnics when you are well."

"Is that a promise?" He gave me a wink and a grin, then pulled me down to balance on the edge of his sofa.

"So warm and dry," he said, indicating my hand. "How I dreamed of the warm, dry hand of a pretty girl during all those wet, cold nights in the trenches. You've no idea."

"Well, you are here now. Back in wet, cold England." I laughed and glanced at the windows. "Except for today, of course."

"England can freeze over, and I wouldn't care, as long as I don't have to go back there." He frowned as soon as the words were spoken and glanced at his comrades scattered around the Library. "You'll think me a disloyal chap, I fear. Or worse—a coward."

I leaned toward him, to check the bandages at the back of his head. "Any man who can survive a bullet is no coward, Oliver. And you have fought just as bravely here in hospital as you did on the field. It's your country's turn to be loyal to you."

Oliver had told me of the day he was shot, weeks ago. Of the strange blurring of his vision, the feeling of being clubbed and wondering why the club-wielding attacker was invisible. The slow fall-forward, each blade of grass in sharp relief against the hard-packed earth, rising up to meet him.

"But what does any of it mean?" he whispered now.

I smoothed the white starched apron over my strawberry-pink uniform. The question required more from me than a simple fetching of water or a cool compress.

"I'm a failure." His voice was still low, and trembled. "I didn't take out a-one of them, to my knowledge. Instead they took out me."

"You sacrificed for what was right and good, Oliver."

He shrugged. "But what difference did it make? What was it all for? Do we really even understand why we're fighting? Those boys in trenches on the other side of the field, firing at us... They're fighting for what they think is right, too."

I sighed. "War is—complicated. I don't pretend to understand."

"Life is complicated."

Agreed.

"But when I get out of here, Sahara..." his voice was a whisper, a private thing for only me. "You and I... we can make it simple."

We'd known each other only a few weeks, and spent every minute in the presence of others, but an unspoken understanding had grown between us. The sense of waiting, of knowing more was to come, as soon as the world returned to sanity, and war was a memory.

He enclosed my hand with both of his, and his steady gaze into my eyes spoke even more than the words.

"Oliver, I..." The admission of feelings lodged in my throat. It had been so long since I'd expressed affection to anyone. Since I'd dared to feel it.

"Just tell me you care for me, Sahara."

I let the heat rise to my face, then smiled. "I care. I care very much."

"Sahara!"

Another summons from her ladyship.

"I need to go." I leaned across, my lips grazing his ear. "I'll return as soon as I can."

Oliver held on for an extra moment, a twinkle in his eye that must have been normal in the days before the war. Voice louder now, for his fellow patients to hear. "You know you're my favorite, right?"

I laughed and pulled my hand away. "Oh, you say that to every nurse."

But I knew he didn't.

Lady Almina was standing at the entrance to the Library, counting men. She turned to me when finished.

"I've just had word of more soldiers coming in."

I scanned the room. "Where will we put them?"

"Exactly." She dusted something from her hands. Talcum powder, perhaps. "I'd like to open up the Mercia Bedroom. Run up there for me, and see what needs to be done to put it in order."

A last glance toward Oliver, who winked again.

Then I found my way to the Mercia Bedroom on the sunny south of Highclere, with its lovely four-poster bed and blue walls.

Lady Almina's generosity, using a cool £25,000 of Rothschild money, had furnished Highclere with expert doctors, including family favorite, Dr. Marcus Johnson, and all the best medical equipment. She was determined to offer a soothing retreat that made soldiers feel like honored guests, even if she had to open every one of the sixty bedrooms on the estate.

The first thing to be done was to open the heavy drapes. I coughed at the dust released. The room hadn't been used in some time.

Three large trunks rested at the side of the room. Recognition sparked. My parents' things. It had been years since I'd gone through those trunks. Two of them, filled with clothes, I had always ignored, but the third was packed with small items they'd left behind when they went to Venice more than ten years ago.

When I was younger, I used to rake through those things, hoping to get a sense of them.

No time for that today. I'd save it for a slow day in our estate-turned-hospital.

For today, I should decide where those previously-ignored two trunks should go, before the room was outfitted for wounded soldiers.

A quick rifling through the contents of first one, then the other, revealed them to be clothing, as I thought. But in the second, my fingers closed around something solid, deep in the fabrics, and I pulled it out.

A beaded headband, which must have been my mother's. I'd never seen it.

It was styled in an old Egyptian pattern—to be worn across the forehead. Woven of golden threads, with beads intricately braided into the pattern, and small droplets of jewels that lay on the forehead above the eyes. In the center, a gold scarab, Egyptian symbol of immortality, hung like a pendant.

Where had she gotten it? It was beautiful, and felt authentic. But it was certainly part of some costume, since it was in pristine condition. Besides, no real artifact of this value would have been stashed in a trunk full of clothes.

On a whim, I attached it to my own forehead.

Then closed up the trunks, surveyed the condition of the rest of the room, and went downstairs.

Her ladyship met me in the hall.

"Sahara, what is that ridiculous—"

"It was my mother's, I think."

She raised an eyebrow, but said nothing more. She typically avoided mentions of my dead parents. "Well? What of the Mercia?"

"The drapes need a good beating, and everything is dreadfully dusty. There are a few trunks of my parents' things that could be moved elsewhere. I'll go through them and donate the clothes. Other than that, the room can be converted quickly."

"Good. Carry on."

TRACY HIGLEY

I carried on. Back to Oliver. He'd have a laugh over my Egyptian-princess look.

He was sleeping when I reached him. Head back against the winged arm of the couch in a deep, noiseless sleep that surprised me, since I had not been gone long.

I pulled a thin blanket over him and almost walked away. But something in his stillness bothered me.

I bent over the couch.

"Oliver?" I hated to wake him...

"Oliver?" My voice pitched higher. "Oliver?" I was shaking him now. With no response.

"Sahara?" Lady Almina's voice carried across the room. "What is it?"

"Fetch Doctor Johnnie! Something is wrong!"

The doctor was summoned, but something was very wrong.

Later, I heard the words *blood clot* and *lungs* but in that moment I only heard the word *gone*.

That quickly. So quickly.

Standing over his still body, I ripped the beaded headband from my forehead, feeling foolish and juvenile, and fighting the tears that proved it.

Lady Almina touched the small of my back. "Perhaps a rest, my dear?" She disapproved of her nurses getting attached. For this very reason.

She had stood beside me at the news of my parents' boat, lost at sea, and I made her proud with my strong and dignified reaction then. I could do it again.

The tears receded. "Yes. A rest." And I sought the solace of my bed.

CHAPTER TWENTY-SIX

I awoke in the solace of my bed. Grateful Lady Almina had given me the time to...

No, that was not right. Highclere, the wounded men, the Great War — it all felt so... distant.

I forced my eyes to flutter open. The light struck my senses and forced an audible groan from my lips. I reached for the back of my head.

A sigh beside me turned me toward the sound, head throbbing.

It was Jack, perched on the side of my bed, leaning over me in concern.

"Jack." My voice sounded raspy, unused. "I dreamed... I dreamed I was in Egypt. Not the digsite. In the New Kingdom, with Tut-ankh-amun's widow..."

But, no, something was not right with that either. I struggled to sit up, but Jack shook his head and gently pushed my shoulders back.

His head was shaved. He was still the bald *not-Jack*. The Egyptian Jack. Ramesses.

My brain twirled, and I closed my eyes to fight the mental motion sickness.

"You've had an injury, Ra-Ne-Hannu. On the road into the desert yesterday, with Ankhe-sen-amun."

Yesterday? Another day lost, with Ay returning soon to use me for kindling.

"You must have been exhausted, to have slept so long. I think you should return to your homeland as soon as you can."

"Is she hurt? Bek?"

Ramesses shook his head. "She was not harmed. Nor the boy. I don't believe anyone meant to harm you either. You were simply caught in the confusion."

I kept my eyes closed, fearing the answer. "The Hittite prince?"

"Dead. Along with all his men."

A surge of pity for Senamun and her failed plan washed over me. And frustration, at the last chance of finding my parents, gone.

I reached back in my mind for simpler times, grasping for the Highclere of my past, even if it came with the other, more painful memories.

Memories of Oliver Bainbridge, dying alone while I played with old costumes.

My eyelids quivered again. Memories collided, reflected each other, then meshed. A beaded headband, tiny jewels, a gold scarab pendant in the center. My mother's headband, found in an old trunk in an unused bedroom at Highclere, but also, also... on my head as I crossed the ancient platforms that lay at the foot of Hatshepsut's Mortuary Temple. Mistaken for Ra-Ne-Hannu.

"What is it?" The Eypgtian version of Jack seemed concerned. "Has the pain grown worse? Shall I call the physician again?"

Something in the way he said it. Something *still* was not right here...

The door burst open before I could complete the thought.

"Ra-Ne-Hannu!"

Senamun crossed the room, hands extended. "You are finally awake!" Her smile seemed teary. She paid no attention to my visitor.

I shimmied myself upward on the cot, ignoring the frown from Ramesses.

He stepped aside to make room for Ankhe-sen-amun.

"I am fine, Senamun. A minor blow to the head. Nothing serious."

She slid to my side and clutched my arms. "I would *never* have forgiven myself if you had been killed!"

I blinked away a few tears of my own, at the unaccustomed connection of a female friend, and returned her grasp. "I am so sorry about the prince."

Her nostrils flared. "That Ay is a vicious beast of a man. He would do anything, kill anyone, in his bid for my husband's throne."

"I am afraid for *you*, Senamun."

She nodded. "I share your fear. That is why you must help me, just a bit more."

I exhaled heavily and glanced at Ramesses, somehow believing he would be on my side. "I don't know, I'm not sure I can be of help. And I should probably be leaving. I need to find... Ahmose and his family."

"I do not understand. Why?"

"Because I believe... I believe they are my family."

At this, Ramesses visibly straightened, with a sharp intake of breath.

Senamun smoothed my hair away from my face. "Then I will send you off to the Great Green with everything you need for the longest journey, I promise you. But first you must go to the Karnak Temple for me."

The Karnak Temple. To see it now, in this time. Unbelievable. But didn't Ay say *he* was going to Karnak?

Ramesses spoke, his voice quiet but firm. "I think it might be best if Ra-Ne-Hannu continues on her way. She has already—"

Senamun swung around, as though surprised by the voice. "Who is this man?"

"This is Ramesses. He has, for some unknown reason, assumed the role of my protector."

Senamun looked between us, and a small smile played at the corners of her mouth. "I see." She patted my hand. "But you are perfectly capable of making your own decisions, of course. One of the many benefits of having no husband." Another sideways glance at Ramesses.

Indeed.

"There is a priest at Karnak. His name is Menna. He has known me all my life, and he is sympathetic to my cause. He believes me capable."

"Capable?"

"I am going to declare myself pharaoh. Like my great fore-mother Hatshepsut, who ruled as a man and needed no one to sit beside her."

Wow. Ambitious. Hatshepsut had been one of Egypt's only female pharaohs, starting out as regent for the two-year-old boy who was a complicated combination of nephew and stepson, and quickly assuming full power. But I knew my history. Unless future generations had managed to completely expunge Ankhe-sen-amun from Egyptian memory, the woman beside me would never become pharaoh.

Unless...

Could I help to put another woman on the pharaoh's throne? What would the consequences to future Egyptian history be? Would everything we already knew be altered? Disappear like smoke? Would anyone but me even remember it?

The questions made my head pound again.

"How will you accomplish this, Senamun? You have no friends here in the palace, no one you can trust. Can one priest truly help you overthrow Ay's influence?"

"Not simply this one priest, but he can help, yes. Menna can send men to fetch Horemheb and whisper among the elite that the Commander is coming from Nubia, to be crowned as my husband wished. And while Ay is distracted by preparing to fight Horemheb, Menna will help me gather those loyal to me, and he will perform the sacred rites to crown me pharaoh."

The idea of taking part in an ancient coup that would rewrite history definitely had its appeal.

But it was a complete detour from my determination to discover more of Ahmose, Ra-Ne-Hannu, and Per-sia. And if Ay himself was in Karnak the trip could put me directly into his rageful path.

"And of course, Menna may be able to help you learn where they have gone."

"Where who have gone?"

Senamun tilted her head. "Ahmose and his wife, of course. I thought you said—"

"How can Menna help me?"

She laughed. "You are so odd, my new friend. You must know Menna is the one who brought them to Egypt."

No. No, I did not know that.

"Someday you will tell me all about where you have come from, Ra-Ne-Hannu. I should like to learn of your Ankh-Land."

Something about all of this struck me funny, and I fought back a laugh.

And could have sworn Ramesses did the same.

He cleared his throat. "I will take her."

"Ah, the protector once again." Senamun smiled with approval at Ramesses. "I am indebted to you, Ramesses, if you would accompany my friend to Karnak to find Menna."

He bowed his head briefly.

So, it all seemed decided, then. Not that I was excited about sticking my neck out once more for a girl I hardly knew, but... seeing Karnak. Crowning another female pharaoh. And finding out what Menna knew of my parents. There really was no choice. I would simply have to avoid Ay, then get back to 1922, as soon as I had my answers.

Senamun stood. "We cannot risk a boat from the palace harbor to the river. I will have horses and a chariot readied for you at the royal stable, and arrange a boat at the Nile's edge. You are well enough to travel soon, Ra-Ne-Hannu?"

I nodded. No sense waiting around.

"Good. I will go to make preparations."

She disappeared from the room without a thank-you.

I tried not to be annoyed. She was royalty, after all, and probably accustomed to people falling over themselves to help her.

I swung my legs over the side of my narrow cot.

Ramesses stepped beside me, grabbed my elbow, and helped me stand.

I peered up at him. "You're certain you're willing to get involved in all of this? I don't even know you."

"I am happy to help."

"I'm not sure how long this whole journey will take." With a sideways glance he didn't see, I watched him carefully. "Too bad we don't have Chefren and his Fiat."

There it was. The brief smile I knew would be there.

I whirled on him. "I knew it! You *are* Jack Moretti!"

He closed his eyes and exhaled. And might as well have confessed.

Once again, I endured that rapid, dizzying shift of everything I thought I knew. Took in Jack's shaved head, his black-lined eyes, bare chest, white kilt.

The dizziness subsided. White-hot anger took its place.

I folded tight arms across my chest. "What is going on, Jack? How did you get here? Do you know how *I* got here?"

"I will answer your questions, Sahara. But not here."

"Yes, here! Right now!"

He eyed the door.

"You were right earlier. I followed you here."

"But—how? Can you—"

"Yes. I can travel backward in time. Just as you can."

My knees wobbled, and I sank to the cot once more.

"And my parents? They could—"

"Yes."

"Why did you follow me?"

"Because I knew you'd get yourself in trouble!" He pointed to my head. "And clearly I was right. Knocked unconscious before you were even here three days!"

I tried to look indignant at his assumption I needed protecting.

But it was the realization of his deceit that swelled into real fury. All I feared was true. Jack was a liar and I could not count on him.

I stood and squared off against him, hit his bare shoulder with my fist. "Why did you lie to me? You had me thinking I was crazy!"

He caught my wrist in his hand, his expression intense, serious.

"I know you don't understand any of this, Sahara. But we must get this trip to Karnak underway. I promise I'll explain more."

"Oh, I know you will."

Every moment of trust I'd given this man taunted me. And yet I let him lead me from the room where I'd been convalescing.

Outside the door, it appeared we were in one of the many palace hallways, which all looked the same to me. Glazed tiles with geometric patterns in reds and blues, wall murals spanning meters that boasted grapevines and flowers, fish and birds. Floors painted in imitation of fish teeming in the Nile. The Egyptians covered every blank space with glyphs and color.

We slipped along the hall. I tried to look confident and yet unobtrusive. Hopefully Jack knew the direction to the stable, because I was severely turned around.

But the maze of the palace halls was nothing compared to the tangle in my mind.

I could travel in time.

Jack could travel in time.

And my parents, perhaps even a sister I'd never met... Once again I seemed to be following in their wake, with no idea of why they were even here, in ancient Egypt, when the last place they'd been seen was traveling to Venice.

CHAPTER TWENTY-SEVEN

November, 1814
Venice, Italy

*R*enae clutched the edge of the rough, wooden table as another pain tightened low across her abdomen.

The slight constrictions had intruded sporadically through the day, but thus far she'd managed to ignore them. The baby wasn't due for another two months. Besides, this had happened sometimes with Sahara, hadn't it?

Two months. How could that possibly be true? Since the day they encountered Giada's employee Joanne at Hatshepsut's Temple and made their hasty plan, they'd been trying to get to this moment. This place. Standing in front of this man. It had taken months.

She let go of the table's edge, a surface that sickened her with its damp, slimy touch. Everything in this city was damp, especially this time of year.

"And that's why we would like to fund your work, and see you create something so spectacular you will never be forgotten."

Alexander's words hung in the air.

The enormous man across the room raised his eyebrows and grunted.

She had known he would be huge. Six feet, seven inches, the history books said. But standing here, in this city of narrow alleys and tiny houses with stunted ceilings, he seemed almost inhuman. Fantastically broad, with massive biceps, a dark mane of wild curls, and a beard that stretched to the middle of his barrel chest. Giovanni Battista Belzoni was a giant of a man.

"So you are saying you will pay me to create this monstrous spectacle? And where would I set this up, this big plan you have for me?" He spread his arms as if to indicate the minuscule house, but he clearly meant the tiny city.

Alexander shrugged. "Not here, not in Venice. Perhaps in Padua."

Renae studied Alex's profile, still so handsome as he neared forty. Did he still have the power of persuasion?

From the back of the cramped house came the bustling sounds of Belzoni's wife, a woman of a substantial size herself. They were quite a pair. Was she making dinner for her guests? It seemed unlikely, despite the heavy odor of onions saturating the air. The couple had been less than hospitable since she and Alexander had arrived.

It had taken nearly a month in 1814 Venice for them to connect with Belzoni, who was abroad when they arrived. This, after the months spent returning from the encounter with Joanne in Egypt, traveling to Highclere to get Sahara settled, and then on to the Venice of 1905, before they could make their way to 1814.

Now, finally, they had come to the moment that could change everything. If they could make it work. But then, Alex could make anything work, couldn't he?

The half dozen or so candles scattered around the inside of the house did little to shake off the gloom of the evening, and did nothing to dry out the dampness of the walls. Was that mold? She swallowed. Greenish fuzz along the base of the floor. It wasn't the Middle Ages, but it might as well have been, considering the cleanliness of the home, and even the odor radiating from Belzoni.

A slow drip of water fell from the ceiling, plopped into one of the beeswax candles, and sizzled like burnt flesh.

A bit of nausea accompanied the low pain in her belly. She needed to get out of here. She levered herself into a chair and touched her fingers to a series of sketches on the table—some kind of hydraulic system. Belzoni had studied hydraulics in Rome. And unless they were successful here today, he would soon move on to Egypt to begin his career there, starting with his proposal for a new machine that could draw water for irrigation from the Nile.

But that would only be the first step, in a series of steps, that would eventually lead to their lives being in danger from Giada Moretti.

Renae wiped the back of her hand across her forehead, freeing the wisps of hair plastered there. From the damp humidity or her own sweat?

They shouldn't be here so late. So close to the baby's birth. They should have gotten Sahara, started the journey back home. But this was the only way.

Belzoni was speaking again. Had she missed something?

She felt so strange, so distracted. As if something momentous was about to happen.

But of course, something momentous *was* about to happen. They were about to change history by convincing Belzoni to stay in Italy.

The ridiculous bundle of bank notes in Alexander's pocket should go a long way toward convincing the man. Probably more money than Belzoni had seen in a lifetime. With the *lira* the new currency of Italy since 1866, it had been fairly simple to acquire a huge amount of discontinued *scudi* bonds in the Venice of 1905. A veritable fortune in 1814.

Alexander was pointing to the sketches. "Surely, a man as talented and brilliant as you, and"—Alex extended his hand toward Belzoni's upper body—"with as many additional gifts, could build a spectacle like the world has never seen."

"And why would you be giving me such a sum of money, to do such a thing?" Belzoni asked.

Behind Renae, the tiny door squeaked open.

Renae turned, with a strange premonition this visitor was not good news.

The hunch proved true. Standing in the doorway of Belzoni's tiny home was the one woman she had hoped to never see again.

Giada.

A slow smile spread across Giada's face as she took in Alexander, Belzoni, and Renae. Then a glance to Renae's belly, and widened eyes.

"Again? Didn't you learn your lesson the first time?"

Alexander stepped in front of Renae, shielding her with his body.

"We don't want any trouble, Giada."

Giada squinted and tilted her head.

"Trouble? Why would I bring you trouble?"

Renae stepped out from behind Alexander and shot the woman a venomous glare. "What do you want?"

"I want what I have always wanted."

"No." Alexander's simple word echoed.

Giada ignored them both to circle the table and extend a hand toward Belzoni.

He looked at her hand as though it were supposed to contain a gift, but was empty.

She dropped her hand. "You must be Mr. Belzoni." Her voice was honey. "I have heard so much."

Alex loomed behind her and hissed in her ear. "You might as well go back, Giada. We won't—"

She turned on them. "Are you certain? It would seem you have much to lose." She extended her hand toward Renae's swollen abdomen. "But not only this new little one. The lovely Sahara as well, spending her summer at Highclere Castle. Seemingly innocent of who and what her parents are."

Renae sucked in a breath, and felt the low ache again, this time sharper.

She forced her voice against the pain. "What do you know about Sahara?"

"Know about her? Why, I've had such a nice visit with her. Strolling the gardens of Highclere, picking ripe peaches from the scented trees inside the greenhouse."

Alexander held Renae's forearm in restraint.

"So, you have found us." His voice was steady. "You have found Sahara. But you cannot force us to do what you want."

"I can. And I will." Giada smiled up at Belzoni as if he were a co-conspirator, then glared at Alexander. "You will make the changes I requested, or I will send someone to England, to destroy your life. The Society will undo everything you've accomplished, and you will have nothing."

"Then we will start again, somewhere else." Alexander's chin was set and lifted.

"And I will send someone to kill Sahara."

Renae gripped the slimy table.

The clattering racket from the back of the house increased, Belzoni's wife swearing in colorful Italian. Perhaps dinner wasn't cooperating.

Another drop of water from the ceiling. Another sizzle. That smell.

Gorge rose in Renae's throat.

Neither she nor Alexander spoke. Was his mind racing, as hers was, trying to unscramble a way in which they could protect Sahara?

The best they could do was return to Highclere, which would take at least two weeks of travel from Venice to England, even if they arrived in 1905 the same moment they left.

Giada seemed to sense her thoughts. "By the time you get there, she will be dead."

At the word *dead*, something snapped inside Renae.

She tore free from Alexander's grip and barreled at Giada like an angry wolverine protecting her pups. Fists raised. Voice howling.

She slammed her forearms into Giada's chest and knocked the woman backward.

Giada stumbled, fell, hit her head against the edge of a chair. She slumped to the floor.

Renae stared and felt only relief.

Belzoni lifted the woman, cradled her in his arms like a child, and peered down on Renae in utter bewilderment.

At that moment his bear of a wife emerged from the back room, dishrag in hand.

She took one look at Belzoni holding Giada, and gave a shrieking hiss.

"You cheating, lying son of a monkey! I will tear your eyes out!"

She snapped the dishrag at his meaty face and indeed, narrowly missed his right eye, then twisted the rag for another snap.

Alexander grabbed Renae's hand, pulled her to the door and out into the cramped and lamplit Venetian alley.

They ran for only a minute or two before Renae pulled him back, forced him to stop.

She bent, bracing her hands against her belly.

"What is it?" There was tension, fear, in his voice. "The baby?"

Renae nodded, unable to speak. Then shook her head. "But we must run."

And yet, where were they running? Certainly they were running to St. Mark's Basilica, the place where they had entered 1814, so they could return to 1905. But what then?

Giada had the power to do what she had threatened, and if she weren't dead in Belzoni's giant arms...

Renae allowed herself that brief wish, but then shoved it away. She had no desire to murder anyone. No matter how justified.

What could they do to prevent Giada from acting on her threat?

"We must run."

And so they did, hand-in-hand as always, through the maze of alleyways and streets. Their feet smacked cobblestones as they passed smoky street lamps and breathed in the wet, salty air of the Venice lagoons.

She begged Alex to stop every few minutes as another pain hit. The pains were closer now, more regular, and it was excruciating to keep moving.

And then in one moment of standing still, hand braced against a stone wall along the narrow street, a sudden rush of fluid down her leg signaled the undeniable truth.

She raised her eyes to Alex's, and saw her own terror reflected there.

"My water broke," she whispered.

Alexander took it in stride, as he always did. "Come, we need to get you off the street."

"To St. Mark's, Alex. We have to make it back to Highclere."

He nodded, a tight nod that spoke volumes. They both knew what it meant to have the baby born here, here in 1814, here where Giada knew exactly where they were.

The spires of St. Mark's loomed above them when the horrible pressure began, low and urgent.

"I can't." She stopped and doubled over, tears flowing. "Alex, I can't run anymore."

They were nearly there, at the corner just before the Square. Outside the Caffé Florian where they'd drunk coffee just this morning. This morning, when everything seemed promising, and they knew today would be the day they made their offer to Belzoni.

But it was still too far, too far across St. Mark's Square, into the basilica, down to the lower levels, where they had first arrived in 1814 Venice.

Alex scooped her up, despite her ponderous weight, and used his elbow to push open the door to the café. He laid her gently on one of the crushed red velvet cushions that ran along the gilded windows.

She breathed, heavy and quick. Searching the café for something to fix her eyes on.

Casanova had reportedly spent time in this cafe. Was there a picture of him somewhere?

Ornate scrollwork, raised and gold-painted around mirrored walls. Parquet floor with its hatched design. Her eyes scanning, scanning.

The place smelled of coffee and warm pastry, just like this morning.

Marble tables, glass and velvet. Cooler—dryer, even—than outside. She could breathe here.

Yes, she could breathe here, and she could have a baby here.

She would have a baby here.

She tried to wrap her mind around it, without panic.

Giada was likely chasing them through the streets. And Renae was trapped here in the café about to give birth. It was like having a high-speed train bearing down on you, and all the while your foot is painfully impaled and bleeding on a rusty nail on the tracks. Terror and pain mixed together, inextricable. Trying to make space in her mind to think, to make a plan. Her mind was blank.

"Not here," she hissed through clenched teeth. "Not here, Alex. We can't let the baby come here, where Giada can find us."

Alex was nodding, but his face showed the panicky expression she remembered from Sahara's birth. As though he could see her foot impaled on the rusty nail, could see the train bearing down, and could do nothing. Could form no coherent thoughts.

Renae's gaze landed on a painting mounted on the wall beside her.

It was a painting of the café, with the artist's name, Tiepolo, etched beneath it. The caption read "The Opening."

Tiepolo. Eighteenth Century, wasn't he? Perhaps painted in the year the café opened. *How long ago? Long enough?*

"The painting." She lifted her chin toward it to draw Alex's attention.

His eyes scanned the artist, the subject, the caption. Then back to her. A quick nod.

"The day it was hung," he said simply.

They both placed their hands on the gilded frame. Bent their heads. Did what they must.

The world was spinning. The pressure unbearable.

Renae feared she would vomit. Feared she would die. Feared for the baby.

And then it settled. The world, her mind, even her body seem to settle into an easier rhythm of *knowing*. Total clarity.

The pain remained, but the train was gone. Everything sharpened into a single point of focus. She opened her eyes, could see she had left 1814. Left Giada behind.

She took a deep breath, pushed away the thoughts of what all of this meant. The knowledge that in the Highclere of 1905, Giada might very well kill Sahara.

But even if Sahara escaped, would Renae ever see her daughter again?

And then she bore down against the pain, and everything else faded away.

CHAPTER TWENTY-EIGHT

1325 B.C.
The House of Rejoicing, Thebes, Egypt

The palace halls echoed with our footfalls, in time with my pounding headache.

Jack turned corners and crossed through stone arches as though he'd lived here for years.

Perhaps he had. It was too soon to know the extent of all his lies.

But I would have the truth from him very soon. His usual evasiveness was not going to continue.

I touched a hand to the hard lump at the base of my skull. Whatever hit me yesterday had not been gentle.

I still had no team of guards following me. What happened to the two men Ay had instructed to watch me?

As we neared the stable, Bek waved from the entrance. His eyes widened at the sight of Jack, and he turned to speak something into the shadows.

We slipped into the dim shelter, and I pulled the boy to my side and whispered against his head. "I'm so glad you weren't hurt in that battle!"

Bek held my hand and searched my face. "You are well?"

I cupped his cheek. "I am well."

Senamun handed the reins of a two-horsed, two-wheeled chariot to Bek. "The boy will accompany you, to fetch transportation on the other side of the Nile."

I exhaled frustration. Bek should stay safe. And I needed to get Jack alone, to grill him.

"We don't need him to—"

"Don't we?" Jack turned on me. "Do you know how to get us all the way to the Temple of Karnak?"

"Fine." The word emerged sullen and petty. I didn't care.

"Ankhe-sen-amun, we will deliver your message to the priest," Jack said, "and learn what we can of Ahmose and his family. But we won't be returning here. It's time for us to move on."

I stared, open-mouthed. Who gave him permission to make decisions on my behalf?

"Ramesses, I can—"

"Why return to danger here? You will learn what you need from the priest, and then you can return home."

He was right. Which pained me to admit. So I didn't.

I squinted into the stable's empty courtyard. "We should leave, before Ay's guards finds Senamun and suspect something." I embraced the girl briefly. "Good luck. I hope it all goes well for you."

She seemed surprised and hesitant, but then returned my hug. "Thank you for everything you have done."

And then we were off, leaving Senamun and the palace behind us.

We reached the edge of the Nile in minutes, and the waiting boat Senamun had arranged, its curved prow high and haughty above the water. The river churned with boats, traveling both directions. Egypt had not bothered with cutting roads through sand or farmland. The Nile was the highway of the kingdom, with a current to chase you north and a wind at your back as you sailed south. We, however, only wanted to get across.

We climbed aboard the narrow vessel, and Jack nodded to the dozen or so crew manning the squared sails and the rudder at the stern.

Safe for the moment. It was time to get answers.

Thankfully, Bek seemed fascinated by the workings of the rudder.

I grabbed Jack by the forearm, and pulled him to the shadow of the boat's great prow.

Where to start? The building pressure in my chest, unanswered questions mixed with anger, threatened to explode into something incoherent.

He put up a hand before I could.

"First of all, I need to apologize."

If he thought an apology was going to fix this...

"Obviously, I have not been honest with you—not here, in this time, nor when we first met."

"Obviously."

The boat shifted from the riverbank. I grabbed the wooden edge that rose from the deck.

"I had no intention of your even seeing me here, after I followed you. I'm just terrible at reconnaissance, it would appear."

I swallowed hard. Outrage was squeezing my lungs.

"As I said, I had a feeling you were not... experienced... at traveling in time, and I was afraid for your safety."

So, one question answered. It was possible to travel back and get hurt. Maybe even get dead.

"I can take care of myself."

Jack sighed, shook his head, and looked away.

"I think my parents are here. Or at least they were here, not long ago."

He said nothing.

"I have to find them."

"I know."

The boat was turning north now, riding the current but with the crew rowing us at an angle, cutting across the blue-green water. The sun was rolling down behind us and warmed the back of my hair.

We stood side-by-side, watching the Luxor temples lit by the sun across the river.

The picturesque sight seemed to loosen the tension in my neck.

"Why didn't you tell me you could... do what I do?"

"Because I didn't know if you could do it. It's not an exact science for any of us. And with no one to teach you—"

"My parents?"

He nodded.

"Can—everyone—do it?" The question seemed ridiculous, but I didn't want to think I was special.

"No. It's genetic."

"Explain."

"It's passed down from parent to child. Typically only *one* parent..."

"But both my parents could do it?"

"Yes." The answer seemed tinged with disapproval.

I turned to him, still leaning against the rail, eyebrows raised.

"It's not... allowed. For two travelers to marry, have a child."

I straightened. "Allowed? By whom?"

"It's complicated."

"Oh, I hope you don't think that's enough of an answer."

Sadness tinged the edges of his smile. "There are many, many rules. Some of them immutable, more like laws of nature we've discovered, about how the traveling works. And some of them imposed. By those who have formed a Society, a sort of self-governing body, to monitor the actions of all of us. And that organization has decided it is unsafe for two time travelers to have offspring, in which the genetic trait is amplified."

Too much information to take in at once. The idea that my parents had defied some shadowy organization to marry and produce me was certainly romantic, but it created more questions than it answered.

"Amplified. Is that an official term?"

"Actually, yes."

"And what does it mean?"

He ran a hand through his hair and scanned the cloudless sky. "Anomalies. There's no predicting, but they can be... dangerous."

I'd let the specifics wait on that statement. Another question was bothering me. "So if I am— amplified—why has it taken all these years for me to do it?"

He glanced sideways at me. "So this is your *first* jump?"

Jump. Like off a cliff. Interesting.

"Well, technically, no. The first was a couple of days ago at Hatshepsut's Temple."

He slapped a palm against the ship's hull. "I knew it."

"You followed me that morning, too! Were you going to follow me back three thousand years as well?"

"I was thinking about it. But then you came walking down the ramp, so casual, and I thought maybe you really were sightseeing."

I studied the water. "I did it once before. Years ago. Accidentally. I thought I was having a hallucination."

He covered my hand on the rail with his own. "I'm sorry, Sahara. I can't imagine how frightening it must have been, with no one to train you."

"Train me?" I yanked my hand away and squared off against him. "I would have appreciated someone at least *telling* me!"

He chewed at his lip. "I thought about that, too. But I was trying to figure out, first of all, if you already knew. Think how it would have sounded if I'd tried to explain, and you had no idea what I was talking about."

I didn't particularly care how it might have sounded. "So you decided to follow me."

"You gave me no choice! I knew you'd get yourself into some kind of danger. And after that obvious ploy with your scarf and our driver, I came back to the American House and, yes, I followed you."

"So why didn't we end up at the tomb here together? In this time?"

"Like I said, it's not an exact science. I arrived here before you, actually."

The confusing answers were only increasing my anger over his deceit. I was sick of playing catch-up on something I should have known from the start.

"And once you found me here? Why the elaborate masquerade?"

He studied the rippling water at the base of the prow. "I panicked. I hadn't planned on letting you see me. I knew you'd be annoyed I'd followed you to protect you. I don't think you even realized how your determination drives you to work too hard, take too many risks, and refuse to accept help."

I bristled at the list of accusations.

"But it was more than that, I knew if you recognized me, you'd eventually realize something else."

I scanned my overloaded brain, but nothing surprising leaped out.

"I knew you'd figure out that if I could also travel in time, it was much too coincidental I simply wanted to write a story about you for the newspaper back home, after my aunt had mentioned meeting you years ago."

The obvious fact hit me in the gut, much like the first time Jack had mentioned his aunt. There was something more going on here, something that felt almost sinister. As though I were being watched. Tracked. The hair rose on the back of my neck.

"So… Giada. You said it was passed through families. Can she—"

"Yes. She was a friend of your parents, through the Society."

"Does this society have a name?"

"Tempus Vigilia."

Tempus Vigilia. Time Vigil.

I had needed to join the Egyptology Club at university. I'd paid dues to the Royal Archaeological Institute when I started my career. This was the first organization I'd been conscripted into without my knowledge.

"How many?"

"How many what?"

"How many are there, people like us?"

"I'm not sure. We don't all meet in one place. We're scattered over the globe. Thousands, definitely."

"Thousands." The word escaped my lips like a prayer.

As shocking as all of this might be, and as prickly as I felt about anyone disapproving of my parents' marriage, or neglecting to inform me of this crazy ability, or covertly following me through time, there was also the undeniable draw toward people that claimed me as one of their own.

"What is it, Sahara? What's wrong?"

I swiped at the unexpected tears. "I've been—alone—for a long time. It just struck me, perhaps I actually belong somewhere."

Again, the hand covering mine.

Again, I pulled away.

No matter how kind, I did not trust this man. How could I? It would be foolhardy and dangerous to let myself feel any connection to him. Better to be wary and to be my own protector.

"Sahara, I only—"

"Save it, Jack. I'm tired of being part of whatever games you're playing."

He grabbed both my arms and turned my body to face his, a breath away.

"You think this is a game for me?"

The low intensity of his voice startled me. I averted my eyes, studied the dark water sliding past.

"Lady?"

Bek stood behind Jack. He looked between my tears and Jack's face and scowled. He'd probably give Jack a good kick in the shins if he believed him to be the source of my emotion. Or perhaps pull out that sling he kept strapped to his waist.

"I'm well, Bek. What is it?"

In answer, he pointed to the approaching shoreline, the outlines of buildings lit by the final rays of the setting sun.

We'd arrived on the east bank of the Nile. For now at least, my questions would have to wait.

Questions, yes, but also a glimmer of hope. Hope that my life was not as isolated as I once thought. Hope, even, that I was part of some larger purpose which had simply been unknown to me.

Within minutes, Bek had secured us transportation—something less pretentious than the gold-trimmed chariot we'd taken from the palace. More like a horse-drawn wagon.

He patted the side of the vehicle. "She won't attract so much attention."

"Good." I climbed aboard. "Maybe we can avoid Ay and his guards."

Jack followed me into the cart. "The vizier? What's the problem with him?"

I lowered myself to a woven mat and shrugged. "He may be trying to kill me for being a spy."

Jack's frustrated exhale spoke volumes.

We jolted our way along what would eventually be the Corniche of Luxor, where Jack and I stood at the rail just a few days ago, overlooking the Nile.

A line of unassuming mud huts slid past in the twilight. Huts that in three thousand years would be eclipsed by the Winter Palace Hotel.

We traveled in tense silence. Impossible to say what Jack was thinking. I sifted through a jumble of anger, distrust, and a longing that only left me frustrated with myself.

As we neared the massive temple complex, the silence of the village gave way to a dull hum, then increased to the distinct sounds of revelry. Dusk was giving way to darkness, but the temple ahead flared with light.

Bek grinned and bobbed his head. "We will see the Tekh Festival. Very exciting."

Oh gravy.

Jack looked between the boy and me. "What's the Tekh Festival?"

"Otherwise known as the Feast of Drunkenness. It commemorates humanity's salvation by beer."

"Okay, I need to hear the rest of that story."

I smiled, despite my agitation. "The god Ra set out to destroy evil humanity by unleashing the warrior goddess Sekhmet to tear them apart. Later he regretted his rashness, so he dyed huge quantities of beer with pomegranate juice and served it to Sekhmet, who believed it was humanity's blood and drank herself into a stupor, then eventually woke up as the beneficent goddess Hathor."

"Nice."

We rode slowly to the west entrance, its soaring, slanted pylons illuminated by the flames of a thousand torches held above dancing throngs. The Temple of Karnak was more a complex of temples, lakes, and courtyards, built up slowly over hundreds of years by many pharaohs, with new sections yet to come. But it was already a wonder.

We disembarked into a frenzied crowd of worshippers, packed tight and pulsing with the beat of unseen drums.

Jack grabbed my hand, eyes narrowed. "We'll never get through this mess."

"Nonsense." I slipped from Jack's grasp and bent to Bek's ear, to ensure he heard me. "Stay here. We won't be long, and we'll meet you here."

A flicker of disappointment in his eyes worried me a bit, but I would have to take the chance.

"Come," I said to Jack. "Let's find Menna."

But the task was not so simple. Festival-goers danced and twirled, stumbled and crashed together, the air vibrating with them. We burrowed our way through, in the general direction of the temple's entrance, but more than once I was nearly knocked off my feet.

Finally, the first entrance pylons. I strained forward, Jack on my heels.

But then a train of dancers, arms linked, sailed between us.

I tried to catch Jack's eye, between the passing figures. "I'll meet you inside!"

Did he hear me?

The crowd surged against me, and I needed to move with it or risk being trampled. I hesitated, then shrugged.

He'd followed me this far. Let him figure it out.

CHAPTER TWENTY-NINE

I fought my way through chinks in the temple crowd and pushed forward until I escaped the main press of people, past the twin obelisks Hatshepsut had erected at the entrance, into the Hypostyle Hall in the Precinct of Amun-Ra.

In later years, this hall would be expanded by the very same Seti in whose tomb I first traveled through time. The hall would become one of the most popular sites in Egypt, with more than a hundred sandstone columns soaring twenty-five meters into the air, each splashed with colorful symbols from roof to base.

For now, it was more of an open court, milling with worshippers going to and from the chapel of Amun in the northwest corner. I could spend a week here, a year even, uncovering all that would be lost to history. Again it struck me, *how little we know.*

I stood on my toes and scanned over the heads of the crowd that surged through the courtyard, searching back toward the entrance. Saw nothing of Jack.

He would have to catch up, or meet me back where we'd left Bek.

At least the crowd made it less likely for Ay to spot me.

Hopefully he was back across the river already, waiting for me to bring Ahmose to the throne room.

I wandered through packed space, recollections of the temple complex's layout in my head, from both books and my own previous visits. Where was I likely to find Menna?

Perhaps deeper into the complex, in the Precinct of Mut. The goddess Mut had eventually absorbed and merged with the warrior goddess Sekhmet. Since today was Sekhmet's festival, certainly there would be activity in those temples.

I pushed through, reaching the Temple of Mut's courtyard, pock-marked with a smattering of black granite statues of the lion-headed Sekhmet. The temple itself was fronted by the Porch of Drunkenness, where by night's end many festival-goers would pass out, to be awakened by drummers to commune with the goddess.

Beyond the central temple, the crescent-shaped sacred lake sparkled in the darkness with the reflection of a hundred dancing torches.

Certainly this was as good a place as any to search.

I paused at the foot of the stone steps. Who could I ask?

A young girl passed, dressed in the white robes and eye paint of a priestess. She glanced at me and slowed.

"I am looking for the priest called Menna. Can you tell me where to find him?"

Wordless, she pointed toward the temple interior.

I nodded my thanks and jostled my way up the stone steps and into the central hall.

The temple was surprisingly empty, with a hollow hush.

A priest bent over an altar toward the back of the chamber, sprinkling something over it that sparked like tiny fireworks with each scattering.

The air smelled of blood and burning animal flesh. My throat seized with disgust.

He turned, his face blank and unresponsive.

"Are you Menna?"

He nodded once, slowly, like some old sage. The deeply-lined face and wispy white hair added to the effect. He wore an odd earring, something like the shape of a serpent, in one ear.

Where to begin?

"I have come with a message from the Great Royal Wife Ankhe-sen-amun."

"A wife no longer." He held a metal bowl of fragrant incense in two hands at his waist.

"Yes, well... That's what I came to talk to you about. She is afraid for her life."

"As she should be."

"She needs your help."

The priest glanced left and right, then leaned toward me.

"What does she desire?" His voice was low and tense.

Did the guy ever say more than four words?

I stepped closer, matching his tone. "She wants you to help her— to declare herself pharaoh."

He drew himself upright. "A woman?"

I rolled my eyes. "It's happened before."

"Yes, but—"

"She wants you to send for—Horemheb. And then spread the news he's coming to be crowned successor, like Tut-ankh-amun wanted."

"And yet she thinks to crown herself?"

"Yes. While the vizier is distracted, or maybe even on the offensive against Horemheb, she wants you to come to The House of Rejoicing with others who are loyal, and make her Pharaoh Ankhe-sen-amun."

He exhaled heavily, and scanned the temple shadows once more. "He is a dangerous man, the vizier. Not to be trifled with."

"So I hear. Ankhe-sen-amun believes he murdered her husband."

"I am quite certain he did."

The words were delivered so matter-of-factly, it gave me a chill. "Do you think he would kill Ankhe-sen-amun?"

"He would not hesitate, if he believed it would serve him. For now, he believes marriage to her is his best way forward. But if that were to change..."

"Ankhe-sen-amun also needs information from you about a man and his family whom you brought from the north. Ahmose and his wife. Perhaps a daughter—"

"I know no such man."

I straightened my shoulders. "There is no danger. She is aware you brought them—"

"I said I do not know them."

His insistence seemed genuine.

But I couldn't simply let it go.

The scuffle of footsteps behind us drew our attention. We both turned toward the entrance of the temple chamber.

Jack strode out of the shadow, his flashing eyes and clenched jaw illuminated in the torchlight.

"There you are!"

"What's wrong?"

"What's wrong is that you didn't wait for me. What's wrong is that you insisted on coming here alone, as if you know what kind of danger you might face."

"Who is this man?" Menna's scowl was something fierce to see.

"This is... my servant. Ramesses. He accompanied me from The House of Rejoicing." I turned on Jack. "Remember your place, Ramesses. You know I wanted to see the Temple of Mut."

His eyes went dark, but he said nothing.

I returned my attention to Menna. "Perhaps you only knew Ahmose's wife, Ra-Ne-Hannu?"

He flicked a hand at me. "I am finished with your questions."

I fought the emotion that made me want to strike him. First the Hittite prince, now this priest. I'd been led on a fruitless chase for the mysterious Ahmose and his family for days, still no closer to the truth.

"If you could just try to remember—"

"Enough!" The wise old sage was gone, replaced with something more hostile than helpful.

Every route blocked.

"Shall I send word to Ankhe-sen-amun with the assurance you will help her?" My voice was tight, words measured.

He lifted his chin. "I shall tell her myself, when I return with you in the morning."

"The morning? No, we are going back tonight—"

Menna chuckled in condescension. "Not unless you are a very good swimmer. You will find no one to take you across the Nile in the darkness."

I huffed and turned to Jack.

He shrugged.

Not helpful.

"I must find Bek, my... other servant. He will find us transportation. I will make certain Ankhe-sen-amun knows you will join her in the morning."

Menna pursed his lips and shrugged.

Whatever. There was nothing more for us here. We were leaving.

I hurried from the temple. I didn't need to hear Jack chastise me for leaving him in the outer courtyard. When we hit the mass of people, I shouted to him.

"If we get separated, I'll meet you where we left Bek." That should satisfy him.

We pushed back the way we'd come, until Bek's shaved head and bright eyes met us. He stood atop a half-wall, waving madly.

"Did you see the Temple? The Sacred Lake? Was the goddess Mut sailing there?"

Bitter disappointment sharpened my voice. "We saw all we needed to see. We're ready to go back across the river."

He frowned. "Return? At night? How will I find someone to take us at night?"

Jack arched an eyebrow at me. "Well, now, that is a surprise, isn't it?"

I glared him down. "Where are we supposed to spend the night?"

"Will not the priest Menna give you beds?" Bek thumbed in the direction of the temples.

I glanced at Jack. "What do you think?"

"Beats sleeping with my back propped against a temple, I guess."

And so we returned, all three, to the Temple of Mut. Sought out Menna. Requested beds. And then went our separate ways—Jack joined Bek to spend the night in the servants quarters, which gave me a small amount of pleasure—and I was ushered to the hall of the priestesses.

I was shown a bed and did nothing but fall into it, eager to sleep.

But sleep did not come.

Instead, I replayed everything Jack had told me about traveling through time. Formed a hundred new questions. Imagined, then discarded, one answer after another. Worded angry accusations for Jack and his secrets.

I rose with the light, more fatigued than the night before.

After washing as best I could and dressing in yesterday's clothes, I picked at a sumptuous breakfast of melons and honeyed bread served in the priestesses' hall, then reconvened with my travel partners in the courtyard outside the first pylons. The evidences of the night's festival were strewn about—snuffed torches, scraps of torn clothing, chunks of discarded food being pecked by birds. It reminded me of the streets of London, the morning after the Lord Mayor's Parade.

Menna joined us moments later. I barely recognized him, dressed in a simple white kilt and carrying a staff as though he were some kind of shepherd. He kept his head bent, clearly not wanting to be seen.

Jack pulled me aside and leaned in to whisper. "As soon as we get across the river, we'll get Bek to arrange us transportation to the tomb. It's time to get out of here."

I kept my eyes averted and said nothing.

Regardless of having missed Ay's deadline to present myself with Ahmose, I had every intention of seeing this thing through. Of watching Senamun crowned as pharaoh.

Of seeing Ay's smug face when he realized he'd been outmaneuvered.

CHAPTER THIRTY

*T*he priest had better travel accommodations for us, and we rode in style in two chariots to the waiting boat.

Bek insisted on riding with Jack and me. "That priest's eyes have the look of a crocodile," he said.

But once in the boat, Menna sat with his back propped against the hull and closed his eyes.

I drew Jack to the other end of the ship. It was time for Part Two of my interrogation.

We stood side-by side at the ship's prow, this time looking toward the western necropolis, now with the rising sun warming our backs. Yesterday's anger gave way to resignation. People are bound to fail you. Right now, all I wanted was information and to understand.

"These rules and laws you talked about. The ones that dictate the traveling. What are they?"

He didn't answer immediately. Then took a deep breath. "There are too many to explain in one trip across the Nile. But briefly… First, there is the Codex. Which is full of all the rules Tempus Vigilia has created over the years, rules we're supposed to follow. And then there are all the principles we've collected from members about how traveling in time works for us. Those have been compiled into something we call the Knowledge Base."

"And who set up all these principles?"

Jack rubbed the back of his neck. "Depends on your beliefs, I guess. God? The universe? Random chance?"

"What do you believe?"

"I don't know. Some kind of higher power, I guess."

I traced a line of splintered wood on the rail with my fingertip. "I go to Sunday services at the American House with the others, usually. But religion, for me, has been more like a warm blanket—somewhere to retreat when I want to feel comforted. Thinking of a God directing me through time is a little... freakish."

"Why am I not surprised that you'd rather be in charge of your own life?"

"Funny."

The boat dipped, spraying a mist of cool river water onto our heads. I wiped the dampness from my cheeks.

"I read a letter from my father to my mother that implied you could only visit a specific time once. Is that true?"

"Yes." He turned his head, eyebrows lifted. "That is true. Also, you must jump at least eighty years backward, each time you travel."

"Eighty years? Why is that a rule?"

"Not a rule. It's just how it is. If you try to jump back to a time closer than eighty years, or within eighty years of a place you've already visited, it simply doesn't work. Perhaps to keep you from gaining knowledge you can somehow use to your benefit. No one really knows."

"So you can't travel back to yesterday and undo a mistake you've made?"

He looked away. "No."

"Hmm." I hadn't thought of the idea of traveling backward in my own life. Of actually going back to 1905 and convincing my parents not to leave for Venice. Perhaps correct a few other indiscretions in my past. But apparently, that was off the table.

What would happen if eighty-one-year-old me went back to check in on one-year-old me? One of those questions that would bother me until I had an answer, certainly. Someone must have tried it at least once. But I'd leave that research question for another time.

"What about going forward? Can you go forward eighty years or more into the future?" I shivered at my own question. I'd been fascinated with ancient history all my life. Being able to see it firsthand was riveting. But to travel into the unknown future... It sounded rather awful.

"No. You can't travel any further than your own life. I suppose because you have to be able to envision a past event, hold a past object. Or perhaps because it simply hasn't happened yet. I don't know. But no one has ever traveled forward."

"But... What if we were to find a person who could travel in time, who had our ability, but was born here in ancient Egypt. If we told him about the future—the future *we* have seen—why couldn't he—"

Jack was shaking his head, smiling. "You're already deep into the questions Tempus Vigilia has been asking for years. But I can only tell you it hasn't been done."

My mind was swimming. I braced my elbows on the ship's edge and pressed the heels of my hands against my gritty eyes.

"You're exhausted." Jack placed a hand against my back.

I straightened, away from the hand.

"I didn't sleep."

"Come." He gently pulled me from the hull, then down to the deck. He sat with his shoulder braced against mine.

"Close your eyes. I'll let you know when we're near the western bank."

I succumbed to closing my eyes, then even to dropping my head to Jack's shoulder.

He lowered his head to mine.

Why was it no matter how hard I tried, I couldn't stop myself from feeling a connection with this man?

"Jack, when we get there, I can't leave. I have to make sure Senamun is safe."

His voice was a whisper. "This is madness, Sahara."

"I know. But I have to help her."

"Why? Why is she so important to you?"

"Because she is alone. She has no one."

The words, though quiet, fell heavy in the morning light. The silence after them lengthened.

Did Jack understand? She'd been abandoned by anyone who loved her, forced to make her own way in the world. How could I leave her to whatever fate Ay had in store for her?

"Why did you follow me to Egypt, Jack?"

"I told you, I feared for your safety—"

"No, I don't mean that. I mean, in Luxor, at the dig. Why did you seek me out?"

He sighed. "I told you. Because I've wanted to meet you since my aunt told me of you, all those years ago."

"But not to write a newspaper story about me."

"No. I'm sorry about that."

"Then, why?"

He inhaled, as though reluctant to tell the story.

I kept my eyes closed, giving him space and time.

"Like you, my parents were not there for me when I was young. My Aunt Giada kept me away from anyone else who was... had my gifts, other travelers. I was mostly alone. Like you."

I barely breathed, his confession came so quietly.

"Years ago, when my aunt visited with you at Highclere, she returned and told me about you. Told me you seemed to know nothing of the abilities you would grow into, abilities she had been preparing me for. She told me you were smart and strong, but with no one to train you, she wondered what you would do. I was fascinated, I will admit. And over the years, I would ask about you occasionally, and she would tell me where you were, what you were doing. And then one day, she suggested I come to meet you myself."

So many things to take apart there, and I sensed it was still not the whole truth. I lifted my head and started with the statement that intrigued me most.

"My abilities— you said I would 'grow into' them?"

"Yes. It typically happens between the ages of twenty and twenty-five."

"So then, in 1914, when I was twenty-four, and found myself suddenly in the funeral rites of Seti I, it was the beginning of the new Sahara."

"Yes."

"Why was your aunt looking for my parents back in '05?"

"She'd lost track of them for some years. Wanted to talk with them about the work she was doing." He drummed his fingers against his thigh. "I am surprised after your accidental trip you went nearly eight years without any other incidents."

"I didn't spend much time here in Egypt for many of those years. I was helping with the war effort."

"Helping?"

I closed my eyes again. "Lady Almina turned Highclere into a luxury hospital to care for wounded soldiers. I was conscripted for nursing duties. To tend to the men—" My voice faltered.

"Who was he? The one who broke your heart?"

I sniffed and dropped my head to his shoulder again. "It was hardly a broken heart. Mostly a flirtation."

He took my hand in his, rested it on his knee. "I think maybe it was more."

"I didn't even know him long. But it was only the second time I'd allowed someone—had let anyone—it was foolish. And then he died."

Jack lips brushed the top of my head. "Not foolish. And you don't need to know someone for long to be sure of what you feel."

True.

"I don't think my parents actually died. I think they left me behind, to travel through time. And I think I have a sister."

Jack was silent a moment, his body warm against me.

"Maybe they had no choice. If your sister was born while they were traveling, the only way they could return to you would be to leave her in the year she was born. She wouldn't be able to go forward with them to her future, to the year they left you."

Could that be true? Some kind of cosmic mix-up?

The sailors were calling orders at each other now.

We climbed up from our position on the deck. The western shore was a stone's throw away.

"Keep your head down when we disembark," Jack said. "Let's try to avoid attention while we find a way to the tomb."

"I told you, Jack, I'm not ready to leave yet. Senamun may still need me. Need us."

I took a few steps away, toward the middle of the ship.

"Sahara."

I closed my eyes, not wanting to hear another reprimand.

"I need to tell you something."

"I'm listening." I folded my arms across my chest, suddenly chilled in the morning air.

"It's part of the Knowledge Base."

"So," I returned to where he stood, "something we know about traveling in time. Not a man-made rule we're supposed to follow, but a... principle about how it works?"

"Right."

"Well?"

His eyes were averted, toward the Theban hills.

"When you traveled backward the other two times—at Hatshepsut's Temple, and years ago, in Seti's tomb—how much time had passed when you returned?"

I thought back. "At the temple? I don't know. But it didn't seem like much. Maybe none."

"And in the tomb?"

"That was odd. I remember Howard was saying something, just before I—disappeared—I guess. When I returned, he said it again, as if repeating himself. But I had the strange sense he wasn't repeating. That I had come back to the same moment. Or to a few seconds before, I suppose."

I could hear Jack's exhalation. I waited.

"Yes, it's just how it is. When we jump backward in time, we can stay however long we like, but when we return, it's to the moment, just a fraction, before we left. And then the moment of our original jump passes us by, and we have not left at all."

"I don't understand."

He brought his gaze back to me, jaw tight and eyes dark.

"We erase our trip backward."

I clenched my teeth. "Speak clearly, Jack."

"By living again *through* the moment we originally jumped back from, but without actually traveling backward, it's as if it never happened. We basically undo everything that happened while we were back in time."

"What? Why?" I struggled to comprehend the implications of this news.

"Again, we don't know why things happen as they do, only that it's the way it works. Our best guess is that it's to avoid tampering with history. We can go back as observers, and even interact if we wish, but when we leave, we will have left no trace of our visit."

"That's good… right? So we don't change something for the worse?"

"Right."

The silence held, and then the reality hit me hard.

"Nothing I am doing here makes any difference. Helping Senamun. It will be as if it never happened."

"Right."

My stomach dropped at the single word, and my throat felt dry.

"The only thing that does matter, is your life itself. We can die here, Sahara."

I turned away, moved away, unable to speak.

"And that's why we need to leave."

"But my parents…"

227

"I know," Jack said simply. "But every avenue has been exhausted, and we have made enemies."

I followed him from the boat, head down, Menna and Bek behind us.

But when we stepped onto the west bank, our escape plan dissolved.

A retinue of Ay's armed guards stood ready to escort us to the palace.

And oddly, the only thought running through my mind was a quote from a long-lost journal.

We hope, of course, to intercept Belzoni before his impressive, yet destructive, work begins.

If nothing done in the past remained, why did my parents believe they could stop Belzoni?

CHAPTER THIRTY-ONE

$\mathcal{W}$e walked ahead of pointed spears, our entire party wordless.

Bek kept his hand in mine.

I stumbled once, scraped my sandaled foot on a rock, then kicked it out of my path.

My trip across the river had yielded nothing about my parents. And now the fruitless errand gave Ay another chance to take me, with another reason to believe me treasonous.

We entered a silent, empty palace.

A servant scurried past.

Menna stopped her. "Why is the palace deserted?"

She flicked a fearful glance at all our faces. "Are you foreigners, that you know nothing of today? Everyone is in the throne room."

A sick feeling washed over me. Everyone? In the throne room?

The guards prodded us forward.

Menna led the way, with Jack and I behind, Bek trailing, and the guards still at our backs.

We approached the throne room, guarded by two sentinels outside, but Menna raised his head and was recognized.

They bowed in unison and opened the double doors to the room.

As in the palace halls and royal bedchambers, here carved wooden columns supported a mural-painted ceiling, and scenes of gods and nature covered the walls in vibrant reds, blues, and yellows.

It appeared we had been forced upon some kind of ceremony, with everyone facing forward, and several figures on an elevated platform at the front of the room.

I strained to see above heads, to no avail.

Jack pulled me closer to him and indicated a break in the crowd.

At the front of the room, looking pale and small and frightened standing beside the hulking Vizier Ay, was Ankhe-senamun. A priest lowered something to her head.

But the headpiece was not the red and white crown of a unified Egypt's pharaoh. It was the feathered Vulture Crown of a Great Royal Wife.

My shoulders dropped and I closed my eyes. So this was how history played out. Poor Senamun.

The crowd parted and the Vizier Ay, wearing the Red and White Double Crown, swept down the aisle, dragging his new wife.

They rushed past us, but not before Senamun saw me, opened her lips as if to speak, then sealed them again and turned away.

I felt like a traitor and a failure all at once.

How had this happened? We left less than eighteen hours ago. There was nothing in the wind at that time of an immediate marriage.

"Menna, can you do nothing?"

Perhaps I had no ability to change things, but certainly the priest could.

Menna turned his head to one of our armed escorts.

"Take her to the Royal Wife's chambers."

The guard grabbed my arm.

"What?" I sought Jack's face.

Jack lunged for me.

But another guard stepped between us, shoulders squared against Jack. "What about this one? And the child?"

"They are nothing. She is the traitor."

The soldier hauled me toward the throne room's double doors.

I struggled, fighting to look backward.

Jack was yelling, elbowing, now grappling with one of the guards.

The other clubbed him with the blunt end of his spear, and he went down.

I didn't resist. There was no point.

Menna disappeared into the crowd and my guard dragged me forward with an iron fist around my upper arm.

My chest thudded in time with the slap of my sandals.

I would say nothing. They had no proof I had done anything wrong.

Well, except for my clandestine meeting with the priest last night, in which I laid out our entire covert strategy.

It must have been Menna who sent word in the night to Ay, to warn him Senamun was plotting against him. Turns out there was at least one person willing to sail across the river at night.

Jack's recent revelation burned its way through my mind. None of this latest disaster made any difference. All that mattered now was that I escaped and got back to the sealed door of Tut-ankh-amun's tomb so I could return home.

The two guards shoved me into Senamun's chamber.

The sun bore through the window and the air felt hot and close.

Senamun rushed me. "You must get me out of here."

Did she not see my armed escort?

She glanced sideways at the guards, waited until they exited the chamber, then pushed on. "That horrible man—I do not have much time. I am unsure whether he will lock me away, or kill me, or simply force me to his bed. And I cannot say which fate would be worse!"

She started her usual pacing, twisting her hands, plucking at her clothing.

"Senamun, I don't know what I can do—"

"Find Menna."

"Menna has betrayed you."

She stopped and spun. Her face blanched. "Have I no friends?" She pulled the Vulture Crown from her head and tossed it to a couch. "Perhaps Bek?"

"He is a child, Senamun. What can he do?"

"I do not know! Somehow he must secret me away, away from The House of Rejoicing, perhaps even away from Egypt. Yes—yes, that is what I will do! I will go far upriver, to the land of Punt. It is a beautiful land, I hear. Rich with resources. I will live out my days unknown by anyone. Yes—I could manage to be an ordinary woman, do you not think so, Ra-Ne-Hannu?"

"Senamun, I don't have any idea how to get you to Punt." Or Punt's exact location. Scholars disagreed about the site of one of Egypt's trading partners. Ethiopia perhaps? In the northern Horn of Africa? I shook my head at the historical questions. I was losing my mind.

The doors burst open and a forbidding-looking woman strode in. She stood much taller than average, with wide shoulders and eyes like black beads.

"Ankhe-sen-amun, Beloved of the Great King, Favored of Hathor, Lady of Grace, your king desires your presence this evening in his chamber. Your women will take you to the bathing pool to begin your preparations."

Three young women filed in behind her and circled to gently lead Senamun toward the door.

Before they got her out, Ay barged into the room, a wicked smile on his thick lips and personal guards flanking him.

Senamun pulled away from the girls and retreated to the low couch, her face still white.

But Ay's attention was on me.

"So, my new wife's accomplice. A traitor, as I suspected."

He drew close, peered into my eyes.

I pulled my head back a fraction, but there was no getting away from that stare.

"Where are you from? Who has sent you? The Nehesyw? The Mitanni? Which enemy has dared to strike a blow at the crowned head of the Upper and Lower Lands of Egypt?"

"She is no one, husband!" Senamun struggled to stand and approached Ay. "A simple friend, visiting from my family in Amarna."

Ay turned his hostile scowl to Senamun.

She shrank back.

"Simple, you say? And yet she crossed the Nile to conscript my priest Menna, to help you. To make you *pharaoh!*" He laughed.

The guards joined his laughter, as though they understood the joke.

"A messenger, only, husband. And clearly, I was... out of my mind... with grief for my late husband. I — I meant nothing by it, no disloyalty."

I could hardly believe what I was hearing. She had never seemed a strong girl, but this complete turnabout, into cowering and groveling, was hard to believe.

Unless one took into account the extreme power of men in this time. Especially one who had been crowned king.

Ay patted Senamun's cheek, but the touch was not affectionate. "I will forgive you, my new wife, for I know these days have been difficult."

He turned on me. "This one, however, has no excuse."

My palms were damp, and my tongue dry in my mouth.

"Kill her."

My knees buckled.

"No!" Senamun's hand went to her mouth.

One of the guards turned on me and caught me before I fell. Then drew a sword.

Ay cut him off with a growl and a slap.

"Not here, fool. You'll get blood all over the floor!"

"Husband, I beg you," Senamun grabbed at his robes. "How would it look to the people if your first act as pharaoh was to begin killing your wife's friends? Surely you want your people to see you as the benevolent king you are?"

Ay scowled, looking between us. Then sighed.

"Chain her up. Until I decide." He flicked his head toward the door. "And not in the prison. Too many loose tongues there. On the roof."

CHAPTER THIRTY-TWO

hy had I ever believed I could rewrite history? The past was the past, and there was no changing it.

It would have been nice to say goodbye to Bek.

But then again, what difference would it have made? This was all basically make-believe.

All except the hot sun frying the top of my head, where I now sat chained to a post in the center of one of the palace roofs.

Only one guard attended me. Not surprising, since the heavy irons he clamped around my wrists would take a Westinghouse drill to cut through.

Beside my hitching post, irrationally, a fire blazed. As if the sun weren't hot enough. I had asked the guard who sat nearby more than once if I could be chained somewhere else, away from the fire.

He ignored me.

A deep fatigue stole over me, aided by the heat and lack of sleep, but more a weariness at reality.

There were no answers here about my parents. Only the truth that they had left me in a deeper way than I ever imagined.

Now their trail was cold, proving once again that any hope of connection was illusory.

The image of Jack going down under the javelin of Ay's guard seemed unreal.

We can die here, Sahara.

And perhaps we would. I had let myself feel something, for Senamun and Bek. For Jack. I acted impulsively, before having all the answers, gotten distracted and let my new attempt at trusting people extend even to Menna, foolishly.

And now I'd probably gotten Jack and myself killed.

So, I was on my own.

But then, when, in the last seventeen years since my parents' death, had I *not* been on my own? Wasn't everyone ultimately alone in the world, and must make their way without relying on others for rescue? Even Senamun was learning this lesson.

I hunched into a cross-legged slump at the ridiculous nature of all this nonsense.

Forget the impossible fact that I could travel through time. But trying to be a hero in ancient Egypt? Thinking something I could do would actually be important? Make a significant difference in someone's life?

That was the *real* impossibility.

I'd spent my entire adult life attempting to do something to make myself feel valuable somewhere. To someone.

Sure, the Carnarvon family had been kind to me. And Eve had been a friend. Howard, too, seemed to at least respect my work.

But what difference had any of my life meant?

This latest surprise—that my actions here in the past meant absolutely nothing—only served to highlight that my entire life was much the same.

What was the point of any of it, really? We live, we die, and what does any of it matter?

Perhaps I had been trying to prove something. To myself, to my dead parents.

The parents who had not bothered to stick around long

enough to inform me I could travel through time. That I could fly like a bird over the millennia, but never touch down, never touch anyone. Walk through the sands of time and leave no footprints.

Though my parents... and Belzoni. None of it made any sense.

The tears trickled, and I swiped them away in anger, my manacled hands heavy.

Enough, Sahara. Self-pity serves no purpose.

At the sound of the clanking, the guard looked up from his seated position in front of the fire, then went back to staring into the flames.

It was time to deal with reality.

I was alone here, but I was alone, period.

If my parents had ever truly been here in the ancient past, they were gone now, and I had no idea where they'd gone. Or *when* they'd gone.

And trying to trust someone else, connect with someone else, was just as irrational as hunting my parents through time.

Hunting through time... I wondered... could I jump backward in time from this moment, to escape my shackles?

I'd need to be touching something from the time period I chose, but the rooftop seemed old enough. And I'd need to know the time to aim for, but maybe I could conjure up the occupants of this palace a hundred or so years ago.

Wait... that didn't make sense. Even if I did manage to vanish myself from this time, I'd only come back to a moment before I left, still sweaty and chained to a post.

These rules were really problematic.

And this guard was probably going to kill me.

Absently, I scraped the heel of my sandal across the rooftop, finding it marked a white line in the chalky stone. I doodled a simple fish, then a sun, trying to push away the cold emptiness that was seeping into my soul.

My father and I had doodled like this. Only we'd turned our little scribblings into a special language. Our very own hieroglyphs. I indulged myself with the memory of him, sitting at his huge mahogany desk in the library, with eight-year-old me standing beside him, pointing to the markings on his blotter...

~

"*Hieros*, Sahara, from the Greek, meaning 'sacred.' And *gluphē* meaning 'carving.' These will be our sacred carvings—a code just for the two of us."

I smiled at the little sun and the tiny fish with the winking eye. "What letters shall these be?"

"Hmm." He tapped his chin with his forefinger. "I think the sun should be an S."

"S for sun?"

"S for Sahara. Because you are the light in my life."

He reached an arm around me and tickled me under the ribs.

I laughed and pushed his hand away. "And the fish?"

"The fish shall be an A, for Alexander, for then you will always have me winking at you."

"We will need twenty-four more drawings."

"Indeed. Do you think we can find that many?"

"Oh, yes. But what if someone guesses?"

"It will only a be simple substitution cypher, that is true. But if we keep the key secret, someone would have to work quite hard to figure it out."

I nodded, knowing instinctively our code was not important enough for anyone to take the trouble, but at the same time it was the most important thing in the world to me.

"I will tell you what, my girl." He wrapped an embracing arm around me, no tickling. "We'll be partners here. You will have the job of coming up with twelve more drawings, and I will come up with twelve of my own, and then we will put them together."

"And if we duplicate some of the same symbols?"

He smiled. "How bright you are, Sahara. I was right to make you the sun."

I ducked my head but grinned.

"I suppose if we duplicate, then we will have to think of more together. That is what great minds do, you know. They think alike, and then they collaborate."

I gravely took the stack of blotter paper and pen he offered and ran off to begin my assignment. I found a spot in the garden under my favorite tree, where I sketched and crossed out, scribbled and paper-crumpled, until I had what I knew were twelve wonderful shapes, reminiscent of the wonderful Egyptian hieroglyphs on papyrus that graced the walls of my father's library.

I brought them to him the next day, when he was at last alone at his desk. Tacked to the wall above his desk was an unrolled length of paper, with years marked out in a long line. A series of stars dotted the line, with shaded areas on each side of the stars. I had asked him once about the chart.

"That's my travel journal," he answered. "Someday you will have one, too."

Today, he looked up from his books and smiled at my outstretched hand.

"Why, Sahara, look at what you've drawn!"

"Is it not good?" I bit my lip.

"It's more than good." He drew a paper from atop a stack of books. "Here are my drawings."

I scanned his twelve, and saw only our little birds were duplicated. But his bird was odd somehow, not quite like… a bird.

"Do you see, Sahara?"

I didn't want to be critical of his drawings, not even the bird.

But his forefinger went to my symbol, and then to his own matching sketch. "Tell me what you see."

"I see… a bird."

He laughed. "Well, that is encouraging, at least. But come, girl, be honest."

"Yours—it is not quite—*birdy* enough, is it, Father?"

He laughed again, this time a big laugh, throwing his head back.

"No, it is not at all birdy enough." He tapped my drawing. "But yours—yours is most certainly enough." His hand brushed hair from my eyes. "Do you know what that's called, Sahara? That's called *talent*. You have a talent for drawing. One I do not have. It's a special gift. One of many special gifts you'll learn of, I'm sure."

I smiled, feeling warm under his praise.

He pulled me to his lap. "Come, let's decide which letter each of our pictures will represent. And then I can start writing you secret letters!"

I giggled. And all was right with my world.

But all was not right with my world anymore.

My father was gone, taking my mother and even a sister with him to some unknown place and time.

My ill-advised attempt to connect with them again had amounted to nothing but danger. And as I had long suspected, it was better to remain independent and self-sufficient, where no one you counted on could die or leave or simply fail you.

It was time to rescue myself.

CHAPTER THIRTY-THREE

At every tick of the clock, in every inhabited part of the world, an unimaginable richness and variety of "history" falls off the world into total oblivion.

~C.S. Lewis, essay on "Historicism"

The sun slanted across my rooftop prison, the heat subdued at last. It hovered above the horizon, lulling me into a worrisome drowsiness. I wasn't going to get out of this place by falling asleep.

And I wasn't going to get out by feeling self-pity.

Fragments of my father-daughter memory lingered. My father's love for me. His wall-mounted timeline and the promise that I would one day chart my own progress through time. Fragments were all I had, really. The past as it truly happened, whatever my parents had done, and the history which I knew and remembered, were not necessarily the same. The sheer volume of information here in the actual *past*, as compared to the known *history* of this past, attested to what a tiny sliver of information we have of anything that has come before. Like the third terrace of Hatshepsut's Temple, unknown to historians in my time, and yet quite real, the past and history were not synonymous. Memories could even be faulty, as my own ignorance of my parents' time-traveling abilities attested. And interpretation of those memories can be skewed.

Perhaps I had it wrong, and they had not given me up so easily. Perhaps the danger I'd felt from Giada Moretti was real, and there was far more at work than I knew, even now. Was it all an unfinished story, in which I tried to assign meaning before the ending was revealed?

Should the future and its decisions be based on such unreliable information?

A movement across the roof drew my eye.

Bek! Popping up from the steps, along the roofline. Striding toward me like he hadn't a care.

My guard grunted. "Be gone, rat. You've no business here."

Bek lifted his hands to the fire. "Just trying to get warm, my friend." His eyes darted to me, then back to the flames. "Before my master and his wife make me drive them out into the cold desert." He jutted his chin toward the north. "They want to see the king's tomb as the sun goes down." He tapped his temple. "Crazy, eh?"

"You think I care about your complaints? You can go die in the desert!"

The guard stepped toward him, arm raised.

Bek shrugged and backed away. "No troubles, friend. We are leaving soon anyway."

With another quick glance at me, he trotted to the steps and disappeared.

So. Perhaps people do not always abandon you. Maybe some of them should be given a chance.

But did Bek have a plan to get me off this roof? Or only a ride to the tomb if I could escape? Could I risk acting without any more information, trusting a child?

My guard bent in front of me, his hairy calves close enough to touch, and stoked the fire. Was the late desert afternoon too cool for him?

Unknowingly, he slid the flat of his sandal across my earlier scratchings of the sun and fish, wiping the roof clean.

I tried again, using a pebble to sketch out a quick copy of the roofline of the palace, with a little fire roaring atop it.

Then I got his attention and pointed to it. "You like it?"

He grunted and leaned over, then glanced at me. "You did that?"

I nodded. "Tell me something else to draw."

He thought for a moment. "A camel."

"Too much detail for this pebble." I pretended to search around. "Hand me a piece of charred wood." I pointed to the edge of the fire. "Not hot," I added.

He hesitated, then shrugged and flicked a blackened ember toward my feet.

I scooped it up with my chained hands, and proceeded to sketch out a camel on the stone.

The guard scooted closer and watched me work.

I finished the camel, and then for good measure, drew a splash of spit hitting the ground in front of him.

My audience laughed at my joke.

"Now me."

"What?"

He pointed to my rooftop canvas. "Draw me."

Just the opening I'd hoped for.

"People are much more complicated. So much shading, and I'd want to get it right." I held up my hands. "Not possible with these."

He frowned, then looked around at our empty rooftop, and shrugged. No doubt believing even if I ran, he could take me out with ease.

And so I was released, and, ember in hand, directed my subject to the best angle.

"Here," I pointed. "With your face to the sun."

And your back to the fire.

I crouched in front of him, and started the broad outlines of head and shoulders, giving him a width in the shoulders and a cut of the jawline that were both a bit generous.

He held his head up, but his eyes watched my fingers.

Still crouching, I paused as though unsure, then stood.

He watched me, but squinted at the blinding sun streaking across the desert into his eyes.

"Do you think I should stop there, at the midsection?" I pointed to the sketch.

As soon as he looked down, with my heart in my throat, I kicked him. Hard, in the chest.

He toppled backward into the fire.

Screaming.

And I ran.

My breath, when it came at all, gulped at air and barely released. I flew down the steps. The sound of his screams bounced inside my head.

My stomach heaved. I had to slow a moment, hand braced against the palace's outer wall, to be sick.

I'd never done anything so cruel in my life. The only thing that kept me from collapsing in a heap was the repeated phrase in my mind... *None of this is really happening.*

It was happening, of course. It was a real man back there, in real pain. Pain I had caused. But somehow I was going to make it never happen. Like a sketch I'd drawn, but one I could erase.

I slid along the palace wall. Should I search for Bek? Was Jack still alive?

It had taken about twenty minutes for my chariot driver to bring me from the tomb to the palace four nights ago. How long would it take to run? Could I even find it?

The possibility of wandering the desert without food or water until I fell dead in the sand was not appealing.

"Pssst."

I turned to the sound.

Bek peered around a corner, waving me toward him.

Oh, this boy.

I ran to him.

He grabbed my hand and led me, wordless, along back palace halls, through to the walled enclosure around the foreigners' quarters.

We passed unhindered through the creaky gate, across an empty courtyard, to what appeared to be a trapdoor in the sand.

Bek lifted the door and pointed into the darkness.

A tunnel, perhaps? I climbed down the steps.

And into Jack's arms.

"Sahara!"

The door dropped shut above us, but not before revealing the close confines of a tiny cellar. Not a tunnel.

Jack's face was against my hair, his breath in my ear.

"I was terrified for you." His words were muffled, with his face buried against my neck. "I knew I couldn't get to you. The best thing I could do was get out here and arrange for Bek to help you..."

"Jack, it's okay. I'm fine." I pulled away.

The slim crack of light around the door illuminated Senamun's worried face.

Bek crossed to the girl, then turned to me. "We have a plan." He spoke as though in charge.

I smiled, despite the situation.

"I have a cousin. He sails upriver, very far sometimes, to trade. He is home in Thebes now, but he will take the Great Royal Wife to Punt at daybreak."

Jack gave me a serious look. "And Sahara, we need to get to the tomb."

I hated to ask any more of Bek, but did we have a choice?

"Bek, can you get us a chariot?"

Jack shook his head. "They are hunting for the boy now as well."

Senamun wrapped a protective arm around Bek's shoulder. "Perhaps if he hadn't kicked the new pharaoh..."

Bek grinned. "Couldn't help myself."

Jack faced me. "I'm the only one Pharaoh Ay isn't gunning for. I need to be the one to get us transportation to the tomb.

Give me about an hour. Then get to the north wall of the palace."

Bek's head bobbed. "Yes, yes. We will take you to the tomb to meet your friends, on our way to my cousin!"

Friends?

Jack shrugged one shoulder.

So, I had to let Jack go again. Trust he would not abandon me. That he'd be waiting for me in an hour.

I studied his eyes, but it was too dark to gauge his truthfulness. He had kept so much back from me, and I sensed there was still more he had not said. Did he have some other agenda, even now?

Hands fisted against my sides and lips tight, I nodded once. It was the best I could do.

Jack embraced me again.

"You had better not get hurt," I whispered.

He held me a moment longer, then disappeared up the steps.

When the three of us guessed our tense hour of waiting had passed, we followed Jack's trip to the surface.

Bek took the lead, each of us resisting a run that might draw attention.

In the open courtyard, we were an easy target. At least guards weren't armed with arrows. But how far could one of those javelins be hurled? The muscles between my shoulders tensed.

"You there!"

I cringed and ducked.

We all kept moving.

"Hold!"

Bek glanced at me, then Senamun, but slowed.

Senamun and I stopped behind him.

I turned and stepped in front of Senamun. "What is it?"

A single guard faced off against us, built wide with a jagged scar across his bottom lip.

"Are you the ones Pharaoh is searching for?"

Uh… no?

Bek spoke up. "I am accompanying the priestess Ra-Ne-Hannu back to the Temple of Amun."

I lifted my head, attempting to look priestess-like.

He thrust his chin toward Bek. "I know you—you're Ankhe-sen-amun's little errand boy."

Bek squared his shoulders, little fighter that he was. "You will address the Great Royal Wife by her proper titles."

Another glance from the guard, this time at Senamun, and recognition.

He lurched toward us.

Faster than I would have thought possible, Bek loaded a sharp stone into his sling, stretched it taut, and flung the stone at his forehead.

The missile found its mark, and the guard *oomphed* and collapsed, like something out of a biblical tale.

But after only a beat, Bek's conquest stirred and groaned.

"We must get out of here!" Bek tugged on my hand.

We slid along walls again, backtracking through hallways.

Was it possible? Would we remain undetected?

Finally, at the north side of the palace, the three of us leaned against the wall, panting.

"Where is he?" I scanned the horizon.

Had Jack already gone into the desert? Traveled home without me?

Or had he been detained—or worse—by the new pharaoh?

Senamun smiled. "You are very concerned for your friend."

I felt myself coloring. "Yes. My friend."

"He will not leave you."

A crunching sound, like wheels on gravel, struck fear into my chest. We pulled back into the shadow of the wall.

But the two horses, and then the small chariot that lurched around the far corner of our section of the palace, nearly brought a laugh to my lips.

Jack had gotten to drive in ancient Egypt, after all.

Not quite a Fiat, but it would do.

CHAPTER THIRTY-FOUR

1325 B.C.
The House of Rejoicing, Thebes, Egypt

*J*ack rolled to a stop, held out an arm, and swung me into the chariot and into an embrace.

I leaned against him, relief flooding me. It had only been an hour. But I had felt the separation keenly. "I wasn't sure you'd come."

He glanced sideways, surprise in his eyes. "I could never leave you behind."

Senamun and Bek climbed behind us.

Jack turned the chariot toward the darkening desert.

Night crept upward from the horizon as we churned up sand in our rush toward the tomb of Tut-ankh-amun. With nothing to hinder the last rays of the sun, they warmed the orange-tan landscape until the last finally disappeared below the rim of the earth.

We had the advantage of a bright moon rising behind us, promising enough light to navigate even in the darkness.

Senamun directed Jack, as though she knew the desert well. It all looked much the same to me, but I would have to trust my new friend. Perhaps she had been making journeys to hidden tombs in the desert all her life.

Hidden tombs...

The words of the supervisor who had driven me to the palace after I arrived came back to me.

"Have the stairs filled in by the time I return."

What if the tomb had already been erased from view, hidden from looters? How would we ever find the door?

On the other hand, what would happen if we stood at the bottom of the door when we made the jump in time, and landed buried under six feet of sand?

And there was still the question of how my parents expected to stop Belzoni, if none of this made any difference at all.

I shook my head roughly, hoping to shake loose the contradictory thoughts. Jack knew more about all of this than I did, but there was no time for questions. I would have to wait. Wait and trust.

Look at me, trusting everyone today.

Jack directed the vehicle to a disturbed stretch of sand Senamun pointed out, and pulled up the reins.

"Where is it? Where is the tomb?"

"Just there." Senamun pointed. "There is a small marker that will remain for the first year."

Jack grabbed my hand and we stepped down into the sand.

I turned to Senamun and Bek. "We must say goodbye now."

Both our escorts frowned, then glanced at each other.

"But where are your friends? There is no one here to meet us. Who will take you?"

I broke away from Jack and crossed to the chariot. Though I had said goodbye to both of them earlier today, I wanted to say it again, with more time given.

"Ankhe-sen-amun," I grasped her cool fingers, "You are an amazing young woman. I hope you will be well, and happy, and live a long life of peace." I turned to Bek, at my eye level in the chariot, and took his hands in turn. "And you, my young friend, are also amazing. So smart and kind. You deserve to be loved well—so well— and to have wonderful adventures and people who love you and a home of your own." My voice choked over the words. "I hope you find all of that."

Senamun pulled the boy to herself, much as she had done earlier today, looked into my eyes over his head, and nodded. "He will."

"Now, you both must go. Find Bek's cousin, and stay safe until Punt. Don't worry about us. We know how to get home from here."

Jack nodded to Senamun and tousled Bek's hair. "Safe travels."

Still looking uncertain, but apparently deciding to believe us, the two circled the little chariot to point southward.

In the distance, torches flared in intervals at the base of the palace. An odd gap in the torchlight drew my attention.

"What is that?"

Not a gap—the light from the torches was blocked—by oncoming chariots.

"They are chasing us!" Senamun clutched at the chariot's frame.

"You must go!"

One last wave, then Bek flicked the reins, and they rode away from the tomb, away from the palace. The chariot wheels kicked up little puffs of dust.

How was it possible none of this was happening, had happened, would happen? I could not work it out in my head. And I didn't like it.

"Ready to dig?" Jack's words broke the sudden, heavy silence of the desert. "We should get out before they arrive."

I spun to scan the mounds and valleys around us. Looking away from the palace and oncoming chariots, as far as the eye could see, we were alone. So strange. I had never been so alone in my life.

And yet, Jack was here.

"I'm ready."

He inclined his head toward the darker patch of sand and the marker. "The ground slopes downward. Hopefully the door won't be far."

I hesitated, biting my lip. "What if it's not the right tomb? What will happen if we try to return from the wrong place?"

"I think... nothing. If we used the wrong tomb and were trying to travel backward in time, to an earlier time, I suppose we might end up there, if it was more than eighty years back. But trying to return to 1922, without touching the place where we arrived, does nothing."

I took a deep breath. "If you say so. I don't want to end up swirling in outer space forever, or disintegrated into dust, or something."

He chuckled. "No, that sounds unpleasant." He held out a hand. "Trust me."

We hurried, hand-in-hand, to the little painted slab that poked from the slope.

With nothing but our hands, we began scooping away the loose sand, filled in only a few days ago.

And only a few days ago, I had dug out this very door alongside Howard Carter.

Within minutes, I could see the beginnings of the carved necropolis seals Howard and I uncovered last week.

The effect was dizzying. All around me was nothing. No excavated trench rising on all sides of me. No dig tents pitched around the site. No tent of Howard's, with his bottles of whiskey buried under spare trousers in his steamer trunk. This was the same door, three thousand years younger. And nothing else was the same.

Jack knelt. "I think this should be enough, to get our hands on it."

"Wait—I—I need to know what to expect."

He sat back on his heels, eyed the oncoming dust storm of chariots.

I couldn't make out yet how many there were. But they'd be here soon.

"When we arrive. We won't be together, will we?"

He studied the sky, a crease forming between his brows. "Let's see. I went out to the site about an hour after I left you. What time did you get there?" He half-smiled. "Well, *here*, I guess."

"I don't know. I left the American House soon after you dropped me off. Drove to the site. Oh, and told Chefren to wait for me with the car. So he should still be there, right?"

"Right. So, I guess I will show up back in '22 about an hour later than you will. Can you wait for me, with the car? I didn't tell my driver to wait."

My brain was hurting again. "But I don't understand. If you reached the site after I did, wouldn't I have already returned? Why follow me at all, if I was already back?"

He frowned up at me where I stood above him.

"Because you hadn't come back."

"I don't understand. You left '22 after me, but arrived here before me—"

"Sahara, please. Leave the questions for later. Let's get out of here."

I nodded. Took a deep breath. Knelt beside Jack.

We reached our hands out together, but then I pulled mine back, an inch from the door.

He glanced back at our pursuers and growled.

"I just wanted to say... thank you. I know you expected me to be angry you followed me. And I was, a little. But mostly I'm grateful. I'm glad you were here, to explain things. To help."

He curled his fingers around mine in the sand. "I'm glad I was here, too."

"Not that you don't still have a whole lot more explaining to do! Unless there's some kind of time travel school I can attend."

He squeezed my hand and smiled. "I'll be there. For whatever you need."

I took another deep breath. My lungs couldn't seem to get enough of ancient air.

"You know, a strange part of me doesn't want to leave this place. I wished I had been able to see more."

"I get that. But Ay and his soldiers appearing on the horizon is a bit of motivation."

"Agreed."

"Besides, ancient Egypt had about three thousand years of history to it. Even at eighty-year intervals, that's an immense amount of time to visit."

I smiled. I would be back.

"Let's go home."

Still kneeling, fingertips touching, we placed two palms on the door.

I placed my mind back in 1922, at the digsite.

We both bent our heads in a sort of strange obeisance to the carved door.

As my head tipped downward, I wished once again the things I had done here, the help I had given Senamun, had not been in vain. That it had meaning. That my departure would not simply erase my arrival.

And then the vertigo, and all thoughts were pushed aside.

As before, the sensation of time slowing, rather than speeding up, overwhelmed me. Floating, with images cascading. No thought, just a detached sort of observation at the images that spun past.

A red-and-white striped tricycle. Something like I'd seen ridden by ladies in flowing dresses in Hyde Park, but much smaller.

Standing in the center of a book-filled room with my parents, our hands clasped to form a circle and my parents bowing to me, as though teaching me a new dance. The scene blurring and then reforming, different somehow.

There was less nausea this time.

And then the images slowed to a stop and fizzled away. A slight jolt, and I felt myself back on solid ground.

My eyes fluttered open, focused first on my hand on the top of the door, fingers still splayed but without Jack's overlapping.

Dark. Cold. Stars out, as they had been when I left.

Knees in the gritty sand. Head pounding.

I stood shakily, brushed off my knees.

My electric torch was nowhere to be seen, and the moonlight was only a tiny sliver tonight.

Throat dry and heart pounding in rhythm with my head, I climbed out of the trench, knowing somehow, impossibly, Chefren would be there at the edge of the digsite, having waited only a few minutes.

But all was dark on the surface. I scanned the area. Had I misjudged where I'd left him?

Had he driven off and left me?

But if he had driven away before I traveled back in time, I would have heard the engine. And if no time had passed now that I was back, he would still be here.

An unreasonable panic shook me.

A sickening disorientation. As if I had been unmoored from time itself. Where was I? *When* was I?

Get ahold of yourself, Sahara.

The digsite was here. Howard's tent. Everything familiar. The only thing missing was Chefren.

I exhaled. No worries. I would simply wait in Howard's tent for Jack to arrive and we would walk back to the American House together. And he would explain.

How long had he said? An hour?

I found my way through the dark to the tent, and then collapsed on the cot. The trip back—no, the entire *day*— had drained me. Forget that, the whole adventure had been beyond exhausting. It would be good to rest a bit before Jack arrived.

My eyes felt as leaden as my joints, and the last image I saw before succumbing to sleep was the way my fingers had intertwined with Jack's on the door's carved necropolis seals.

CHAPTER THIRTY-FIVE

1325 B.C.
The House of Rejoicing, Thebes, Egypt

enae puttered about the villa, gathering up the odds and ends they would take from this place, packing them into a small satchel.

Though she forced her body to move slowly, her mind whirred.

Egypt, and this small home in the foreigners' quarters, had begun to feel like home. But it wasn't home. And it was time to leave.

They never dreamed when they left Venice they would be here for so long. But it had been difficult, standing in the Karnak Temple complex, hands on the Luxor Obelisk in 1737, to exactly pinpoint the day they would arrive. Concerned they would arrive too late and find the tomb sealed, they aimed early, and were surprised to arrive only one day before Tut-ankh-amun was dead.

Though now, at last, with the seventy days of the king's mummification completed, they could finally climb back up the shaft of time, not all the way home, of course. But at least to the home they'd made for themselves in Venice.

She lifted the lid of a hinged chest and removed a tiny alabaster jar of scented perfume and a matching alabaster comb, then placed them into the satchel. These finds would be added to someone's collection back in Venice. Perhaps her own, or perhaps she would give them as a gift. She hated the antiquities black market, selling items like this with no idea of their provenance. But these were tiny things, likely to have been lost to the sands of history anyway. So technically, she was contributing to, not subtracting from, the wealth of Egyptian artifacts that existed in the future.

She left the bronze mirror on the low table for the next visitor.

Thoughts of Venice, and of Italy, filled her with homesickness—a feeling that surprised her, given Venice was only a stopping point.

But it was Persia's home.

And that meant it had to be theirs.

The soft sounds of a harp in the garden outside the villa soothed her tight nerves. She finished packing and placed the satchel on the bed, then sat and took in for the last time the terra-cotta walls, the reed mats and tan bricks beneath her feet, the dark wood furniture. The scents that had grown so familiar —coriander, saffron, cumin—were nothing like the scents of Italy.

Yes, even though she had stayed mostly invisible and not gotten involved with the local people, she would miss this place. But they had come for a purpose, and that purpose was about to be achieved. She would not stop now.

Footsteps in the courtyard, then Alexander slipped under the lintel, followed by their daughter.

Renae smiled. How beautiful Persia had become, turning into a woman before their eyes.

Had it truly been seventeen years since that night in the Caffé

Florian in Venice, when Persia arrived in the fraction of time between 1814 and 1720?

"All taken care of?"

Alexander nodded. "She's disappointed, of course. But I told her we have things to attend to, and that we're leaving tomorrow. That we have important business in our home country and must return."

"Do you think she will be alright? "

Persia slipped from behind her father, crossed the room, and touched her fingers to the satchel Renae had been packing.

"I hope so. If she stays out of his way."

Alexander had gained the begrudging respect of the vicious Ay, but they all knew the man would not stop at violence to achieve his goals.

Her husband braced a hand against the doorframe. "She wishes we would wait for the Hittite prince to arrive. I told her I wished the prince's father would've believed us and sent him back with us."

Persia leaned against the bed. "You should've seen her clutching at Father. You would've thought he was *her* father. "

Renae glanced at the girl for some sign of jealousy. Ankhe-sen-amun was not much older, and it would have been understandable for Persia to be envious of the unexpected relationship between Alexander and the widowed queen. But Persia was smiling at her father, as though proud he could make anyone love him.

And he certainly could.

Is Sahara as generous?

It was a frequent habit, comparing Persia with the fifteen-year-old Sahara she remembered. Wondering how much thirty-two-year-old Sahara was like her sister.

Hopefully, Sahara had only grown in spirit, in a generosity and compassion Renae had tried to instill in her from an early age.

But Persia and Sahara were very different. Sahara was like

her father. Serious, bookish, so intelligent. Focused and committed wherever she set her mind.

And Persia... Persia loved life with an all-out love, grabbing at every experience she could, laughing at the way the world responded.

I suppose Persia is like me. Or at least like I once was.

Before she had lost Sahara.

Renae shook off the morbid thoughts. She had not lost Sahara. More like, misplaced her. Or more accurately, it was *they* who had been misplaced. And now perhaps, they would find a way to find each other.

It would have been amazing to be here, at this time, with both her daughters. But the only way Sahara would ever come here is if the three of them left.

Alexander held out a hand. "It grows late. Are you ready?"

"I'm ready."

They slipped through the courtyard, and then the palace halls, sensing the growing darkness as the sun lowered toward the desert horizon.

Outside the palace, Alexander had already arranged a chariot to drive to the king's newly-finished tomb.

It had to be tonight. They had waited until the tomb was nearly full, and ready to be sealed. Alexander carried his collection, one of which would be left in the tomb, along with a piece of papyrus he had so carefully inscribed. They couldn't leave the items too early, or their clue would be spotted, and perhaps removed. They couldn't wait any longer, or the tomb would be sealed, and it would be too late. And if they didn't leave, she would never find them.

They rode in silence, with Alexander's clucking to guide the horse faster.

Almost there, Persia said, "Do you think it will work? I would so much like to meet my sister."

Renae reached across to clutch Persia's hand where it rested on her thigh.

"It will work."

She spoke with the certainty she did not feel, and yet she must continue to give Persia this hope, otherwise the girl would retreat backward, into the lifelong guilt that plagued her.

That night in Venice, with Giada on their trail, they had used the painting in the Caffé Florian to travel backward, and had landed in 1720, the year of the cafe's opening. Renae had assured Persia repeatedly over the years that it was not, *could not*, be her fault she had been born in 1720. It was not her fault she could never accompany her parents forward to a century that had not yet happened at the time of her birth, and that the eighteenth century would always be her home. But still, Persia felt responsible that her parents could not travel back to 1905 where they had left Sahara, without leaving Persia behind.

"I still don't understand," she had said so many times over the years, "why one of you couldn't have returned, just to tell her what happened."

And Renae had answered the same each time. "You know why, Persia. If your father had gone back to Sahara, he would never have been able to come back to you. It was an impossible choice."

"But we could have simply met up somewhere else, in the past."

And Renae would shake her head, and say what she always said. "We will never separate again, Persia. Your father and I will never take the chance of losing each other, or losing you."

And it had always been true. Neither of them were willing to separate, nor leave a baby, a toddler, a young child in the past, to go back to Sahara. It was too much risk. And so they made this plan, to find another way to be reunited with their older daughter.

But if the plan did not work, Renae could not say if they would continue to refuse separation. Although they could lose each other easily in the millennia of times and places, as the years went by she grew less willing to be apart from Sahara. Persia was no longer a child. Perhaps a day would come when they would feel like she could be left on her own in the eighteenth century.

But now is not the time to think of such things.

Now was the time to think of the plan and of the risk they were about to undertake.

This clue they would leave for their daughter could ruin so many things. Could drastically shift the lives of so many people. Ordinarily they would resist such interference, but their heartbreak had grown over losing Sahara and they simply couldn't stand it any longer. With each passing year of Persia's life, they saw more of what they had missed. Thankfully, they were able to come here, to the time of Tut-ankh-amun. In all their adventures, they'd never been within eighty years of the date. It was their best plan, and they'd been waiting seventeen years to see it come to fruition.

Alexander pulled the small chariot to the side of the worn path, still too far away from the tomb to make it out. "We'll wait until darkness falls fully before we approach."

He'd brought a torch, oiled and waiting to be lit by a flint. When the glow across the edge of the desert waned, he lit the flame and beckoned them forward.

A few scattered laborers worked nearby, but the valuable items—the gold, the jewels—would not be placed in the tomb until tomorrow, and there was little risk of tomb robbers tonight, with only ordinary household items having been piled into the antechamber. The gilded burial chamber walls that housed the granite sarcophagus in the burial chamber itself had already been sealed behind a wall of hieroglyphs. It was into the crowded antechamber they would place their message.

They held hands down the steps, trying to appear reverent to anyone who might be watching, as though they had come to pay their respects.

Down, down, down. Sixteen steps, then along a passageway that ramped downward yet further. Then into the antechamber that lay in front of the burial chamber.

Alexander waved his torch around the room in slow arcs, and

they each took in the overloaded space, crowded with so many treasures. He pulled the papyrus from a pouch inside his tunic, then pulled out a small coin and held the two together between his thumb and forefinger.

Once again that longing for home swept Renae. But their time in Venice would be short, long enough only to prepare to travel yet again, to the place they hoped Sahara would meet them.

If the objects they left in this tomb ever found their way into their daughter's hands.

Alexander held the items out to Renae. His eyes were soft, compassionate. Hurting, just like her.

She took the papyrus and the coin silently. Felt the dry crispness of the one and the smooth engraving of the other. She crossed the antechamber to the back corner, where a painted wooden chest sat, intricately covered with battle scenes. Inside lay personal items, jewelry, even sandals, that had belonged to the dead king.

Quietly, almost reverently, she placed the papyrus on the rounded lid of the chest, then laid the coin on top of it.

Risky. So risky. They had never done anything, since discovering their ability, with such potential to disrupt history.

A wave of mixed emotions nearly crumpled her. Would Sahara ever touch these items?

So distant in the future. She would be thirty-two now. Was she even alive? Would she know?

Despite the unanswerable questions, it was the closest Renae had felt to her daughter in seventeen years. It was like pulling out a faded photograph of someone you missed terribly. Not the same, but better than nothing.

Hours later the trio found themselves at the Karnak Temple, standing in the dark before Hatshepsut's twin obelisks, ready to travel again. Renae took one of Persia's hands in her own.

Again the nostalgia. The memories of doing the same with Sahara, when she was too young to remember.

They had made a mistake with Sahara, not explaining who

she was, who they were, what she might someday be able to do. And then it was too late, and they were separated, and they had never known if she had become like them, had developed the ability to travel through time. She had no one to teach her, no one to train her, no one to explain.

The omission was a sharp ache in Renae's side that never abated.

They had not made the same mistake with Persia. She had known everything from the start, since she was old enough to understand at all. At seventeen, it still remained to be seen whether she would develop the ability to jump through history, but in the meantime they could take her with them, and make sure, if they ever lost each other, she would know all she needed to know to survive.

Alexander handed their travel satchel to Persia, his coin collection and Renae's trinkets safely tucked inside.

Persia strapped it across her chest, the only way it could move through time with them, and took her father's hand so the three formed a tight circle around the obelisk.

They pressed their foreheads against the stone, then bent their heads.

And as they let ancient Egypt tumble away, Renae prayed this crazy plan would work, and Sahara would somehow find them at their next stop through the history of the world.

CHAPTER THIRTY-SIX

November, 1922
Valley of the Kings, Egypt

"Sahara."

My mouth felt filled with pebbles, and a persistent fly was buzzing at me.

"Sahara!"

Sharp breath in, eyes open, blinking.

A swimming feeling in my head that was starting to feel commonplace, as my eyes focused on white fabric above my head, stretched taut.

I swiveled my head and looked up at the one calling my name.

"Howard?"

I heard him exhale heavily, as if in relief.

"Thank God."

"What's going on?" It was bright outside the walls of Howard's tent.

Oh, for glory's sake. I'd slept through the night. Jack must have been confused when he returned and I wasn't waiting with Chefren in the car.

Howard was pacing, a hand braced across his forehead, shielding his eyes.

"Howard, what's wrong?"

He stopped and stared at me. "What's wrong? Sahara, you've been gone without a trace for more than four days! We all thought—we all thought you were—"

My chest warmed at the real emotion I heard in Howard's voice. He had been worried about me.

But—*four days?*

"Where is Jack?"

Howard was still staring. "Jack? Jack Moretti? That reporter?"

I nodded and swung my legs over the side of Howard's cot.

"I don't know. In a Luxor jail cell by this time, maybe."

"What? Why?"

"Because they think he killed you!"

Oh my.

I stood quickly, then put a hand out when my head started to spin.

Howard darted forward and grabbed my hand to steady me. "Are you hurt?"

"No. No, I'm not hurt. I need to find Jack."

"Sahara, what sort of tommyrot has been going on here? Everyone has been searching—"

"What day is it?"

His mouth gaped. "Saturday. But where—"

"I'll explain later, Howard. Right now I need to make sure Jack isn't in trouble."

He huffed and shrugged. "Fine. I'll have Omar drive you to the river. I can't leave the site right now."

I nodded, squeezed his arm in thanks, and sped from the tent.

Saturday. I'd been gone since Monday night.

Omar had me at the ferry in less than ten minutes. Had I truly just made that trip yesterday in an Egyptian chariot?

I gripped the rail of the ferry and watched the water lap beside it. I couldn't force my pulse to slow.

How had this happened? Jack told me I would return to a moment before I'd left.

But I didn't. I had... retained... the time I'd been in the ancient past. I had been missing from 1922. Jack must not have done the same thing, since he'd apparently been under suspicion about my disappearance for the past few days.

It did explain why Chefren wasn't there last night when I returned.

So... Jack must have returned to the same moment he left. Was Chefren still there with the car, waiting for me? What did Jack do when he found I had not returned?

"Because you hadn't come back."

Jack's explanation for why he followed me to ancient Egypt.

I shook my head, postponing the puzzle. I needed to talk to him. None of this made sense.

It was a short trip from the ferry dock to the Luxor police station. The desk clerk knew nothing, but fetched a superior from a back room.

The man emerged from an office and inclined his head at me. "You are Sahara Aldridge?"

"Yes. Yes, I wanted you to know I am fine. There is no reason—"

"How can I know you are this woman, as you say?"

I patted my clothes, my trouser pockets and the breast pocket on my workshirt, but already knew I'd brought no identification.

"Alsahra'?"

I turned to the voice. "Ahmed!" I breathed out relief at the sight of Ahmed Gerigar, the digsite foreman.

The police officer turned to Ahmed and pursed his lips. "This is Sahara Aldridge?"

"Yes, yes," but Ahmed was already hugging me.

I returned the hug, eyes watering at the second person to welcome me back with such joy.

"Where have you been, *sayida*? We have all been so worried."

"I'm sorry I worried you, Ahmed. I will tell the story sometime. But right now I'm looking for Jack Moretti. Do you know him?" I glanced at the officer. "Is he being detained here?"

The officer shook his head. "Not enough evidence against him for now." He shrugged and held out a palm toward me. "Or at all, I suppose. But we told him to stay in his hotel until we cleared him to leave."

His hotel.

I nodded to both men, fled the police station, and hailed the first *caliche* driver I saw in the street.

"Sheikh House Hotel."

My heart still pounded and I willed the wheels to roll faster. It was as if my brain had stopped functioning. I couldn't think about anything until I saw Jack.

Hopefully I'd remembered his hotel correctly. He'd only mentioned it in passing.

A quick check at the front desk for his room number, two flights up, and I was knocking at his door.

"Coming."

I closed my eyes. Never had a voice been so welcome.

He opened it slowly, as if not excited about whomever might be on the other side.

When he saw my face, he didn't speak.

But his shoulders dropped, he breathed out like he'd been punched in the gut, and he looked like he might cry.

And then he wrapped me up in his arms and didn't let go.

"I'm sorry, Jack. I—I don't know what happened."

Another hotel guest emerged from the room next door. She gave our embrace a scowl as she passed.

Jack pulled me into his room and closed the door. "I don't understand what happened, either."

We crossed the room and sank into a small settee near the window.

"The night you had Chefren drive you to the digsite, when you didn't return, I was afraid something must have happened. That's why I followed you to the tomb, and then through time. To make sure you got back safely. But then after we left together, and you *still* weren't here, I hoped you got tired of waiting for me and left. It seemed strange, but I wasn't too worried."

He stopped and gripped my hands, as though concerned I would disappear.

"But then the next day, you were nowhere. And then Chefren was questioned because someone saw him pick you up at the American House."

Minnie Burton, no doubt.

"He told them he'd taken you to the digsite and you'd promised to only be a moment, but then you never came back. For the first day or so it seemed like they were suspecting Chefren of foul play. But then your time spent with me came to light, and they pulled me in and started into the questions."

"I'm so sorry that happened. I went to the police station before coming here. They know I'm back, so there should be no more problems for you."

He waved my statement away as if inconsequential. "I know they're watching me here during the day, but last night I was able to sneak away. I figured if—if somehow—you'd managed to come back to your real time, four days after you left, that I would find you there last night, the exact amount of time you were in the ancient past and gone from 1922. It was the only thing that made sense." He exhaled and swallowed. "When you weren't there…"

I squeezed his hand.

"I thought I'd failed you—that I didn't protect—All I could think about was what you said about being lost in outer space, or disintegrating into dust." His voice choked.

"Oh, Jack, that part was all my fault! I *did* get back last night. When Chefren wasn't there, I went to Howard's tent to wait for you, and promptly fell asleep! Howard woke me up this morning. From his reaction, it was quite a shock to find me there."

"I must have just missed you last night."

We sat in silence a moment, each of us in our own thoughts.

"But, Jack, I still don't understand. How did it happen?"

He smiled gently, searching my face.

For what, I didn't know.

"Did you want it to happen?"

"I don't understand."

"When we were together in the past, ready to leave. Were you wanting to come back to the night you left? Or were you thinking something else?"

I pondered a moment. "I was wishing it hadn't all been in vain. Wishing all that happened there would not be erased."

"And so it wasn't."

I was tired of saying I didn't understand, so I said nothing.

"Sahara, you are special. You have a special gift."

My father's words, so long ago.

"You have the ability to come back *after* you left, rather than before. To leave the past as you affected it."

I laughed. "Truly? So, all of it, with Ankhe-sen-amun, getting away from the Pharaoh Ay. Taking Bek with her to Punt. All of it became... *real?*"

"Yes."

But his 'yes' was not as happy as I would have expected.

"What's wrong?"

He rubbed at the back of his neck. "It's a heavy responsibility, Sahara. Not just everything good you did remains there, but *everything*. It all happened."

I struggled to put that fact into place.

The soldier I'd pushed into the fire.

I winced and closed my eyes. What else?

"And it's not just what you *did*, but also what you caused or prevented."

"Meaning?"

"Well, for example, perhaps in the previous history, Ankhe-sen-amun and Ay had a child together. If so, that child no longer exists."

It was my turn to exhale like I'd been hit. What had I done?

"But you—" I searched his face. "You came back *before* you left. So it was like I was there, but you weren't? How does that affect the past?"

"Impossible to say, I suppose." His brow furrowed. "Something tells me you would have still saved Ankhe-sen-amun without me."

"And did I? Did I save her?"

"I've searched the history books, these past few days—I knew you'd need that question answered—and there is no mention of her, after her failed attempt to marry the Hittite prince."

"So, perhaps I did *some* good? But... why me? Why can I do this?"

"I'm guessing it's because both your parents were travelers."

"Because I'm... amplified."

"Yes. There is a trait, that some have."

I waited. Why was he always so reluctant with information?

"I haven't told you yet. But there are two types of travelers. The vast majority of us can only return to the moment before leaving and erase our own travels. We're called Observers."

"Tempus Vigilia."

"Yes, observers of time only. But others"—he gripped my hand—"others are called Revisionists. The changes they make to the past actually alter it."

I took that in for a few moments, not really knowing what to do with it, and then my hand went to my mouth, stifling my sharp intake of breath.

"My parents. They believed they could keep Belzoni from his work in Egypt. That's why they went to Venice."

Jack's face drained of color. "Do you understand what this means?"

"One of them was a Revisionist, too. That's the only way they could have stopped him."

Jack rubbed the back of his neck. "Quite a heritage you have, Sahara. Both your parents are travelers, one of them a Revisionist."

"Why didn't you tell me about these *Revisionists* before?"

"They're practically myth and legend. No one talks about them much. And you should know... Using this ability is... frowned upon."

"By your secret society, right? And all their rules?"

"Tempus Vigilia is *your* society, too."

"So what does 'frowned upon' mean?"

"Outlawed. Restricted. Penalized."

"Great." I should ask what penalties I could be expecting, or how Tempus Vigilia would even know what I'd done. I didn't. "But it seems like I can control it, right? It didn't happen the other times. It was only this time, because I was wanting it to happen." I straightened. "So, that's simple then. I'll just never cause it again."

Jack nodded, but seemed unconvinced.

"What?"

"I don't know. Somehow, this seems like a gift you are supposed to use."

"So you believe someone is controlling all of this? Has some higher purpose?"

"I do."

"And what is it?"

"I have no idea."

We both laughed. And the laughter felt like healing. We were here, we were safe, and we were together. I wanted that to be enough.

But it couldn't be. A few kilometers away, Howard was waiting for an explanation.

An explanation that needed to be good enough to keep me on the digsite team that was about to make the greatest discovery in the history of Egyptology.

CHAPTER THIRTY-SEVEN

When we ransack the past in search of ammunition rather than illumination, we predictably find what we are looking for, but we rob history of its power in the process. History loses its potential to surprise and unnerve us, ultimately to teach us anything at all.

~Robert Tracy McKenzie

November 24, 1922
Valley of the Kings, Egypt

They came, two-by-two, through the desert twilight, to the flickering torches at the entrance of the tomb of Ramesses VI.

Howard and I flanked the square-cut opening, smiling and greeting each as they approached. Herbert Winlock and his wife, Helen. James and Frances Breasted. Albert and Mary Lythgoe.

Howard's chest looked near to bursting out of his dapper tan pinstripe suit with snow-white waistcoat, and not even his large mustache could hide the toothy grin of a boy given an early Christmas.

I ran a shaky hand down the length of my dress, the color of wine and rubies, a splurge in Cairo when we'd gone to fetch Porchy and Evelyn a few days ago.

Where is he?

Nearly all the dinner guests had arrived, filing into the narrow tomb for a celebratory banquet we'd somehow arranged in only hours.

But then there were dusty headlights, bobbing over the dunes, and there was Jack across the sand, alighting from the car wearing the same light suit as the day we met, the same cobalt blue tie that matched his eyes.

Minnie Burton, on the arm of her husband Harry and wearing a fluffy concoction the color of ripe peaches, reached for my hands. "Oh my dear, how stunning you look!"

I returned her grip and smiled. "Thank you, Minnie. You are lovely tonight as well."

She tilted her head, lips pursed. "I would say that glow in your eyes is the torchlight, but I'm thinking perhaps it's the young fellow coming in behind us."

I laughed and pulled her closer, to whisper against her pale cheek. "Shall we let him believe it's the torchlight?"

Harry Burton was clapping Howard on the shoulder. "Ready for a party, old man? You certainly deserve it."

Howard dipped his head, that grin still fixed. "We'll see. We're not there yet."

But we were practically there.

In the twelve days since Jack and I had returned to 1922, news of the stone steps and carved door in the Valley sparked across news channels, setting presses afire and reporters massing. Thankfully, all that attention had Howard too preoccupied to ask more questions about my odd disappearance.

We brought Porchy and Eve from Cairo two days ago, arriving back in Luxor to find Howard's longtime friend, Arthur "Pecky" Callender, summoned for his engineering expertise, already clearing the upper layer of rubble.

This morning Pecky began directing the clearing of the stairs down to the ancient door, until the nine bound captives of the Necropolis Seal once again revealed themselves at the top.

And then, only a few hours ago, there it was. The unmistakable cartouche of the boy-king Tut-ankh-amun, carved into the door of his tomb.

We had found him. After so many years. We had found him.

At Jack's approach to the party entrance, I smoothed my hair behind my ears for the hundredth time.

His eyes locked onto mine, then broke away and traveled the length of me, taking in my face, my red dress, my matching T-strap heels.

A fluttery spaciousness tickled against my chest, shortening my breath.

Jack took my cool fingers in his warm hands, pulled me toward him, and kissed my cheek. His voice buzzed against my ear. "You're like a gorgeous long-stemmed rose, blooming in the desert."

I breathed through parted lips, warmth spreading to my limbs.

"Inside, you two." Howard nodded his head toward the tomb. "Time to get this started." His look was less than friendly for Jack. Reporters had truly become his nemeses in the past two weeks. The camera slung around Jack's neck didn't help.

Jack extended a hand to let me precede him into the tomb, then fitted his palm perfectly into the small of my back as we entered.

Only an occasion as extraordinary as the finding of an intact royal seal would have convinced Howard to throw this lavish a party for colleagues and their wives inside the entrance to KV9, the tomb of Ramesses VI, Twentieth Dynasty Pharaoh.

The entrance corridor was long and cool, intimate in its table setting for twelve, with three sets of mirrored silver candlesticks and smoking ivory tapers casting flame-shadows against wall murals of green tendrils intertwined with clustered lotus flowers. Multiple corridors led downward into two chambers, but our party would confine itself to the area just inside the wooden grille.

The tomb hummed with laughter and conversation and smelled of bread and wine.

"Here they are!" Porchy pulled himself to standing, gripping the pearly-smooth linen tablecloth for support, then lifted a cut-glass goblet of sparkling wine toward our entrance.

The rest of the group rose from the table as one, chairs scraping against the stone floor, and lifted glasses.

"To Carter and Aldridge. Names to be remembered."

Howard took a glass from the tray of an Egyptian server and held it aloft. "And to Lord Carnarvon. Without whose generous patronage and unfailing optimism we would not be here."

There were cheers all around, our names hailed, and I felt my face grow pink, but I placed a hand over my heart and bowed slightly to the room in gratitude.

Jack and I slipped into seats at the table, beside Eve and her father.

Since arriving in Cairo Eve had talked of little else but her new beau, ironically called Sir Brograve Beauchamp, a British politician who just a week ago had lost heavily in a bid for a Parliamentary seat, and whom Eve was working hard to console with daily telegrams.

"Even with the lost election, Pugs thinks he's bound for great things," she whispered.

I listened to her latest update with pleasure. It was good to see her happy. But even engrossed in Eve's love life, I was ever conscious of Jack's nearness, of his knee touching mine under the table, of the heat of his arm near my own.

On the other side of Eve, Lord Carnarvon was leaning forward. "And how long are you staying, Mr. — Moretti, is it? Waiting for your big scoop, I suppose? Or is your interest here more... personal?"

I plucked a heart-shaped strawberry from the tray in front of us and fussed with the green cap.

Jack leaned past me. "I am indeed fascinated by Egyptology,

your Lordship. But you've sized me up right, I'll admit. I've developed quite a fascination for a certain Egyptologist as well."

Our end of the table tittered with amusement. Henry Winlock actually winked at me.

"Well, I've always said Sahara was made for the desert." Porchy rested an arm around his daughter's chair and chuckled. "Lady Carnarvon wanted to bring her out as though she were a *debutante*, a few years after her parents were gone. Can you imagine? Our trowel-wielding Sahara, dressed in a ball gown and parading at court?"

I laid the strawberry on my china plate and felt for the napkin in my lap.

"I can indeed imagine it." Under the table, Jack's hand squeezed my knee. "Sahara would have made a charming debutante."

"Yes. Well." Lord Carnarvon sniffed and straightened. "Glad she has such a champion in you, my good man. Did you say when you were leaving?"

"I'll be needing to get back to Philadelphia soon. But of course I'll be waiting with the rest of the world to see what's on the other side of that door."

Jack's plans were not a surprise to me, but my fingers tightened around the linen napkin.

The conversation moved on without us.

Jack spoke quietly. "I'm sorry, I hope I didn't embarrass you."

"No, it's fine. I—I just wish you didn't need to leave." And I wished he would ask me to go with him. Not that I would. Or even could. I'd only known the man for three weeks, for glory's sake.

But still.

"And I wish I could join you, traveling from tomb to tomb, for a touchpoint in history where you might find your parents."

I shrugged. "I'm not in any hurry to do that."

Jack leaned forward to study my face. "I thought that was your whole intent in... traveling... the first time." His voice had lowered to a whisper. "To figure out if it would be possible to intersect with them before they died."

I laid the crumpled napkin on the table. "Except they're not dead."

Howard was standing at the head of the table, clinking his spoon against his wine glass.

I turned in my chair to face him, my shoulder to Jack.

There were speeches and explanations of upcoming plans. A bit of arguing over who would be involved, what photographs taken, how it would all be protected from both the press and would-be thieves. A rant from Howard on the importance of gleaning every bit of historical information as we progressed through the project.

The voices droned on, but my thoughts moved to Jack's question about my own abandoned project.

Yes, I had wanted to find my parents before they died. To warn them, even. But that was back when I was naive about what it meant to have the power to change history.

That fire, the face of the guard I shoved, his screams, it all poured back into my memory, like a dousing of river water. I shivered.

My parents didn't need saving. They didn't even need me, since they had Persia. So I should stop mucking with time. At most, I should confine myself to being an Observer. But perhaps even observing was dangerous. I couldn't bear to bring harm to anyone else, family or not. The idea of being special—of being *amplified*—it was simply too much responsibility.

The meal began to wind down, and I slipped outside into the coolness of the desert evening to bask in the final glow of the sun.

Jack followed, as I knew he would.

"Your favorite color." He lifted his camera to the horizon. "Inky ribbons of clouds across the terra-cotta canvas of a Luxor sunset. Wasn't that it?"

I sighed. "Indeed." A shame the photograph would capture the outline of cloud and desert only, and not the colors.

He turned the camera toward me.

I shook my head and pushed it away.

"You okay?" He circled my waist with his arm.

I leaned my head against his shoulder, still so appreciative of his being taller than me, and rubbed my arms to ward off a chill.

"I'm fine."

"Just needed to get away from people?"

I smiled into the twilight. "No, actually. I'm enjoying the party."

"Is this my Sahara? First she's dressed like a movie star, now she's having fun at parties?"

I elbowed his chest. "People can change."

Yes, I had changed, at least a little. I'd begun to suspect that the careful walls I constructed to keep the past from repeating itself were built on a false foundation. That perhaps some people *could* be counted on when you needed them. Trusted to not reject or abandon you.

Jack tightened his grip on me. "Yes, I suppose the sudden revelation you can travel through time would change a person."

"It feels as though the entire universe has changed. Or at least my understanding of it."

"Feeling that cosmic destiny now?"

"Perhaps. Maybe there is some higher purpose, some higher power, in all of this. I've always thought of history as a line drawn across a paper, with an arrow at the end, extending time into infinity, into eternity. But now I wonder if perhaps that's all wrong. Maybe we live on the storyline, can even travel back and forth on the line, but there is some sort of author to all this story, an author who is standing *outside* the line drawing. Outside the story itself. Existing in the Eternal Now."

"The Eternal Now. I like that."

The first star heralded the advent of another clear desert night. The distant silvery wink seemed close enough to touch and invited deep thoughts.

"If there *is* an Eternal Now, then I think we are foolish to let half-understood tiny fragments of our past define us. We hoard our memories like antiquities collectors, then romanticize or vilify them in turn. We study and make much of all the fragments, believing we can determine truth and therefore understand the past."

He shrugged. "But self-knowledge—clarity about where we've come from—they're important to understanding our present, don't you think?"

"Important, yes. But those fragments of our history can only take us so far. At some point, studying our past should liberate us, rather than define us."

"And are you liberated?"

I laughed. "I'm not sure. Probably not yet. I do know that much of what I've believed about myself, about who I am, has been built on something false. Nothing is as I thought. So now it's time to figure out who Sahara Aldridge truly is."

"Sounds like you're ready to leave the past behind, and step into the future."

The future... yes, the future was as wide as the Egyptian sky.

Whether Jack and I had a future, it was too soon to know, and perhaps I shouldn't even be asking the question. There was the problem of his mysterious aunt. And the feeling that Jack still held secrets. Not to mention that a romantic relationship was "forbidden" by Tempus Vigilia.

Whether my ability to travel through time meant I had some kind of purpose or destiny... well, that was one more mystery remaining to be discovered.

But then, weren't unanswered questions my thing?

A trace of celestial light shot across the Libra constellation, that cluster of stars ancient Egyptians called the Scales of Truth.

There was still a mystery to solve. And perhaps I was just the girl to solve it.

EPILOGUE

*H*ow distant it all feels now.
And yet how recent.

Time has such strange ways of playing with us, elongating days but shortening years. Giving us moments that seem to last a lifetime, and lifetimes that last only a moment. It's a fickle playmate, and even now I'm still learning to mistrust its games.

But you asked for my story, and so I've partnered once more with Time to tell it, to give you this first installment at least, this journal of how it all began. Should others stumble onto this story, they will wonder at my vantage point of a century passed. But you, my dear, already know that part.

We were on the verge of changing the world, those of us who gathered to celebrate that night. None of us could have predicted what would follow, when the tomb was finally opened. By the time the 1920s sputtered to a bleak end, no part of culture went untouched by "Tut-mania." Everything from the gilded geometric architecture of Art Deco, to the flapper fashions of beaded headbands and sheath dresses, to the Mummy Curse that spawned a perennial Hollywood craze. The world was obsessed with King Tut's Egypt.

And the impact on me, on my story, was no less explosive. Not because of the treasures we were about to unlock, including that small painted chest in the corner of the antechamber, filled with Tut-ankh-amun's sandals and robes and jewelry.

No, it was not the chest's contents that rocked my world. Instead, it was the little personal cache left on top — a scrap of papyrus, with a message written in symbols, held in place by an illogical coin.

But the rest of my story is best left for another day. I still had much to learn. About myself, about Time, even about Jack.

And how sometimes the only way to heal a wound is to cut it open once again.

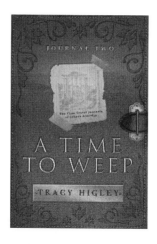

SOMETIMES THE ONLY WAY FORWARD IS *BACK*.

Sahara Aldridge, a young Egyptologist in 1922, is chasing down the trail of her parents through the unknown corridors of time.

But when all clues point to Ancient Rome as the next place to search, Sahara retreats into the safety of her archaeological work, cataloguing treasures from the newly-discovered tomb of Pharaoh Tutankhamun.

As the discovery of the intact tomb propels the world into a frenzy of "Tut-mania," the ever-present Jack Moretti is there to help, but what is his agenda?

And it appears Tempus Vigilia isn't going to leave her alone. The secret society has sent others, tracking her movements and asking too many questions.

Now it seems her family is in danger.

Sahara must once again put her career on hold, to find what she has lost.

But will Ancient Rome hold the answers, or only one more reason to grieve?

Purchase *A Time to Weep* at

https://tracyhigley.com/buy-weep

I THINK YOU'LL LOVE THIS FREE STORY!

Hello Reader Friend,
Would you like a free adventure?
When you sign up for my mailing list, you'll receive a free ebook, *Theft on the Nile*. It's a classic murder mystery (about an hour's read) that I think you'll love, my gift to you!

[Bonus: you'll run into Sahara again in this story!]

You'll also be in the know when there are free books, new releases, and discounts on past titles.

Get your free ebook right here:
https://BookHip.com/ZFAPAXS

Dear Reader,

Thank you for taking an adventure to ancient Egypt with me! I hope you greatly enjoyed *A Time to Seek*.

You can find lots more about ancient Egypt on my website, along with travel journals of my trips there.

And in case you're curious, here's more than you want to know about me...

I've been writing stories since the time I first picked up a pencil. I still have my first "real" novel—the story I began at the age of eight during a family trip to New York City.

Through my childhood I wrote short stories, plays for my friends to perform (sometimes I had to bribe them), and even started a school newspaper (OK, I was the editor, journalist and photographer since no one took that bribe to join me). Then there were the drama years of junior high, when I filled a blank journal with pages of poetry. {{*sigh.*}}

In my adult years I finally got serious about publishing fiction, and have since authored nearly twenty novels.

When I'm not writing, life is full of other adventures—running a business, spending time with my kids, and my favorite pastime: traveling the world.

I started traveling to research my novels and fell in love with experiencing other cultures. It's my greatest hope that you'll feel like you've gotten to travel to the settings of my books, through the sights, sounds, smells, colors, and textures I try to bring back from my travels and weave into my stories.

I'd love to hear your thoughts about *A Time to Seek*, or ideas you have for future books I might write. Get in touch with me at tracy@tracyhigley.com.

Now, onward to another adventure!

HOW TO HELP THE AUTHOR

I hope you enjoyed *A Time to Seek!*

If you're willing to help, I would really appreciate a review on Barnes & Noble or Amazon.

More than anything else, reviews help authors spread the word about their books.

It doesn't have to be long or eloquent – just a few lines letting people know how the book made you feel.

Thank so much!

BOOKS BY TRACY HIGLEY

The Seven Wonders Novels:

Isle of Shadows

Pyramid of Secrets

Guardian of the Flame

Garden of Madness

So Shines the Night

The Time Travel Journals of Sahara Aldridge:

A Time to Seek

A Time to Weep

A Time to Love

The Books of Babylon:

Chasing Babylon

Fallen from Babel

The Lost Cities Novels:

Petra: City in Stone

Pompeii: City on Fire

The Coming of the King Saga:

The Queen's Handmaid

The Incense Road

Standalone Books and Short Stories:

Nightfall in the Garden of Deep Time

Awakening

The Ark Builder's Wife

Dressed to the Nines

Broken Pieces

Rescued: An Allegory

Made in the USA
Middletown, DE
17 November 2023

42941067R00175